FEAR THE DEMON WITHIN

Ed Cain stood inside the closed front door, felt the adrenalin starting to pump, a raging torrent inside his own body that rushed and roared, pounded relentlessly at his senses. Deafened, he could not be sure whether there was laughter amidst the noise. Tensing, grinding his teeth, clenching his fists, swaying unsteadily because the hall was tilting from side to side, starting to gyrate. An instant uncontrollable rage, a boiling fury that would have been vented on the woman standing outside – had he been capable of movement . . .

Also by Guy N. Smith in Sphere Books

FIEND
MANIA
THE CAMP

THE UNSEEN

Guy N. Smith

SPHERE BOOKS LIMITED

A SPHERE BOOK

First published in Great Britain by Sphere Books Ltd 1990

Typeset by Fleet Graphics, Enfield, Middlesex
Reproduced, printed and bound in Great Britain by
William Collins, Glasgow

ISBN 07474 0345 7

Macdonald & Co (publishers) Ltd
Orbit House,
1 New Fetter Lane,
London EC4A 1AR

A member of Maxwell Macmillan Pergamon Publishing Corporation plc

For Anne Marriott

CHAPTER ONE

The cathedral city had its rush hour just like any other city. Ed Cain sat behind the wheel of his Volvo, was aware that the tickover was a trifle too fast. You noticed things like that when you were caught up in a traffic jam and it added to your rising frustration. He deliberated over whether or not to switch the engine off, decided against it because the vehicles in front would probably start to move any second; another few yards and then stop again.

It was raining, a fast drizzle that made the wipers squeak their own annoyance as they attempted to clear the windscreen; cutting a wide swathe, slowing as though they might give up the incessant struggle for vision. It was uncomfortably mild for February, Ed turned on the cooling system, would have let a window down if it had not been for the drizzle.

He could not see whether the traffic lights at the centre junction were on red or green, or even functioning at all because a cement-mixer two vehicles ahead blocked his view. A cumbersome obstruction, he cursed it beneath his breath. Heavy vehicles were banned in the city centre but this one was probably on its way to the new shopping precinct complex whose construction was way behind schedule on account of the severe weather in January. The machine had every right to be here, it was no good getting worked up against it.

Christ, the lights must have changed by now! Probably back to red because cars were jamming the yellow box and holding everybody up. Impatient drivers adding to the confusion. Ed lit a cigarette, he was trying to kick the habit, had cut down from twenty to ten a day but he felt he was entitled to one now. Calm the old nerves, the classic excuse.

That mixer was having an hypnotic effect on him. He must have been staring at it for a full minute before he realized it; his eyes following the grumbling, rotating barrel. Up and round, going up again, spelling out the black lettering on the faded orange paintwork: GRINDLE CONSTRUCTION LTD. A sense of pride filled him because they were customers of the bank he managed, had an overdraft of a million which more than paid the staff salaries. Which was one reason why he stopped cursing the readymix truck. All the same he would be glad to see it rumble forward, hopefully turn right because he was going straight across.

Great, we're on the move at last! Ten yards perhaps and then the brake lights in front were reflecting on the wet road surface. The mixer was up to the lights, next change and we're all across. He wrenched his gaze away from the churning concrete container, looked hopefully for a winking flasher; right or left, it did not matter which. There was none, maybe the driver would signal late or not at all. Because I don't want to follow you all round the ring road. Ed could see the traffic lights now, a frowning red in the gathering dusk of a wet spring night, almost as though they had a personal grudge against him.

He drew hard on his cigarette. Frustration was bad

for the heart, he had read somewhere, pumps the adrenalin and you don't get a chance to burn up the energy sitting in a car. Still watching that groaning cement cylinder, a constant unhurried movement regardless of whether the truck was stuck in a traffic queue or trundling along a main road. You had to train yourself to be like that, an automaton, if you wanted to survive the stress factor.

He forced a change of mood, a smugness. He was entitled to it, only last week the *Financial Times* had reported that Ed Cain was the youngest bank manager in England. And that was some achievement at thirty-two, not just a branch out in the sticks with a staff of three where the manager was a glorified clerk and ran the lunch hour till, but a major High Street office with an assistant manager and twenty-nine clericals, even a messenger to open up at 9.30 am and close the doors at half past three.

In a moment of vanity he glanced at himself in the driving mirror. A boyish face, brown wavy hair, alert blue eyes. A whiz-kid if you liked, that was all right by Ed. A fortuitous whirlwind career, a 'face that fitted' and a bit of luck thrown in. He had passed all his Institute of Bankers examinations first time, his preliminary training had been a kind of crash course; three months counter work, they had told him he was wasted there. An early junior appointment, a spell in the regional head office, a sub-manager and now a major branch and a salary of twenty-five grand a year. Against all the odds. He had married Judy just after his eighteenth birthday; she was sixteen then and her parents had tried to stop the wedding going ahead. Two kids; he hadn't opted out of anything to further his career. Becky was ten, Richard fourteen. And Ed was still climbing the ladder, he had another thirty years to go.

Blaring horns from the rear jerked him out of his reverie. The way ahead was clear, the lights on green, and now it was himself who was snarling up the traffic. Back down to earth and straight across the junction, the Volvo surged forward like a sleek and powerful panther in its jungle habitat. Slowing, braking because he was in the queue up to the big clocktower island. And immediately in front of him was that cement-mixer.

Jesus Almighty! He let the window down, threw the remains of his cigarette out because he did not crave it any more, which was an encouraging sign. The two cars ahead of him must have turned off, he just hoped that the mixer would head south at the island. It might be another ten minutes before they reached it, there were roadworks now, single file traffic and another glowering red light.

Usually, unless the weather was really bad, Ed walked to the bank, a distance of less than half a mile from the privileged rented house in the quiet backwater of the cathedral close. The old part of the city, fifteenth century half-timbered houses that leaned across the pavement, alongside the park, or through it if he had the time to spare on a sunny morning. A miniature lake with its flock of tame mallard quacking to be fed and a pair of Canada geese which had flighted in last autumn and stayed. Down a narrow alley which emerged into the cobbled square, business premises, even the modern bank, in keeping with their surroundings. Idyllic, the best of both worlds, you tried to kid yourself that beyond the market square it was the same, that the council had not yielded to pressure to erect a shopping complex, that there were no housing estates with rows of identical boxes, no busy ring road. But you knew they existed, that the city had grown and expanded, sprawled beyond the old boundaries whilst attempting to retain its atmosphere of quietude. You accepted the conurbation because it paid your salary.

The light was on green, bright and hurrying you. Come on, I can't wait to change again. The mixer bumped up a ramp, showered some grey water on to the road, sprayed it upwards. Ed used his screen washer to clear his vision. Thirty yards, a good unbroken run before the traffic bunched again. He saw the clocktower; 5.40, he would be home by six with luck. What was twenty minutes? A long time when you were stuck in traffic.

He got to thinking about the house. Prestigious in the charming close with its beautiful cathedral dating from the 12th century, once a wooden edifice that had been razed to the ground and then rebuilt. Held by the Royalists in the Civil War, it was besieged and taken by the Roundheads, defaced and then restored. Once called the Field of the Dead, where violence and killing had taken place, it was now a holy place to which tourists from all over the world flocked on a summer pilgrimage.

The majority of the close houses were occupied by clergy, innumerable canons and prebendaries, a deanery and a bishop's palace with its walled garden. Occasionally when one of the houses became vacant and there were no immediate clergy to occupy it, it was leased to an 'outsider'. Perhaps there was a shortlist of applicants, Ed Cain had no idea, only that number nineteen had become vacant and his predecessor had chanced to mention the fact. Rent is dead money, was one of Ed's sayings but he had ignored his own advice, applied for the property and, weeks later, had been interviewed by the dean. The rent was nominal, it seemed that status was of far greater importance; a host of restrictions and formalities. No residents' cars to be parked outside their houses during the daytime, noise to be kept to a minimum. You were expected to attend Sunday services. One dog was allowed per household but had to be exercised *outside* the close.

For Ed there was no problem, he was granted the tenancy of number nineteen on a five-year lease; if his career continued at the same rate of progress as hitherto then he would be moving on then. It might work out just right. Judy liked the house, the setting. The children weren't bothered. Socially it was a good move and much of bank business came from socialising.

The island. Ed saw a gap in the oncoming traffic, eased into the flow. Moving into the centre lane so that he could filter into the northbound flow. Christ, that bloody mixer was in front of him again!

A dual carriageway and the lumbering vehicle was picking up speed, its grinding cylinder spewing out cement water so that he had to use the washers again. It was signalling, moving across to the central carriageway filter, beating him to it.

He waited again; this was a treacherous cross-over, blinding headlights and spray, you had to wait your chance. He wondered where the Grindle's driver was headed, maybe he had taken a wrong turn and had to get back into the city centre. Or perhaps somebody up on one of the new estates was having a concrete floor laid. Which was unlikely at this time on a Friday night.

His banking brain strayed to Grindle's accounts. The overdraft was due for renewal next month. No problem, they could have two million if they needed it. He hoped they did.

The cement-mixer made it across to the side road opposite. Ed had to wait for two cars, then caught it up again. There was a minor junction ahead, he signalled early; the mixer's right-hand flasher indicated that he was turning right also.

Ed found himself watching that rotating barrel again. He had the impression that something was wrong, something which did not fit with his symmetrical oriented mind. The thing was slanting at an angle, leaning backwards, too! Instinctively the bank manager's foot eased off the accelerator pedal, the Volvo would have dropped back except that the truck in front was slowing down. Turning left into the cathedral close!

Now who the hell wanted ready-mixed cement in the close? The bishop, of course. Ed recalled that there was an extension being built on to the rear of the palace, he had noticed Grindle's boards up outside, the fact had not registered until now. If the bishop needed readymix then he could have it any time he wanted. Except Sundays, naturally!

There was a ridge in the road outside the entrance to the close, a 'sleeping policeman'; far rather that a vehicle's springs or chassis was broken than that it exceeded the statutory 5 mph within those holy boundaries. Ed was anticipating the jolt but apparently the driver ahead of him was unaware of it. Or else he treated it with contempt due to the size and weight of his own vehicle.

Ed saw the truck lurch as its front wheels hit the raised tarmac. *And then it seemed to stop, to rear up like some unwieldy cart horse attempting to unseat its rider*!

A cry of terror escaped Ed's lips. He braked, tried to push the lever into reverse but for some reason was unable to do so. He saw the great beast in front up on its hind legs, its saddle girths snapping, its rider fighting to stay on its back. The barrel was spinning, faster now that it was unleashed, vomiting that revolting gravelly spew, showering the windscreen of the car behind it but mercilessly not obscuring the driver's vision.

For a second or two everything seemed to stop, a hermetic film still freezing the action. The mixer was airborne, hovering in spite of its huge weight. Then it moved, slow-motion so that Ed saw every twist and turn, a trapped victim in a night-time air raid watching a doodlebug heading straight for him.

Seconds during which you clung to precious life, praying that it was all a dream, or if it wasn't then the thing would either fall short or else overshoot you. Bracing yourself, not even able to scream.

Treacly gravel sludged on the windscreen, left a gap for Ed to see through. The barrel was speeding up, hurtling. And then it hit the Volvo, steamrollered the bonnet, flattening it into a ramp as it rolled, a systematic sheet metal robot on a production line in a car factory.

Sudden darkness, the artificial glistening lights were gone. Ed felt the car's bodywork compressing, tried to draw his legs up, grappled with his seat-belt fastener but to no avail. Human meat in an upholstered sandwich, unable to breathe. He heard a cracking that might have been bones or metalwork and then there was total silence.

His final sensation was of a sticky wetness washing over him as he slid slowly into a bottomless abyss.

CHAPTER TWO

Norma Pringle peered from behind her living room curtains at the scene of devastation outside her front door. Her capacious body trembled with a mixture of excitement and anger as she glanced behind her to check that Pretty, her ageing tabby cat, had not slipped out of doors. Not that Pretty ever went outside but she had to be sure. She reached across, switched off the light; nobody would be able to see her from outside now and if they thought they were coming *here* to use the phone then they had another think coming!

Norma was approaching sixty and her once attractive features were lined with bitterness and grief. She had been widowed almost fifteen years and she had not forgiven the Church hierarchy for trying to evict her from the canon's residence. She presumed they had admitted defeat as she had not heard from them for two years now. A bunch of hypocrites, Peter had served them faithfully from the day he was ordained but apparently he was dispensable. Kick his widow out into the street and appoint another canon; or so they had thought: She had stuck it out and over the years had become a recluse, seldom going out of the house except for her Friday shopping expedition into the city and she made that as brief as possible. She didn't need people, any more than she needed the God who had treated her so cruelly. So long as she had Pretty's company she was fine. Her once slim figure had expanded as she sought solace in food; she cooked three meals a day for herself and her cat and lately she had taken to tippling a couple of generous whiskies in the evening before retiring. She repeatedly told herself that she was perfectly happy with her lot in life and had come to believe it.

A crowd had gathered, faceless ghouls huddling at the entrance to the close, it was impossible to recognize those shadowy silhouettes but Norma had a bet with herself that Canon Holland was amongst them, gloating and rubbing his chubby pink hands together. He wouldn't come forward to see if he could help, he would stay back and relish the carnage. Like herself; except that she had a good reason for doing so.

What was the close coming to, allowing cement-mixers to infiltrate its peace and quiet on a spring evening? Of course, it was on its way to the bishop's palace to further the building of that unsightly extension. The bishop was a law unto himself, nobody would question him. Whoever was in that crushed car was almost certainly dead. And, like Peter, they were dispensable. Nothing must stand in the way of the bishop's empire-building.

Norma found herself willing somebody to bang on her door, yelling for her to open up so that they could call an ambulance. Come on, one of you! Rehearsing her reactions in her own mind, stepping back from the window and listening to their frantic knockings. Maybe she wouldn't pretend that she wasn't in, she would yell out 'go away, don't come crying to me for help. You didn't help my Peter!'

But nobody knocked on her door. The cement-mixer

had rolled to a standstill, crushed a length of pavement and demolished a flight of stone steps. It seemed to have veered off that car instead of running right over it. And then she heard the wail of an approaching siren.

The ambulance arrived first, backed up to the wreckage of the car, the two-man crew standing in the road because there was nothing they could do until some cutting equipment arrived to free the trapped victim. He would be dead, anyway, crushed beyond recognition, there was no doubt about that. So there was no hurry.

A man in grimy overalls staggered out of the shadows towards them. The truck driver, he seemed dazed, was demanding something. Norma saw the flare of a match, the way he cupped his hands as he leaned forward to accept a light for the cigarette he craved. Then everybody was waiting again.

Three minutes later a police car arrived, its blue light flashing, escorting the fire-engine which followed it. A huddle of uniformed men was busy dragging some bulky gear up to the Volvo. Steel cutters doubtless, Norma decided, and pressed her face against the window pane in an effort to see what was going on.

The crowd was swelling; a policeman gesticulated angrily, ordered them to get back. Even the precincts of a cathedral had its ghouls; Norma knew that virtually every window overlooking the accident had an audience and she despised the hidden watchers. She had a valid reason to be a spectator, they were just gloating.

A grinding, tearing noise had her wincing, clenching her fists until her fingernails gouged the palms of her hands. A flurry of dazzling sparks from the fire crew's equipment like sparklers at a bonfire party dazzled her. They were going to have to saw the wrecked car up before they stood any chance of rescuing the mangled corpse inside.

A pause, a consultation between policemen and firemen, and a man in civvies with a trilby hat pulled down over his face. The latter was obviously a doctor waiting to pronounce the crushed driver dead.

More sawing, then pieces of twisted metal were cast to one side, bouncing on the road. The rescue team were almost there.

The ambulance men had a stretcher ready, the others were carefully dragging something clear of the car. Norma strained her eyes, wanted to see what it was. *Who* it was. An indiscernible shape was lifted on to the stretcher, a blanket tossed over it as it was borne towards the waiting ambulance.

Disappointment for Norma Pringle; and then a surge of excitement. Because suddenly she *knew* who the dead man was, did not have to see his bloody remains to identify him. It was that bank manager fellow who lived at number nineteen!

She laughed aloud, let the curtains fall back into place and switched the light on. The cat in its basket by the fireplace stirred, looked at her quizzically.

'Yes, my darling, it's *him*.' Norma stooped, stroked the tabby and made it purr. 'You know, the man who has that nasty labrador dog which chased you across the cathedral lawns just before Christmas. Oh, my sweetie, how marvellous! He's dead now and you can bet that his wife and those abominable children will be moving away now and taking that beastly dog with them. Apart from the bishop and the dean, I wanted it to be him. I recognize the car now. And the bishop killed him!' A shriek of near-hysterical sadistic laughter rang out. 'If the bishop hadn't ordered the cement lorry then the bank manager would be still alive. Anyway, bank managers have no business living in the close, poor Peter must have writhed in his grave the day that chap moved in. Not that I've any time for the clergy but between the lot of them they've got just what they asked for . . . '

Ed Cain felt himself starting to surface from that awful pit of darkness. It seemed that his fall had been checked, like he had hit something soft and now he was floating gently upwards. Confused, he did not try to understand, could not remember what had happened. Just that he was stirring out of a deep sleep, not properly awake.

Then he was lying still. He could not see anything, all around him there was impenetrable blackness. He did not try to move, just lay there. Distant voices reached him but he could not hear what was being said; people talking urgently, a harsh grinding noise that came and went, then came again.

Time meant nothing to him, he was comfortable and very sleepy. Probably he was at home in bed after an exhausting day. So just rest, it will be time to get up before you realize it.

He felt hands touching him, exploding his body. Judy probably, she often stroked him in the middle of the night. Sometimes she was aroused, in the mood for love-making. But not tonight, darling, I'm too tired.

Now he was being lifted up. That puzzled him but he made no attempt to resist because he did not have the strength; it was probably all a dream, anyway.

A sensation of moving as if he were in a vehicle of some kind. That could not be true, he was warm and snug in bed, he could even feel the sheets against his body. He tried to stretch out a hand to feel for Judy, making sure that she was there beside him, but his limbs refused to respond. Because he was bloody exhausted. Judy was there all right, she always was.

The bedroom light was on, he sensed its brightness beyond his closed eyelids the same way in which he was aware of it on those occasions when Judy read late into the night and he slept by her side. A disturbance because he was aware of the absence of darkness but his eyelids were too heavy to open. It didn't matter, it meant that Judy was there, engrossed in a novel. So everything was perfectly normal.

He must have slept heavily again because that feeling of movement disturbed him. Not a vehicular one this time but like somebody had lifted up the bed and was carrying it across the room. But if that was the case then it was all a figment of the sleeping mind because the bedroom was not large enough for them to carry it this far. He felt the bed being lowered, hands groping for him again. *Please*, darling, not tonight. Maybe a quickie in the morning if we're fresh enough.

Those lights were brighter than ever now, searing through his eyelids, hurting his eyeballs. Tossing, trying to writhe. He thought that perhaps he was ill, a virus of some kind that had taken him as he slept, one of those awful 'flu bugs that used to creep up on you when you were a kid. Fevered nightmares, walls and ceiling threatening to close in on you, crush you. He was sure he was sweating, his body felt awash with liquid.

But he could neither move nor open his eyes. *And now everything was becoming very frightening.*

He was naked, he was sure of that fact. Judy must have removed his pyjamas. But how and *why*? Hands touching him, indistinguishable voices like distant whisperings. Things being attached to his body, he did not know what they were, tried desperately to grab for them, tear them away. But the effort was all in the mind, he knew his limbs were immovable.

Ed tried to speak, attempted to move his lips to ask what the hell was going on, what they were doing to him, but even if his mouth moved his vocal chords were unable to function. Those lights were hurting, he wanted to turn his head away, bury his face in the pillow.

It was impossible to relax, impossible to wake up. Trying to think, to remember. Yesterday? Today? He must have gone to the bank unless it was either Saturday or Sunday. A day's work . . . going home . . . no, he had not walked because he had a vague recollection of taking the car into town for something. Something for Judy. Driving out in the rush hour traffic, waiting impatiently for the lights to change . . . A vehicle that held everybody up because it was slow and lumbering. A cement-mixer . . .

And then it all came flooding back to him with awful reality.

He was turning into the close, the mixer was taking the raised ramp too fast. The revolving cylinder was starting to come away from its moorings . . .

No!

A surge of panic, trying to get away from the oncoming missile as it bounced and rolled towards the car. Drawing up his legs, tearing at the seat-belt fastener but it refused to come free. Screaming in his tortured mind. He saw the Volvo's bonnet start to flatten, concrete spewing all over the windscreen. Then the car was flattening in on him like those bedroom walls and ceiling did at the height of a fevered waking nightmare.

Only this time Ed did not sink down into that black crater.

He could see even though there was darkness all round him. The steering column had buckled against his chest, pinioned him to the twisted seat. His legs were trapped beneath him and the arm which had attempted to unclasp the safety belt hung uselessly at his side. He was bleeding, he could feel the treacly warmth of oozing blood, taste it in his mouth. The mixer had changed direction, gone elsewhere; he didn't give a shit where.

Strangely there was no pain, just a numbness, a cramped sensation that was having a morphine-like effect on him as it spread. He head people moving about, heard them starting to cut him free, particles of metal showering all over him like sawdust. Conscious and yet unconscious as they dragged him free, lifted him up on to a stretcher and draped a blanket over him.

He recalled the ambulance trip, the way the doctor and the uniformed man administered to him. Injections, bandages. He had not been aware then but he was now!

Suddenly, terrifyingly, he saw himself as he was now in the same way that he had been able to recall what had happened to him. First a sense of vertigo because he was at a great height, right up against the dazzling white ceiling looking down upon his own body draped in a shroud with two white-cloaked and masked surgeons working feverishly on him.

And Ed Cain knew without any doubt that he was dying.

Frighteningly aware, divorced from his body yet still part of it, he fought against panic. Everything was so terribly real that he did not even hope that it might be some nightmare borne in a tortured mind. His astral body had come free of his physical one, had deserted it because death was imminent. He began to fight against it, sheer desperation amidst the shock and hopelessness. No, I don't want to die. I can't! Please God, for Judy's sake, Becky and Richard, too. They *need* me.

The theatre was no longer a dazzling whiteness, rather a soft glow that became a golden aura like evening sunlight playing on the walls. A warmth where before there had been coldness. A sensation of being sucked right up to the ceiling and then he would pass through it. And after that there would be no return.

It was akin to the slipstream of a passing juggernaut on the motorway, pulling at you, trying to drag you beneath it. Resisting but there was nothing to clutch at because he had no hands, no body. Only the will to live.

Screaming but there were no words, no sound. A leaf caught by a gale, being drawn upwards. Then, without warning, the invisible force slackened its hold on him and he felt himself floating like a child's kite when the wind has suddenly dropped. A sailing boat becalmed, abandoned.

He was confused for a second or two, staring down on the lifeless form that was his own body, seeing the tallest of the surgeons straighten up, shake his head. The man was speaking behind his mask, lips ruffling the material. Ed could not hear what the other said but he guessed, knew. 'He's dead!'

No, I'm alive. Wait, please. I'm coming back.

The return was so easy, like sliding down a polished fairground shute, descending towards that lifeless human body. A moment of euphoria and then a sense of awful foreboding. He had fought and won yet something was wrong! And in that instant of uneasy realization he was aware of the golden glow darkening; the stark whiteness returned, dimmed. And gave way to unending blackness.

Judy Cain had been in the small hospital ante-room since 7.30. Dark-haired, her usually pale complexion was ashen, her perfectly moulded features screwed up with anxiety. Her slim figure was taut, head buried in her hands, fearing the worst. Ed wouldn't make it. He had to, please God let him be all right!

She was vaguely aware that she still wore her plastic kitchen apron with the slogan 'Head Cook and Bottlewasher' emblazoned across it, a joke gift from the children last Mother's Day. She had rushed straight from the kitchen when she received news of Ed's accident, turned the cooker down low and told Richard to keep an eye on the casserole. Not that any of them were likely to eat it now.

She thought about removing her apron. No, it didn't matter and, anyway, discarding it would reveal the black dress which she wore beneath it. A funeral dress. She bit on a piece of loose skin on her forefinger, tugged at it, with a feeling of helplessness and hopelessness. They had told her to sit here and wait. Listening for approaching footsteps down the corridor; they were constant, nurses passing by on some errand; returning. Sometime, sooner or later, those footfalls would slow, the door handle would click open. 'Mrs Cain . . . '

Ed's all right, he's going to make it, don't tell me otherwise because I'm not listening. They had brought her a cup of tea, strong with sugar in true hospital tradition. She didn't take sugar, hadn't for ten years, but she never even noticed its sickly sweet taste. She didn't want tea but she drank it for something to do.

Footsteps again, heavy male ones this time, slow and deliberate. She had steeled herself for the opening of the door long before it did.

The newcomer was obviously a surgeon, tall and grey-haired, a long white coat hiding whatever he wore beneath it. Austere, rimless glasses, trying to smile reassuringly but maybe he wasn't used to smiling. But smiling had to be good news. Or rather, not *very* bad tidings.

'Your husband is very poorly,' he said as he lowered himself into the empty chair by her side. 'At one point his heart stopped but we managed to restart it. He's on a life-support machine. Critical but stable.'

'Oh!' Relief because there was still hope. A vestige of it. An urge to cry but it wouldn't do any good. 'I see.'

'We can't tell you any more at this stage. If you want to sit with him, you can. But he's unconscious.' We can't stop next of kin sitting in but they're a bloody nuisance, his expression said. 'If you wish to go home then we'll call you if there's any change in his condition. You understand?'

'Yes.' There were a lot of questions she wanted to ask, details of Ed's injuries but they were irrelevant to the overall position. 'You . . . you think there's a chance?'

'There's always a chance,' he smiled again, refrained from adding 'whilst there's life there's hope'. 'We are doing everything possible, Mrs Cain, but at this stage it is impossible to ascertain if there is any brain damage. We shall know more in a day or two.'

Judy sat there after the other had gone. She had to go home because of the children. She didn't know whether she would have stayed on if she had been childless. Probably not. She didn't want to see Ed. Yet. He might be clinically dead, the machine was merely keeping the faintest bodily functions going. A switch controlled her husband's life; they could not turn it off without her consent. That was what it was all about, they had not spelled it out yet because they were playing a waiting game. For them it was a routine, something that happened frequently.

This was life at its cruellest; one minute everything was fine, the next you were shattered. She experienced an urge to go into the cathedral and pray but she didn't. Because the children were waiting for her.

CHAPTER THREE

Judy reminded herself every hour of every day she had to be thankful just for having Ed alive. His very survival after that terrible accident had been a miracle in itself; her prayers had been answered and she had prayed in that cathedral itself for his return. God had granted her that, she had nothing to complain about; she had her husband, Becky and Richard had their father.

Or did they?

It was June now and that terrible March evening seemed years away. Maybe it was, there were lines in her smooth skin and only yesterday she had noticed flecks of grey in her dark hair.

The week following the accident had seemed an eternity, days and nights blended unendingly. Sleep was snatched in an armchair and then only because of sheer exhaustion. She had forced the children to go to school because she couldn't bear them hanging around the house in the daytime. Richard had his 'mocks' next term, his GCSEs the following year. Whatever happened he had to continue with his education. Becky had another year to go at the primary school.

Mr Craddock, the surgeon, had warned Judy on

the Monday that she might have to make a decision whether or not to switch off the life-support machine, they would not be in a position to advise her until tomorrow. Which meant that they would tell her that there was no hope, that Ed could be kept alive by artificial means but would never recover. In which case she would have given them the go-ahead; she had prepared herself for that because that was surely what it would come to.

Doctor Lawson, their GP, only a couple of years off retirement, called every day. To comfort her, to try to persuade her to accept some sleeping tablets. He was non-commital where Ed was concerned. Tuesday would be Decision Day.

During Monday night the miracle happened. Judy walked the children into town on Tuesday morning, then went direct to the hospital. Waiting there for Craddock, the sister informed her that he was with Ed, that he would not be more than a few minutes. She was strangely calm, in a way this was therapeutic, like funerals. Finis. Tell them to go ahead, switch the machine off, walk right out of here. Later she would break down.

'Good morning, Mrs Cain.' Craddock managed a smile, one that had a hint of self-sastisfaction about it. 'Good news. Your husband can come off the life-support machine. It's going to be a long job, weeks, maybe months, but there's no brain damage, he's the luckiest man alive. He's being transferred to Ward Five, you'll be able to see him in ten minutes or so if you care to hang on.'

Judy's brain reeled, she found herself thinking that perhaps she had misheard, misunderstood. Until the nurse escorted her into the casualty ward and she saw Ed. Her mind spun again, she almost screamed, thought she was going to faint. *Oh, my God!*

Well, it had to be Ed, they wouldn't have any reason to fool her. A kind of embalmed mummified human shape with blue eyes staring vacantly out of the face bandages. Ed's eyes, brilliant blue. The nose she didn't recognize amidst the stitches. Nor the mouth with its toothless gums.

'There'll have to be more surgery,' the nurse was watching her carefully, 'and dentures, of course.'

'Ed?' Still disbelieving, looking for a reaction in those vacant orbs.

There was none.

'Ed?' She found fingers protruding out of a plaster cast, squeezed them gently. They were as cold as corpse flesh. If she could have found a pulse she would have felt for a beat. Her hand came away, she almost recoiled and yelled, 'that's not my husband. If it is then you've made a mistake and he's dead!'

A noise came from those mangled lips, a sound that was something in between a groan and a hiss. Hostile.

'You'll have to be patient,' the nurse had not departed yet. 'It may take some time but Mister Crawford is certain that there's no brain damage.'

An hour later Judy left the hospital. A fleeting thought that it would have been preferable if Ed had died on the machine. No, that was selfish, because she was frightened of what she had seen. Like the surgeon had said, she had to have patience.

Patience that was still being put to the test three months later.

'Can we go and see Dad?' Richard had asked on the Tuesday evening. She could see the likeness to Ed suddenly, something which others were always remarking upon. Brown wavy hair, blue eyes; it ended there. Now.

'No, I'm afraid not,' her voice trembled, she hoped the children did not notice it. 'He's not well enough to have visitors yet. Except me. And it's best if I don't go too often or stay for too long.' Coward!

'Aw, Mum!'

'Perhaps in a week or so.' When they've . . . repaired him. Made him look . . . *human*!

Well, the plastic surgeons had somehow rebuilt Ed into something resembling his former likeness. And the physiotherapist got him walking again. They assured Judy that in time he would be almost back to normal.

But he had changed.

The day before they sent her husband home Judy had gone into the cathedral and prayed that everything might come right. Not just physically but psychologically. The first time she had kissed him since his accident had been a frightening experience. Not because of the lip injuries but because there had been no response. He knew and understood, he was even talking again with a voice that was like a deep cave echo of his former one. His eyes stared into hers, seemed to be mocking her.

Now he was back home.

Perhaps Cling, the ten-year-old yellow labrador, had felt neglected these last months. Perhaps that was the reason for his behaviour, Judy told herself, the children tried to convince her husband that it was. The day Ed returned, even as he was helped in through the door by Judy and Richard, Cling stood in the hall, bared his teeth and growled threateningly.

'Cling!' Damn the dog, as if I haven't got enough to cope with without you playing up!

The growl died to a whimper, a whimper of *fear*. The dog turned, curled its tail between its hind legs and slunk into the kitchen. From that day it had refused to enter the lounge where Ed had his bed, where he spent his days, the room into which Cling would sneak at every opportunity that presented itself and curl up on the sofa.

'He's been missing you,' Judy told Ed unconvincingly.

'Well, as long as he stops in the kitchen that suits me fine,' Ed snapped, 'and I don't want those kids in here, either!'

'Children,' she would have to stop referring to them as 'children', particularly Richard, but that was irrelevant at the moment, 'I'm afraid you'll have to do your homework in your rooms for the time being. And if you want to watch television, watch the portable upstairs. Or I can bring it down into the kitchen if you would prefer it.'

'Mum, we . . .'

'I'm sorry, but your father needs a lot of peace and quiet. He'll be sleeping a lot of the time,' hopefully, 'and he mustn't be disturbed.'

That night Judy Cain had wept. She was also suddenly afraid of the man who had once been her loving husband. But, as Craddock had said, she would be patient.

Doctor Lawson called daily to see Ed and it was at the end of the first week that he took Judy's arm and walked her down the drive with him because he had something to say which he did not wish Ed to overhear.

'It'll take time, Judy.' Lawson was a bulky man, could be abrupt with malingering patients, kindly with those in need of sympathy. 'You've experienced a miracle, you can't hope for a second one right away, can you? He's mending but the psychological healing will take longer than the physical mending. But it'll come right, take it from me. Oh, and another thing, he isn't damaged sexually so you can look forward to marital relationships again, hopefully before too long. Help him with it if he needs it.'

Two days later Lawson's words echoed in Judy's terrified brain.

Becky and Richard were at school, Cling had gone out into the garden to lie in the shade of the weeping willow the way he often did on scorching hot days, and Judy was in the kitchen preparing a tuna salad for lunch when she heard Ed call her. The fact that he wanted her, needed her, was encouraging in itself for since his return home he lapsed into long periods of silence.

'Coming, darling.' She hastened across the hallway, scarcely dared to hope that this was the breakthrough for which she had been longing, and opened the lounge door. 'Ed, I . . . '

Then she stopped, almost recoiled and nearly fled at the scene which greeted her. She clung on to the door handle, might have fallen otherwise. There was Ed, on the sofa where she had expected him to be, naked and offering her a full view of his innumerable scars like a large scale map of mountainous countryside with every contour detailed. And he was fully aroused, stroking his erection purposefully and smiling with an unholy lust.

'It's been a long time.' There was an intensity in his piercing eyes as they focused lustfully on her. 'Get your clothes off!'

Judy swallowed, felt her stomach balling. They had enjoyed a marvellous sexual relationship up until that terrible night. Since then she had barely given it a thought, did not need it; if it had not come back then she would probably have managed without it. A subtle seduction would have been delightful but without any warning she was confronted with a demand for physical sex, one which would be sheer lust, animal mating.

'I . . . I . . . ' She swallowed, stepped back a pace.

'Come here!' A kind of growl, Ed's eyes seemed to bulge in their sockets and he was rubbing himself faster. 'What's the matter with you?'

She walked forward unsteadily, saw his hands reaching out for her. An unbelievable strength and mobility after the weeks of painfully slow recovery, a driving urge that overpowered his stiffness and injuries. She did not resist, even went through the motions of helping him as he tore at her garments. A button bounced and rolled across the floor, her bra fastener snapped as he ripped at it clumsily. Then she was naked and being dragged on to his reclining body.

The penetration was painful, she hoped that the cry which escaped her lips might be misinterpreted as one of pleasure. Muscles which had softened with the months of inactivity responded as he powered upwards, thrust deep into her. His dentures were clenched with the effort, his body was shiny with sweat and there was a rumbling in his throat which frightened her.

His fingers fastened on to her small breasts, hurt her as he pinched and squeezed, pulling her face down close to his. *Oh, God, this wasn't Ed, it was some carnal beast in his rebuilt body!*

No way was she able to generate any response, it was all an act on her part, an ordeal which she endured because it was a duty that was expected of her. Perhaps next time it would be different; his sexual feelings had returned and he was unable to cope with them. Next time . . .

He was starting to climax. His hands relinquished their grip on her bosom, slid up to her slender neck, encircled it. She was gasping for breath, there was a haze before her eyes and the room was gyrating crazily. His thighs bucked, almost threw her, and without uncoupling he dragged her down, rolled over on top of her, his weight crushing her. Any second she would pass out.

Dimly she was aware of a dog barking, a crescendo of canine noises, ferocious growls. Fighting against suffocation and then suddenly Ed's strangulating grip released its hold and she was gasping for air. He had come free of her, pushed her to one side, was shouting incoherently, lashing out with an arm that had had its plaster cast removed only a fortnight ago.

'Bastard!' He swung a punch and the yellow hairy creature that had leaped upon the sofa was sent sprawling. It rolled over, stood at bay snarling.

'Cling!' Judy recognized the labrador, had never seen the animal enraged before. A placid, lovable creature, it now stood with jaws agape, saliva stringing from them, starting to bark again. 'Cling, whatever's the matter with you?'

'Bloody dog!' Ed raised himself up on an elbow, looked around as though seeking a weapon of some kind. 'I'll have the bastard put down!'

'No, Ed!' A shocked protest, seeing the dog turn and slink out of the room, low on its belly. 'You'd break the children's hearts, mine too. Something must have upset him, perhaps it's the heat.'

'He's been growling at me ever since I came home.' Ed's fury had subsided, he seemed very tired. 'All right, I won't do anything this time but just keep him out of my way. We'll buy a kennel and he can stop out in the garden.'

'He can live in the kitchen.' Judy was trembling, had forgiven Cling for the yellow hairs which covered carpets and furniture during the moult. 'But, please, Ed, don't do anything drastic.'

'Well, he'd better watch it. And another thing, those kids had better be a lot quieter. That record player of Richard's is getting on my nerves.'

'I'll ask him to keep it low.' She began retrieving her scattered clothes. Her bra was ruined, her blouse was torn. The warm wetness which was seeping out of her on to the insides of her thighs was suddenly repulsive. She wanted a bath, to cleanse herself; her body felt soiled and abused. And her neck was hurting, it was going to be very stiff. The ordeal had shaken her, it was as if her husband had been intent on strangling her. *Rape*, there was no other word for it, and for one awful moment she found herself wishing that Ed had not come off that life-support machine.

He was lying back, eyes closed. Exhausted. She looked down on him and again found it hard to believe that this was the man who had only months ago been a loving husband and caring father.

'I'm making a tuna salad for lunch.' She had her clothes on and had moved off the sofa, fearful lest he reach out and pull her back.

'Later,' he muttered. 'Right now I need to rest.'

Becky had piano lessons on Tuesdays after school. The routine was for Judy to collect her and take her to Mrs Carrington who lived at the far end of the close. Mrs Carrington, a widow in her sixties, supplemented her pension by giving private music tuition.

'I have to do a lot more practice at home,' Becky said when Judy fetched her at 6 o'clock. 'Mrs Carrington says that unless I do then I won't pass my Grade One.'

Judy pursed her lips. The piano was in the front room where Ed was currently living. Since his homecoming playing in there had been out of the question but surely he was well enough now. All the same, he had protested about Richard's stereo upstairs. But maybe that was different; the piano was all part of Becky's education, you could not deny her the right to practice.

Ed was lying on the sofa reading the paper when they arrived home. Richard was upstairs in his room and had, thankfully, not turned on any music yet.

'Becky has to practice the piano.' Judy was aware of the nervousness in her voice. 'It's important if she's to pass her exam in the autumn.'

Ed glanced up from his paper, seemed to have difficulty in focusing his eyes. For an instant it was as though he had not recognized them. Perhaps he had not heard. Judy chewed her lip, glanced at the upright piano on the other side of the room.

'I see.' Ed's gaze returned to his newspaper and he carried on reading.

'All right, just for quarter of an hour then.' Judy handed the child her leather music case. 'Then it'll be teatime.'

Judy went through to the kitchen, took a pizza out of the fridge. Something nice and easy, convenience food but at least it had a wholemeal base and that eased her conscience a little! As she put it in the oven she heard Becky starting to play.

Becky was practising the scales. She sounded nervous, hesitated; began again.

'For Christ's sake stop that bloody racket!'

The roar of anger halted the girl in mid-scales. Judy heard the piano stool crash to the floor, a flutter of music sheets and then feet running across the carpet. Even as she ran into the hall the door of Richard's room opened and his footsteps vibrated the landing floor. Oh, God, here we go again!

Judy stood in the lounge doorway, Becky clinging

fearfully to her. Ed was on his feet, his face a mask of rage, his cheeks suffused with blood.

'Ed, please! Becky has to play. She . . . '

'Then she can go and play at Mrs bloody Carrington's!' he shouted. 'For two pins I'd smash that piano up for firewood!'

Judy recoiled, pulled Becky behind her, and then Richard was pushing past her. The boy was tall for his age, strong and athletic, played soccer and rugby for his school. Now he was tight-lipped and his fists were clenched. Judy tried to pull him back but he tore free of her grasp and approached his father.

'That applies to you, too.' Ed stabbed a finger at his son. 'Any more of that rock crap from you and your record player's scrap!'

'Becky has to practise the piano.' Richard's voice shook with rage. 'I've turned my stereo off for *your* benefit but this is different. She's going to practise and you can like it or lump it!'

Judy saw Ed's arm move, was powerless to intervene. That same damaged limb which had almost strangled her had found strength again where there should have been weakness. The fist balled, took Richard full in the mouth and sent him staggering back, sprawled him on the carpet. His lower lip opened, began to ooze blood.

With a scream Judy went to him, knelt down by her son, Becky crying and clutching at her. Ed turned away, sat down on the sofa and picked up his paper, continued with his reading. For him the problem had been resolved.

And in the hallway Cling was barking furiously but the labrador made no attempt to enter the room this time.

CHAPTER FOUR

Ed Cain was both confused and frightened beneath the abrasive exterior which he presented to his family and anybody with whom he came into contact. A defence system which isolated him, gave him time. Time in which to sort himself out.

The nights were the worst, the half-waking recurring dream which had him writhing and tossing in his divan bed in the lounge. Judy had tried to persuade him to sleep upstairs but he had said maybe next week. Always next week; tomorrow was too soon. His mobility had returned, his visits to the physiotherapy unit in town had been reduced to twice a week instead of daily. Physically he was almost back to normal. If only those nightmares would relent.

They were always the same. He experienced those soaring sensations accompanied by a feeling of vertigo. Floating up to the ceiling, bracing himself because he was sure he would bang his head against it. He never did, he always stopped a few inches short of it and no matter how hard he tried to avert his gaze he found himself looking down. On his own slumbering body.

Seeing it, wanting to return to it, feeling the pull against his desires and if he did not fight it he was certain he would be swept upwards, out of the house and through the night sky above, lost forever. Panicking, screaming but no sound came from his astral lips until finally he found himself floating back down to a reunion with his flesh and blood.

Even the darkness did not hide that view of his body from him. Lately he had wondered if it really was his, at times it seemed foreign to him but his fear was that one night he would not be able to return. Ed Cain had died peacefully in his sleep, an obituary in the local paper and nobody would be really surprised.

Doctor Lawson called frequently, told him that he was almost fit enough to return to work. That was something else Ed was procrastinating over because banking seemed a facet of his life with which he had lost touch. He wondered if he would be able to rehabilitate; he read the financial news daily, attempted to familiarize himself with the stock market. At times it was easy, on other occasions he had to struggle to understand the rudiments. As if his brain switched on and off.

It was all due to the accident, of course. They had told him that there was no brain damage but he had his doubts. But worse than the prospect of going back to the office was his terror of what he might do to Judy.

That single physical union had been breathtaking, electrifying, he had never experienced anything like it before. An orgasm magnified a thousand times, he had totally lost control. At its peak he had wanted to kill her, to strangle her, to copulate with her as her life left her slender body.

He had not touched her since, he was terrified that next time he might not be able to pull back. If it had not been for Cling's ferocious intervention he surely would have murdered his wife!

God, he hated that dog, it seemed to sense whatever lurked in his brain. Lately it had taken to keeping out of his way, lying under the kitchen table or beneath the willow in the garden, hackles raised, a low growl in its throat whenever he came into view. No chance to forget, to try to return to normal, the labrador was a constant reminder of his condition. You're sick, boss. You're *dangerous*. And Ed nurtured a desire to kill the animal, brooded on it.

Maybe he had a brain tumour; the idea had only come to him recently. Bangs on the head were capable of starting a growth. It was festering inside his skull, growing by the hour. But he was afraid to mention it even when he had his final check over by Craddock.

'You're fine now, almost as good as new,' the surgeon was just too casual, almost dismissive. 'Get back to work, get back into the swim of things. Moping around at home will turn you into a chronic depressive. Any further problems then consult your GP and he'll refer you back to me if necessary. But I assure you there is no cause for concern now.' Because I want to mark this one up as a success, I don't want to spoil it by investigating too deeply. And, anyway, I've got a round of golf in an hour.

Ed did not mention the nightmares because that would have meant going back to that fateful night. Anyway, surgeons did not concern themselves with dreams.

Which was why he started back to work on the following Monday morning.

The bank itself seemed hostile, like an extension of that operating theatre. This is the next step, we're testing you out. Surroundings that should have been familiar but were not, a remembrance but it was vague. Faces that he had to check out to make sure, a cautiousness that was another part of the defence system with which he surrounded himself.

He made it all come back, worked on it. Houghton, the accountant, had been doing the managerial job during Ed's absence, looked haggard and ill at ease. I've done my best but it's been hard work, don't bollock me. Certainly not bank manager material, the grey-haired man had reached the peak of his own capabilities on the promotion ladder.

Ed closed the door of his office, sat at his desk and consulted his appointments diary. Christ, you'd have thought that they would have given him a day just to acclimatize himself. 11.30: John Cutler. Cutler? A name that was familiar but the face eluded him. Only when Ed consulted his files did the features, the case history come back to him. Fuck it, what a way to start his comeback!

John Cutler was a whiz-kid businessman; shrewd but shifty, one move ahead of everybody else. Or so he thought. The man knew the company laws inside out, was now on his second limited company inside two years. His electronics business had gone to the wall for sixty grand, left his creditors in the lurch. The following week Cutler Car Phones Limited had risen out of the ashes; another name, the same rented office. The bank had lost out to the tune of £10,000 and now he was back wanting overdraft facilities for his latest enterprise.

'When a public corporation defaults and leaves you holding the baby, you have to move on, there's no point sitting with your head in your hands crying over spilt milk,' John Cutler smiled, obviously undeterred by his previous catastrophe. 'My aim is to pay off the creditors as well as building up the new business. And I can promise you this one's a winner. Here, look at these advance orders.'

Ed took the file, stared at it whilst his brain found the right gear and clicked in. The computerized sheets were impressive; if you were the type easily impressed. Car phones, a status symbol for the executive, their benefit was debatable. But if you couldn't afford the real thing then Cutler supplied you with a *dummy* at a fraction of the cost of the genuine article. A yuppy toy, a handset and a coil, a hidden tape that made the right noises. Not only could you be seen to be using a phone in your car but you could also be *heard*! And there were nearly £70,000 of orders received for the product before manufacture had even started.

'We'd like to start making them by the middle of next month.' John Cutler was in his mid-thirties, a stone overweight as a symbol of his affluence. His recent bankruptcy had left him undeterred and unscarred. 'If the bank could lend eighty grand I can provide security up to fifty. But, Ed, you can see for yourself, it's a cert, a bank manager's dream.'

The use of his first name irritated Ed. He could not remember whether he and this smirking young man sitting opposite him had been on familiar terms before. If they had been then Ed was slipping. The fellow nauseated him, a wide boy who knew how to manipulate supply and demand and resorted to the loopholes in company law when things backfired on him. The bank stood to lose if the scheme turned sour; they also stood to gain if it was a success when the outstanding loss from Cutler's previous company would be wiped out. Ed's banking brain had found top gear.

Part of the security being offered was a term life policy worth a hundred thousand which would only be any good if John Cutler died in the meantime.

'I'll put the proposition up to the Regional Director,' Ed said. Passing the buck. He could have thrown it right back at the man sitting opposite him but he didn't. There was a much better way, a germ of an idea which he filed away in his brain to mull the details over later. The RD would sanction the overdraft, Ed would recommend it. He recalled that Cutler was a member of the golf club, remembered seeing him in the bar on occasions but had never played with him. Ed's eyes narrowed. He felt his hatred for the other man rising, pumping adrenalin. He clenched his fists beneath his desk as his body tautened. For one brief second he had to resist the urge to punch Cutler in the face, then he was back under control.

'It stands a good chance,' when the bank manager spoke his tone was soft, there was no hint of the contempt he felt for the customer. 'We'll know by Friday. If they agree the figure, how about a round of golf to celebrate?'

Cutler's euphoria showed in his eyes, the way his flabby hands lathered non-existent soap. 'That sounds absolutely marvellous, we'll celebrate on the course and in the clubhouse afterwards.' A laugh that was almost childish in its exuberance. 'What a splendid way to end the week!'

Ed thought, you stupid prick, and now it was his turn to tremble.

Ed remained in his room with the door closed for some time after Cutler had left, staring at the frosted glass partition, seeing shapes moving to and fro outside in the main office. A bustling of clerks, mostly female, a background cacophony of typewriters and computers. A world which he shied away from.

The Cutler file was put in the pending tray. Houghton would instruct the security clerk to type up the application. That was all academic, Ed was already making his own plans and they were arousing him. Oh, Jesus Christ!

A hesitant tapping on the door interrupted his thoughts. Glancing up he saw the opaque silhouette of a dark-haired girl wearing a blue dress. It might have been Judy except that she was too tall, the hair long instead of short.

'Yes.' A clipped command to enter, his heartbeat speeding up.

Lisa Smith had been managerial typist and secretary at the branch before Ed's appointment. An attractive girl, she did not wear a ring although it was common knowledge that she had a boyfriend, a married man who was enjoying the best of both worlds. And at twenty-two she was obviously quite content for the relationship to continue that way; she had no aspirations towards domestication. 'Shall I take your letters now, Mr Cain?' She smiled, closing the door behind her.

Ed nodded, his eyes tracing her slim figure up and down, in his mind seeing what lay beneath the thin summer dress. 'I . . . er, yes, that's fine, Lisa.'

Routine correspondence, there was a basketful, which Houghton had left. Overdrawn notices, a renewal of overdraft appointments pending. Ed's mind had found its banking channel, experience taking over. Oh, God, he could see Lisa's cleavage as she leaned over the desk scribbling shorthand on her jotter. And once again she might have been Judy, that afternoon when Ed had called her into the lounge and had so very nearly strangled her as his lust escalated beyond his control.

His voice was functioning like one of those hidden tapes in Cutler's dummy car phones, words that spilled out; leaving it to experience, his banking memory functioning without any logical support whilst his concentration was focused on the girl in front of him. He saw her naked beneath him, felt himself pushing deep into her. Everything was speeding up, his fingers were encircling that neck, tightening around it. His breathing was fast, those words, whatever they were, were reduced to an incomprehensible mumble.

'I'm sorry, Mr Cain, I didn't catch that last bit.'

He had to have her, here and now, there was nothing he could do to stop himself! He felt his body, vibrant and pulsing, begin to straighten up out of the chair, fingers flexing in anticipation of that female body; small breasts with erect nipples, sliding up to that soft neck. Lisa was scribbling something on her pad, her eyes lowered. Unaware.

Ed's teeth grated, he started to move round the desk, arms beginning to stretch out to grasp her, to tear at her clothing.

And then there was a sharp rap on the door, he heard it easing open.

A guilty schoolboy caught in the act of a tuck shop theft, he started, leaped back for his seat. The girl's head was turned towards the doorway, there was a stocky grey-haired man framed in it, a large pipe weighing down his lower lip.

'Mr Kemp!' All Ed's anger and frustration was loaded into the chief cashier's name, venomous surprise at this sudden intrusion.

'Excuse me.' The elderly man was unruffled, almost arrogant, as he shuffled into the office, some papers clutched in an extended hand. 'These passport applications needed to be witnessed. Mr and Mrs Weatherby, they're waiting.'

Charlie Kemp had just completed forty years service, was due to retire in the autumn. Most of his working life had been spent at this very branch where he had progressed to the position of chief cashier in 1959 and had remained in that post ever since. A loyal servant, eccentric and sometimes bad-tempered, he was a law unto himself even where young ambitious managers were concerned. He always took quarter of an hour extra at lunchtime and smoked his pipe on the counter, contrary to regulations. He resented having to knock on a managerial door but if he was compelled to then he entered without being invited to do so. Like now.

Cain's features were ashen, somehow he managed to drag his gaze away from Lisa Smith who was looking embarrassed, sensing yet another confrontation between these two men. Last time it had been Cling, now it was . . .

'*Kemp*!'

'The Weatherbys are getting impatient, I couldn't keep them waiting any longer.' The chief cashier gave the customers an unrivalled service, in the eyes of many of them he was the boss here.

'You knock and wait before you enter my office!'

'Fair enough if there's no customers waiting. Are you going to sign these or shall I tell the Weatherbys you can't be bothered?'

For one moment Ed thought that he was going to strike the older man. His fists balled, somehow he stopped himself. A moment's silence, an intake of breath that was held, expelled. He closed his eyes, opened them again. Charlie Kemp was still holding those papers out towards him.

'Give them to me!' Cain snatched them, scribbled a couple of illegible signatures, thrust them back.

'Thank you.'

'Mr Kemp.'

Kemp turned back expectantly. 'Yes?'

‘There’s a matter of a cash shortage on the counter whilst I’ve been away. Sixty pounds short on number seven till. As chief cashier that’s your responsibility.’

‘I mustn’t keep the Weatherbys waiting a minute longer.’ Charlie Kemp quickened his pace towards the door, outspread feet that would have been comical in any other situation. ‘Call me when you’ve got a moment and I’ll go through the respective cashier’s till book with you.’ The door clicked softly shut behind him.

‘Are you sure you’re all right, Mr Cain?’ Lisa’s voice trembled, she prayed that there was no more dictation, that she could return to her typewriter in the outer office. The manager wasn’t well, he had come back to work too soon.

‘I’m all right.’ Cain nodded to her. ‘That will be all for now, thank you.’

Alone again. Sweating. Trembling. So close, he had an awful lot to thank Kemp for even if he hated the old bugger. But it hadn’t solved the problem, only postponed it. Which was why he tidied his desk, locked the drawers and let himself out into the banking hall. Nobody questioned the comings and goings when you were at managerial level, you could even take whole days off on supposedly legitimate business without having to account for your time. Maybe he was going out to do some shopping, or taking an early lunch. It was nobody’s business except his own.

And Ed Cain knew where he was going, what he had to do to satisfy the lust which obsessed his mind and body.

The station car park was deserted which made Ed Cain feel all the more conspicuous. Row after row of parked cars, the selfish bastards had even pinched the disabled bays. He glanced about him, a sudden feeling of guilt, but nobody was watching him as he headed towards the row of public phone boxes.

From a distance he saw the stick-on labels, the scrawled telephone numbers adorning the insides of the booths, even on the brick pillars under the awning, a kind of vice supermarket. Pain or pleasure, at my leisure. Small and pretty. Dusky beauty. Blonde bombshell. A host of numbers to ring. After dark the vice girls crawled here from their sleazy brothels and advertised their wares. Either the telephone company or the railway sent a man to clean the stickers off the next day. Perhaps today he was busy or sick. Ed pulled open a heavy glass door, squeezed into the cubicle. The finger that dialled was shaking; he half-hoped that there would be no reply, but the call was answered almost immediately. Directions and an address; the fee was thirty pounds and a condom was compulsory.

The girl called herself Suzy and could not have been more than twenty. She was attractive in a slovenly sort of way, Ed decided, but when the urge was on you this strong you didn't really care. Dark haired; like Judy. Or Lisa Smith.

He followed her upstairs into a small bedroom where a soiled blanket was spread over the bed in the corner. No preliminaries, Suzy was stripping off and expected him to do likewise. Then she rummaged in a drawer, produced a small foil packet and sat beside him on the edge of the bed.

Her breath smelled of nicotine and something else which he did not recognize. Probably drugs.

'Here, let me,' she laughed, tore the foil and leaned across him with the condom between her fingers. 'Christ, you're desperate for it, aren't you?'

That was when he pushed her roughly back on to

the bed, grabbed her breasts as he rolled on top of her.

'Hey, hang on!' There was a vestige of fear in her voice. 'You've got to wear that . . . '

Suzy's words died away as his fingers closed over her throat and in the same movement penetrated her. She writhed and bucked under him and he grunted his pleasure as he bore hard down on her. Her arms flailed, her legs were kicking wildly and there was sheer terror on her contorted face.

It was during those few minutes of unbelievable pleasure that Ed Cain shed everything except his physical body and its pulsing sensations. It was as though he was hovering above the bed looking down on the mating, apart from it and yet enjoying its pleasures. He saw his own scarred form, fired with a strength that belied those weeks of slow recovery, steel fingers that squeezed the prostitute's frail neck so that her flesh purpled and her eyes stood out like inflated air bubbles.

Her struggles grew more feeble by the second, his powerful thrustings faster and faster. Now her eyes were closed, her limbs were draped limply on the stained blanket. A sharp sour smell permeated his nostrils but it only added fervour to his efforts. His vision was blurred, he was not sure whether he was coupled with the unconscious girl or merely a masturbating spectator. It did not matter; nothing else mattered.

His climax was an explosion that rippled his sweaty body, had him grunting in the manner of a savage beast. He felt his strength beginning to ebb from him as he sank down on to the lifeless form beneath him. Drained, totally spent, the desire to sleep was too strong to resist.

Sometime later, the cheap clock on the dresser

showed 4.30 pm; he stirred. His first thought was that the girl lying beneath him was Judy; it came as a shock when he realized that it was not his wife. Backing off her, then stark terror as his memory began to function.

He tried to revive Suzy but eventually accepted that she was dead. A moment of blind panic but he fought it off. It could have been Judy, or Lisa Smith, lying there; he was fortunate in that respect.

Murderer!

He dressed with difficulty because his hands shook uncontrollably but in the end he managed it, checked to ensure that he had not dropped any damning evidence. He was calmer now. It was just a call girl, it would probably make the newspapers but not the headlines. Prostitutes were murdered frequently, it was a job hazard for them. They were expendable in this modern society.

He eased open the front door of the council flat, peered out. Some children were playing on the grass outside but there was nobody else in sight. He let himself out, began to walk swiftly away.

Ed Cain was within a hundred yards of the close, the cathedral spires towering up into the cloudless sky above him, when he slowed his walk; stopped. He saw again the naked dead hooker, her sprawled body but not her features. She could have been anybody, his lust respected no social barriers. It was satisfied now, but for how long?

It would return, that was a certainty, and he would be powerless to resist it. But the most terrifying prospect of all was who would be his next victim.

Somewhere in the furthermost reaches of his mind he heard laughter, an insane mocking that echoed and vibrated, had him clasping his hands over his ears in a futile attempt to shut it out. Then came a headache of migraine proportions that staggered him, tunnelled his vision so that it was with difficulty that he managed to find the driveway that led to number nineteen. Judy was waiting for him, her features strained with anxiety, and he collapsed into her arms and wished that he could tell her how sorry he was that he had not died on that fateful March evening.

Instead, by some terrible miracle, he had been spared so that others would die. In the distance he was aware of wailing sirens, police or ambulance, he did not know which. A kind of continuation of that inner laughter, a sound of madness and death of which he had become the focal point.

CHAPTER FIVE

'It was damned stupid going back to work,' Judy handed Ed a cup of tea, noted how strained, how ill he looked. 'I thought Doctor Lawson was being optimistic, you should have waited another month at least. Well, you can stay at home for a bit now.'

'No,' he shook his head. 'I'm okay, I'll be fine by morning.'

'You're always worse in the morning,' she eyed him carefully, hesitated, and then said, 'I think you should sleep upstairs with me tonight. There's no reason for you to sleep downstairs now.'

'All right.' His recent aggressiveness, moodiness, seemed to have gone, he was just weak and very tired. 'I'll sleep upstairs and, as a compromise, I won't go into the office tomorrow. But I have to go in at the end of the week because I have an important engagement with a customer.'

'We'll see how you are in a couple of days.' There was relief in her voice. Even if Ed didn't look well at least he seemed more . . . human. In a roundabout sort of way today had done him good but it might be dangerous to push it too far. Richard was upstairs in his room and he hadn't got his stereo blaring out; Becky was doing her homework. A lull in the storm.

Except for Cling, the dog was cowering beneath the kitchen table and from time to time he gave a low growl. That was the most disconcerting factor of all. You could kid yourself that everything was fine but the labrador reminded you constantly that it wasn't.

Ed was back on the life-support machine. He was aware of the wires attached to his body, the bright lights which dazzled him even with his eyes closed. People were moving about, conversing in hushed tones, a hub-bub of whispered conversation.

'He won't make it!'

I will. I did before and I will again. A sense of weightlessness, so familiar recently and he braced himself for the inevitable. Any second his astral body would part from his physical one, floating gently upwards. Vertigo at first, then fighting against that magnetic pull that threatened to whisk him away from life on earth. An exhausting battle but he would win and then return to his flesh and blood. Any second now . . .

But this time it did not happen. At least, not in the usual way. There was no movement within him, just a slight stirring as though this time his spirit was determined to remain with him. Restless; he wanted to open his eyes but the lids were too heavy and he did not have the strength. It was frightening in a way because it was not following the pattern of recent months.

What the hell was going on? Movements around him but somehow they were not reminiscent of the medical team, in fact those low voices had ceased altogether and it was as though the surgeons had gone away and left him. He's dead, we can't do any more for him.

No, please!

Something brushed against him, so soft and gentle that it might have been a gust of wind through an open window. So *icy*. He shivered and now his fear was mounting. What was it that was touching him?

He felt it on his eyelids, exerted what strength remained in his weakened body to keep them closed. I don't want to see it whatever it is!

It was close to his nostrils now, he could smell it, a strong fetid odour that had no place in this hospital theatre where everything smelled of cleanliness. Suffocating, holding his breath.

Then he tasted it, retched and thought he might throw up, might drown in his own vomit. Its cold foulness was on his lips, stagnant sewer gas trying to gain entrance, brushing to and fro. He sensed an anger, a frustration.

Oh, my God, whatever it is it's trying to find a way inside me!

Had he been able he would have clasped his hands over his ears, anticipated its presence there before it stroked a lobe. *And he could hear it, a rushing sound that reminded him of a roaring mountain torrent, foaming and seething, icy from the snow capped peaks high above. And then he heard the laughter, that same maniacal cackling that had stopped him in his tracks a short time ago. Peals of hideous mirthlessness, frenzied insanity.*

He thought it had left him, was surprised that it had not entered him by way of his unprotected ears. Then he felt it again, an obscene touch on the lower regions of his body. No, not *there*!

An unholy invisible pervert, it played with him as if trying to arouse him, a thing of filth and degradation attempting to seduce him. Fighting it with every vestige of willpower he could muster, angering it so that it slid round and tried to prise his buttocks apart.

Finally he knew that it was inside him, had

breached his frail defences, had been taunting him from the beginning. He felt himself tensing, would have screamed hysterically had his vocal chords been functioning. A feeling of fullness, distended bowels that were unable to relieve themselves. A bloated stomach, a tautness around his chest as though he suffered a bout of chronic indigestion. But the physical sensations were as nothing compared with the madness that seized his distraught mind.

An arousement, an urge to kill. He saw again Suzy's limp body, the neck blue and swollen, lusted for her. An insatiable urge that was driving him mad because he was unable to fulful his carnal desires. Writhing within himself, aware that his muscles remained flaccid and useless, a torment that was eating him up and throughout that laughter mocked him.

Whereas previously he had always returned to possess his own body it had now been taken by an unknown unseen entity that controlled it.

In his tortured brain he was screaming at it to be gone, succumbing to it. Shuddering, alive again with an alien unholy power.

And then, in the midst of Ed's agony, the surgeons were back. He was aware of human hands grasping him, shaking him, a voice that was strangely familiar.

'Ed! Ed, wake up!'

Struggling to surface through an opaqueness beyond which there was blinding light. A shapelessness which merged into human features and became recognizable. *Judy*!

'You've had a nightmare.' She stroked him gently. 'It was a bad one.'

He lay there staring at her, saw her slim body through the crumpled negligé, feared lest he might lust for it. But he only felt weak, drained mentally and physically, glanced around the bedroom in case that awful thing was still there.

'Just a bad dream,' he smiled weakly.

'Like you have most nights,' she pressed her cheek against his own and he felt the wetness of her tears. 'Which is why you've been sleeping downstairs all these weeks in case you disturbed me?'

He wanted to tell her everything. Maybe twenty-four hours ago he would have done so in a similar situation. But it was too late now, after Suzy. He lay back, closed his eyes. Whatever it was that had entered him, it was gone now. But he knew it would be back.

And downstairs Cling was barking.

CHAPTER SIX

'I really don't think you're ready to play golf yet,' there was a note of resignation in Judy Cain's voice; she knew she had no chance of stopping her husband from doing anything he was determined to do. A protest really, nothing more.

'The physio said I should take up a sport,' Ed picked up his bag of golf clubs. 'Not that I'm that keen on golf, it's a social thing really. When I get to fifty I'll take up bowls. If you don't mix, you don't get the business, other banks are waiting like vultures to snap it up.' Which was true. Golf was prestigious, a status symbol. You mingled with executives on the course and in the clubhouse afterwards, got one move ahead of your rivals. Ed wasn't particularly keen on golf, at times he found it rather boring. As a bank manager you learned certain tactics; you had to be good enough not to make a fool of yourself whilst at the same time everybody loved to beat their bank manager. Being a good marginal loser was the secret, let your opponent think he had just pipped you. And as a bonus he would stand you a round of over-priced drinks later.

Judy followed him out to the car. Another Volvo, the insurance company hadn't haggled and it had been delivered last week.

'Are you sure you don't want me to drive you, Ed?' Now that was a damnfool question to ask, it had slipped out.

'I'll be fine.' He didn't snap at her, kissed her on the cheek.

She tried to tell herself that everything was returning to normal. Maybe that nightmare had been the last hurdle. She glanced quickly behind her, saw Cling standing in the hallway watching. His hackles were up, there was probably a low rumbling growl in his throat. Stupid bloody dog! She watched Ed drive away, went back indoors. Today was yet another milestone, her husband was back behind the wheel. He'd be all right, but she would be on edge waiting for him to come home. Thank goodness that extension at the bishop's palace was completed, at least there would be no more cement-mixers trundling in and out of the close.

She wanted to get back to her decorating, the spare bedroom was still in a state of chaos from last March. Today, she told herself yet again, was the day when life returned to normal.

She stroked Cling and he wagged his tail. It really was time he accepted the fact that his master was home again and not some stand-in stranger.

All the same, she was grateful for Cling's company when she was alone in the house. The police were still hunting that prostitute's murderer, they had warned all women in the city not to go out alone after dark. Judy shrugged, after all this was a cathedral close, not some red light area and call girls were always at risk. Nevertheless, there was always a lurking fear at the back of your mind.

Ed Cain laughed softly to himself, flipped through a typewritten document that had the Regional Head

Office rubber stamp on every page. Cutler's application for an overdraft had been turned down. The bank weren't taking any chances, they were cutting their losses and running.

Ed stuffed the papers into a drawer. His eyes narrowed; they were still going to play golf. And celebrate.

The golf course was on the outskirts of the city, bordering an area of common land. The club was an exclusive one, there was a waiting list, you needed recommendations as well as status. Unless you were a bank manager. Or a slippery company director who knew how to manipulate people as well as company law.

'Good morning, Ed!' Cutler was dressed in flannels and a blazer which sported a public school badge.

Probably acquired by devious means, Ed did his best to smile, or else just a straightforward bloody fake. The other looked a prig, a real wanker.

'Any news?' Cutler's anxiety showed. He had phoned the bank earlier in the morning but Ed had instructed the telephonist to say that the manager was in a meeting. No way was he going to spoil the party.

'Fine. No problems.'

Relief showed on John Cutler's fleshy features, it had been a nail-biting three days. 'I thought they would snap it up.' In an instant he was suave and confident again. 'It's a real winner, I promise you that, Ed. Your own car phone for fifty quid, how to influence your friends and business acquaintances in one complete package, spare tapes included!' He laughed. It sounded juvenile. 'You should get one yourself, the *real* thing, I mean. Tell you what, I'll do you a generous discount on the latest model. If you don't use it for anything else you can always call the missus up from the motorway to check that your grub will be on the table when you get home.'

'I'll think about it,' Ed tried to keep the contempt out of his voice.

'You do that. My goodness, there's a lot of folks on the course for a Friday. Not that I've ever played on a Friday before. What's it to be, nine holes?'

'Suits me.'

'Splendid fellow,' he was practising his public school accent again. 'And then it's back to celebrate. I reckon this calls for the old champers, eh?'

Ed forced another smile. This prick was getting on his nerves. But not for much longer. He felt his pulses begin to race. 'Come on, we'd better get started or we'll be here till dark.'

The golf course was meticulously maintained, clumps of rough dotting its mown grass. Grass-hoppers were chirping, they grated on Ed's nerves.

'You tee-off?' Cutler giggled. 'Sounds rude, doesn't it?'

Ed hit a long ball, watched it bounce and roll towards a clump of rough. His keen eyes noted the couple on the next hole, a retired colonel, Ed couldn't remember his name, and a grey-haired woman wearing a tweed skirt in spite of the heat. They were busy searching for a lost ball.

Cutler sliced his stroke, skewed the ball thirty yards to his left. One would need to play very badly, below novice standard, to let him win, the banker thought wryly. But today there was only going to be one winner.

'A host of orders have come in since we last talked.' It was evident that the game itself was of no interest to Cutler. 'We're going to have to go full steam ahead to cope with production. Before long everybody will have a dummy car phone and they'll all be kidding one another. We'll soon pay that overdraft off, you'll see.'

'And your creditors?'

'Of course.' The smile disappeared momentarily from the other's sweat-streaked features. 'I told you they would be paid out in full. The bank, too.'

Ed stubbed his ball, sent a chunk of turf in the wake of the mishit ball. 'Damn it!' His clumsy swing was true, on target for that sloping bank of thick wild willow herb and lush bracken. The ball bobbled, disappeared from view.

'Off form, are we?' Exuberance rather than a deliberate taunt.

Ed's knuckles whitened around his club. He turned away so that his companion could not see his expression. 'I've been ill since March, this is my first outing.' He didn't have to excuse his play, it came instinctively. But ultimately it would not matter.

There was an added arrogance about John Cutler, a swagger as he followed Ed across to the rough. Not only had he talked the bank into lending him more money for his latest enterprise but it was on the cards that he was going to show this whizz-kid manager a thing or two about golf. Maybe even flog him a car phone as a bonus.

Ed climbed down the sloping bank, spotted his ball almost immediately atop a clump of springy grass, set up as though Fate had ordained it. He pursed his lips, saw his companion standing on the rise above him.

'Found it?' Cutler was staring in the opposite direction, watching that elderly couple.

Ed Cain looked up. There would never be another God-given opportunity like this if they went the full eighteen holes. He did not reply, the other wasn't listening, anyway. He lifted his club, saw the bulky outline above him against the bright sunlight, swung at the perching ball with every vestige of strength he could muster.

A sharp click, the ball was a streak of scintillating white; a lethal missile.

A sickening thud.

For a moment Ed thought that he had missed. Cutler was still in that same position of relaxed obesity, stomach protruding over the waistband of his ill-fitting grey flannel trousers, blazer buttons taking the strain, leaning on his golf club as if it was a shooting stick. Possibly the latter kept him upright for those agonizing seconds during which Cain rushed up the incline, his heart pounding wildly.

Then Cutler moved, a lurch that swung him round to face his attacker and the bank manager gave an involuntary grunt of satisfaction. The businessman's features came into view and for a fleeting moment Cain thought that the other had developed an additional eye. Between the two orbs protruded what appeared to be a third, several times larger and starkly white, fixed unerringly, accusingly, on the smaller man. It was encased in a crimson rim that widened and oozed twin trickles down the sides of the upturned nose. Then, slowly, sedately, John Cutler sank down on to the turf, limbs spreading out in a posture of relaxation, rolled over as if it was his intention to sleep in the heat of the day.

Except that he was dead, killed instantaneously, deliberately, by a golf ball precision-driven with the force of a rocket launcher.

Cain stood there, had to check an almost overpowering impulse to rush forward and use his golf club to smash that head into an unrecognizable scarlet mulch. He saw the blood, smelled it with flared nostrils and again he heard that manic laughter inside himself. Shrill peals of crazed triumph. So easy. So bloody easy!

He dropped his club, it was too much of a temptation, took a step forward and had to stop himself forcibly. The bastard's dead, he never even knew what hit him!

Ed thought that he was going to faint; his eyesight blurred, he was aware of the sweat on his body dampening his shirt and trousers. Fighting for cohesion because this was only the beginning. He could not run and leave John Cutler the way he had left that whore.

Taking deliberate deep breaths, expelling them slowly, getting himself under control. And only when his breathing had returned to normal and his heartbeat had slowed did he walk out into the open.

The colonel and his wife were hunting for another missing golf ball in the undergrowth some distance away. Cain cupped his hands around his mouth, knew that the cry had to be authentic; a hint of panic, the right degree of helplessness. When he shouted he thought it came out right and by the time the others had joined him he was on his hands and knees beside the corpse going through the motions of massaging the dead heart.

The woman gave a piercing shriek and collapsed in a faint, to lie there unheeded as her husband peered forward, pushed his glasses up on to his forehead. His hooked nose twitched, he stared in hopeful disbelief at the scene before him.

'I say,' he lisped and dribbled frothy spittle from the corner of his mouth. 'Good gracious, the poor fellow looks in a bad way. We need help . . . '

Cain continued to kneel there, heard others coming, golfers who had sensed from a distance that something was wrong. A cluster of bodies, hustling one another in gruesome curiosity as much as a desire to be of assistance. Muttered shocked oaths, the unconscious colonel's wife went unnoticed.

For Ed it was an act that came naturally. Only he

had known the moment he drove that ball where it would land; nobody could prove otherwise. He might even kid himself that it had been an accident after all.

Except that he knew it wasn't and he did not want to believe that it could have been. Because his skin was goosepimpling and beneath it an unrelenting euphoria pumped the adrenalin.

He was still sitting there apparently in a shocked daze when the ambulance came bumping its way across the golf course and he offered no objection when it was suggested that he might be in need of sedation.

CHAPTER SEVEN

The city's annual Festival was due to begin the following week. A fortnight devoted to tourism, shop-keepers praying for fine weather and hoping for a bonanza, the fair was back and looking to recoup the losses it had sustained over a wet Whitsuntide. Banners and buntings decorating the street, a multitude of cheap souvenirs on display everywhere. Even a special pull-out full-colour supplement in the local newspaper which relegated the sensational head-line of BANK MANAGER KILLS COMPANY DIRECTOR to the second page.

The coroner's court had returned a verdict of acci-dental death on John Cutler, there was no evidence to suggest otherwise. A tragic accident that could have happened to anyone. Just one of those things.

Ed Cain had taken a few days off work, he was relieved to discover that he was genuinely suffering from shock. Maybe the tranquillizers had helped.

He experienced a period of subdued depression interspersed with bouts of concealed euphoria because he seemed almost *normal.* A nagging fear that the police might arrive and charge him with Suzy's murder, a state of mind that bordered on guilt, and that was a good sign. No more insane laughter inside his head, it had probably been tinnitus, doubtless a side effect of his accident or even a build-up of ear wax. He delved deeply into his ears with cotton buds and found some wax. Next week he would make an appointment with Graham Lawson and have his ears syringed. He liked Lawson, their relationship had stretched to an occasional fishing expedition on the river bank.

Yes, Ed told himself, he should take up fishing again, it was so relaxing. It was a sport where you didn't run the risk of killing somebody. And mostly you returned the fish you caught back to the water.

He almost felt at peace with the world. If only that bloody dog would stop cringing under the table and growling at him he could safely assume that he was over it. Whatever *it* was.

On the Thursday night he made love to Judy. Or, rather, she seduced him. Her tiny slim fingers found him under the bedsheets, began rubbing in an attempt to arouse him. It wasn't easy, he feared what an erection might bring. In his mind he saw that dingy whore's room with the soiled blanket covering the bed, Suzy sprawled lewdly, lifelessly. He fought to dispel the vision; it was just a bad dream, it had not really happened. Cutler's death had been an accident, really. And that laughter *was* caused by wax in his ears.

Judy flung the sheets back and straddled him, and as they met he found she was soft and wet, the way she always was before . . . his accident. Loving, not lusting, taking their time, pausing when they were both close and trying to delay their orgasms. Finally a skilful combined climax that was the result of experience in marital love-making, afterwards lying in an embrace and kissing gently until they fell asleep.

Normality *was* returning.

He decided not to go into the bank on Friday. A

kind of lethargy that might be a staying-at-home syndrome developing after his lengthy recuperation. Relaxed, content to sit about in the house or lie on the lawn in the summer sunshine. Damn Cling, he's the only one that's spoiling all this.

After a salad lunch in the shade of the weeping willow, Judy came out from the kitchen to inform him that Houghton was on the phone. Ed felt himself tense, shrugged off a feeling of guilt like he used to get when he was a boy and feigned illness to stop off school.

'What the hell's he want?' Ed grunted, struggling up into a sitting position, brushing grass clippings off his bare torso.

'How do you expect me to know?' Judy retorted. 'He's not likely to tell me, is he?'

'Sorry to disturb you, sir,' Houghton sounded apprehensive, his usual subservient manner when speaking to authority. 'Are you feeling better, sir?'

'Yes, thanks, I shall be back in the office on Monday.' Get on with it, you creep, get to the point. 'What's the problem?'

'No problem, sir,' Houghton hastened to assure him. 'Everything's ticking over nicely. I just rang to let you know that Canon Holland called in at lunch-time to leave two complimentary tickets for yourself and your wife for the Festival opening service in the cathedral on Sunday. I wondered if you felt well enough to go, the bank usually likes to be represented. If you don't feel well enough . . . '

'We'll go,' Ed snapped. 'Get the messenger to drop the tickets in here when he goes out on his afternoon round.' He dropped the receiver back on its cradle and under his breath said, 'Fuck him!'

'Who?' Judy was coming down the stairs. Four-letter words left her unmoved. Richard used them repeatedly, claimed that he had picked them up at his primary school. More likely he had learned them from his father.

'Canon bloody Holland.' Ed jerked his head in the direction of the neighbouring house, a nineteenth century property with its long herbaceous garden bordering their own. 'The bugger has two tickets for the bank manager and his wife. Because the stipendary accounts are with my branch, not because I'm his next-door neighbour, I can assure you. A walk of twenty yards and he could have popped them through *our* letter-box. Oh, no, he shuffles all the way into town to take them into the bank! Stupid fucker!' There was venom in his voice now.

'What do you expect?' She noted with some concern that twin red spots had appeared on her husband's cheeks, he might fly into another of those uncontrollable rages. It was a frightening prospect. 'He might have meant to deliver them here but found he still had them in his pocket when he went to the bank.' An explanation off the top of her head, she had to defuse this situation.

'That's a bloody laugh!' Ed's voice was raised, his head was thrust forward angrily. 'If that had happened then any *normal* person would have delivered them on the way home. No, the bastard is still seething because I won't have the hedge cut lower so that he can play Peeping Tom when you sunbathe in the nude. The fucker's miffed because he can't drool over your tits and cunt!'

'Ed, please!'

'It's a fact,' he clenched his fists until the knuckles whitened. 'Ever since we had those few words last autumn I've been expecting a letter from the dean and chapter *ordering* me to cut the fucking hedge. But I won't and Christ help anybody who tries to behind my back. *I'll fucking kill them with my own hands!*'

'All right, we won't have the hedge cut and that's final, I'm with you all the way on that.'

'But we're going to the Festival service.' Aggression; don't you bloody well dare say we're not!

'Of course, we are, I'm looking forward to it.' Which was a lie. She managed to smile, hoped that he did not notice how she was trembling.

Ed seemed to relax, went back out into the garden. He felt weak, shaken; it didn't do you any good working yourself up like that. But he couldn't stop himself.

Suddenly he was clasping his hands to his ears, thought that that terrible laughter was beginning again. But it was only Cling growling his dissent because he was forced to vacate the position he had taken up in the shade of the willow during his master's brief absence.

It seemed that the world and his wife had converged on the city that sunny June morning. All the official car parks were full by 9 am and the side streets were lined with cars. The centre itself had been cordoned off as had the cathedral close, and regular and special police patrolled the pavements; today would be relatively peaceful but from tomorrow onwards the pubs would be open all day and that always led to trouble. Like fourteen carnival days without a break.

Admission to the cathedral was by ticket only, the privileged and those who had applied for seats months ago. Crowds thronged the spacious lawns outside, mostly foreigners here to witness a spectacular English ceremony.

Ed watched from the bedroom window as he dressed in a sombre but fashionable suit. People milled, tried to find a space for a picnic breakfast; already a carpet of unsightly litter was beginning to accumulate, it would be the same in every street.

'All they achieve is to turn the place into a dustbin,' he sensed his depression returning, wished that he had told Houghton to take his missus to the service. But it was too late now.

'We pay our rates to have it all cleaned up.' Judy was in bra and pants reaching a navy blue dress out of the wardrobe. 'We'd better get a move on, we don't want to be late. The procession starts from the palace in quarter of an hour.'

Ed stared out of the window, did not reply. He felt himself tensing as he saw the ambulance carefully pushing its way through the crowds, a policeman moving people back on to the pavement. It stopped by the raised ramp leading to the entrance to the close.

The very place where it had parked whilst they had cut him out of the crushed Volvo that night. As if it had come back to claim him because he had cheated death.

'Ed, what is it?' Judy sensed that something was wrong even though his back was towards her. The rigidness of his body, the way he was breathing. 'Ed?'

He did not answer, just continued to stare fixedly out of the window. She moved across, saw his pallid, strained features, followed the direction of his staring, frightened eyes. And saw the ambulance.

'It's just on standby,' she swallowed, felt the memories of that March evening start to seep back into her system. 'A routine, they have ambulances where there are crowds, just as they have police. In case somebody faints in the heat or the crush.' Or gets killed.

'Yes,' he answered and with an effort turned away. He tensed, half-expected Cling to start barking downstairs. But the only sound was Becky's transistor radio crackling and grating tinnily in her room. 'We'd better get a move on, we don't want to be late.'

Police were clearing a path through the crowds from the palace entrance to the west doors of the cathedral. Already a cross-bearer was leading the choirboys out into the close, their red and white surplices in gaudy contrast to the black and white of the clergy; canons, prebendaries and then the bishop himself, tall and austere in his mauve raiments and mitre, bearing his mace. His very presence was awe-inspiring, reduced the clamour to a ripple of whispers like a calm sea lapping a distant shore.

Ed pushed his way through the mass of spectators, forged a path for Judy to follow. A verger on one of the side doors moved to bar his path, recognized him and stepped back.

Ed found his gaze drawn irresistibly upwards, a feeling as if somebody had called down to him in a hushed whisper. Stone figures, lifesize, a gallery of carvings; the Apostles, kings of England and a saint. All watching him with accusing stares. How dare you enter this holy place, you who are possessed with evil spirits! *Murderer*!

An urge to flee, he might have done so had not Judy been pushing him from behind, whispering, 'Go on, Ed, the procession's already on its way.'

Guilt. They *knew*, he could not deceive them and they were angered because he sought refuge in God's house with blood on his hands. He felt slightly faint, and as he glanced back he saw the ambulance. It had moved into the close, was waiting to take him away.

Then he was inside the cathedral, an awesome gloomy place where his footsteps echoed and an organ was playing softly somewhere. Heads turned in the pews in the main aisle, faces that were pale in the dim light yet their features were indistinguishable.

Watching him.

'Row forty-three, it's way up yet,' Judy whispered, pushed him gently.

His steps were unsteady, he thought he lurched, was unable to make out the numbers on the ends of the pews. The seated congregation were whispering, a rush of indistinguishable words but Ed knew what they were saying all right. '*That's him, the bank manager who killed a chap with a golf ball, claimed it was an accident. He murdered a whore, too!*'

'Here we are.' Judy caught his sleeve, pulled him back. 'Seats nine and ten.'

Which meant that those already seated on this side of the empty space in the middle had to hunch up to let them squeeze past; irritated by this disturbance, shadowy faces with disapproving expressions.

Ed sat down, closed his eyes briefly. It was cold in here, the sweat already chilling his flesh. He shivered. I ought not to have come, I should have left it to Houghton and his vinegary missus. He squinted through half-open eyelids, afraid because he sensed a hostility in the atmosphere. It's all in the mind, they can't know because they're all strangers. But those figures on the west front knew, all right!

He continued to sit there ill-at-ease, out of the corner of his eye saw Judy lean forward, rest her head on her hands. Praying, a custom when you entered a holy place. Maybe she was praying for him. He almost laughed aloud at the idea.

The organ was louder, rising to a crescendo. A kind of march like the entry of the gladiators into the arena. Heralding death. Ed remembered the ambulance again and wondered if it was still there. It was sure to be. Waiting. For him.

The procession glided wraithlike down the centre aisle, heads bowed when they came into view of the altar. Then they were filing off, the choir to its stalls, the clergy to their ornately carved chairs, the bishop to his oaken throne. Distant figures glimpsed through a forest of spectators who had paid for the privilege of viewing from afar whilst outside thousands sweltered in the hot sun and listened to a relayed broadcast of the proceedings.

An opening hymn, Ed vaguely recognized it but made no move to follow it on the service sheet. He glanced sideways at Judy, she was miming the words. In case anybody was watching her.

'Let us pray.'

At the sound of Canon Holland's voice, Ed made a futile attempt to curb his anger. This was a bad place to pump your adrenalin, like getting all steamed up in the car in a traffic queue. They were keeping the bishop until last, obviously, like the star performer at a pop concert. The tannoy was crackling, a bad connection somewhere, the words harsh and unintelligible. Which, Ed laughed silently, was fine because they were a load of shit, anyway.

He felt something pulling at him. Not Judy tugging at his sleeve to attract his attention, something that was not physical yet much more forceful. His heart missed a beat, a sense of dizziness. Vertigo; like looking down from a height . . . *and seeing your own body. Or else looking up, like he had wanted to do in that awful nightmare and was unable to, and seeing . . .*

A stone carving.

It was high up, way above the stained glass windows. He squinted, tried to make it out. Not a king. Nor an Apostle. Nor a saint. It was female.

A winged angel.

And it was watching him intently.

Curious rather than hostile as though it only partially recognized him. Haven't I seen you somewhere before? I'm sure I have.

The figure was caught in a shaft of bright sunlight. It was naked. A slim body, had a worn appearance that was nothing to do with the stone it was carved from, rather a posture of weariness, almost dejection. Perfectly proportioned, the nipples erect on the small breasts, the thighs slightly apart but the shadows hid that which Ed found himself searching for. She was teasing him.

He had to force himself to look at the head, and as his eyes alighted on those features he recoiled from the shockforce that came down at him. There was no mistaking that face, he wondered why he had not recognized it in the first place, it was as though it had undergone a sudden change, a sculpture that had become living flesh and blood.

It was Suzy up there, risen from her deathbed where he had left her and now her expression was hardening into one of recognition. Murdering bastard!

An address was coming over the tannoy, crackling words, fizzing as if the system might set on fire. Canon Holland was saying something; the dean and chapter's stooge, the front man. The fall guy. Ed was tense, standing, his whole body electrified with lust and anger. Anger at the canon, the dirty old bastard was talking about upright living, the hypocrite! Cut your hedge down so that I can get a hard-on watching your wife in the nude, Mr Cain. He's looking at you, Suzy.

But Suzy, for it surely was her high up there, had eyes only for Ed Cain. Contempt, malevolence. You murdered me, Ed!

Sure I did, and I'd do it again. He was aroused, trembling. If only I could get to you. Tell you what, *you* come down here to me.

Ed sensed something touching him. Judy's extended hand, her fingers gripping his sleeve, trying to pull him down into his seat. 'Ed,' a whisper, 'sit down!'

No, I can't. He shrugged her off but she caught hold of him again. A ripple of movement, heads were turned in his direction. What's up with that fellow? Sit down.

Ed felt the power of that stone carving up above which had suddenly come to life. A force that hit him like a laser beam, and with it came the beginning of his terror. *For that laughter was starting up inside his head again just when he thought he had overcome it.*

A maelstrom that sucked at him, a puppet at the mercy of a dark power, which had singled him out for vengeance. Her voice reached him, harsh and vibrant, drowning out Canon Holland's nasal tones. It most certainly was the whore, arisen from the grave, because he recognized her harsh accent, even harsher now with an uncontrolled fury. '*Worship me as you worship your God, Ed Cain. Remove your clothes and kneel before me. Naked!*'

Everything around him was a blur in this gloomy place. Faces that swam, merged into rippling paleness, expressions of surprise and indignation. And Judy was trying to pull him down, using both hands in her embarrassed desperation. 'Ed, for God's sake!'

'Let go of me, you bitch!' He struck out with the flat of his hand, felt it make solid contact with her cheek, a resounding crack as it jerked her head back, almost sent her sprawling across the knees of those seated beyond her. Gasps of shocked horror, that manic laughter was rising to fever pitch. Loudest of all was Suzy's screaming for him to unclothe himself and kneel before her. The congregation was muttering, 'That's him, the bank manager fellow who killed that guy with a golf ball and tried to fool everybody that it was an accident.'

Ed was tearing at his jacket, struggling to get his arms free, entangled in his frantic haste, swaying on his feet. An urge to grab for the erection inside his trousers because the feeling there was overpowering but his arms were trapped behind him. Now Judy was standing up, had hold of him, her distorted face smarting redly where he had hit her.

He heard her say, 'Oh, my God, he's taken leave of his senses!' And in the background Canon Holland droned on, tried to get his dreary message across. Cast off the mantle of unrighteousness and walk in the Path of God.

Eyes uplifted, Ed saw Suzy's contorted stone features, a harlot yelling for her client to unclothe himself and plead with her for the mercy she would not show. A sadist about to vent her wrath on a pervert who had angered her and was rendered helpless by his own compulsion. Mocking laughter vibrating inside him like a pending migraine.

That tightness was back in his chest, a torso-crushing vice and darkness hovered before his eyes. Blackness that was alive with lurking evil. I have to get out of here! There's an ambulance outside waiting for me but I'm not going back on that machine where that thing is waiting to claim me again.

He stumbled, lost his footing, slipped and fell, tumbling Judy with him. And somewhere close by he heard a hushed excited whisper. 'He's had a heart attack.'

Ed was still conscious, struggling only mentally now because his physical strength was ebbing fast. Hands were reaching out for him, he was powerless to resist as they dragged, half-lifted him, laid him on the cold marble of the aisle floor. His eyes flickered open, stared upwards, and he saw Suzy way up in the roof. She was smiling the way she had been when he first noticed her, just a stone angel with shadows cloaking her inhibitions.

The canon had not paused in his lengthy address, his voice now louder, clearer, as if the fault in the loudspeaker on that ornate pillar had somehow rectified itself. ' . . . walk in the valley of the shadow of death.' Gloating, you should have cut that hedge, Mr Cain, so that I could lust after your wife's body as you've lusted after my beautiful angel.

Fast authoritative footsteps that echoed purposefully, coming this way. Ed tried to turn his head but he could not move. A figure knelt over him, a head wearing a flat peaked cap came into his range of vision.

'Take it easy, pal, and let's have a look at you,' the ambulance man said. Judy's strained features shimmered in the background. She mimed something with trembling lips, dared not ask the question.

Ed was aware of a coldness, his sweat-soaked shirt chilling and causing him to shiver.

'I don't think it's anything serious, but I can't be sure.' There was relief in the uniformed man's voice as his gaze flicked from Judy to his companion. 'Probably the heat. Anyway, we'd better take him in, get him checked over.'

The other man had brought a stretcher, now they laid it out on the floor, lifted Ed gently on to it. 'Don't you worry yourself, mate, you'll be okay.'

Ed tried to speak but the words would not come, got caught up somewhere in his throat. People were leaning over their pews, straining to see. A breed that thrived on tragedy, an unexpected bonus, secretly willing it to be a heart attack. Don't disappoint us, mister.

A re-run of an old television programme, one you dimly remembered from years ago when you had an old ten-inch black and white. Ed saw the ambulance through a shimmering haze, backed up on to the ramp like a dog trying to mess on somebody's doorstep. Rear doors wide, another crowd pushing forward in the hope of catching a glimpse of that still figure on the stretcher. He *is* dead, isn't he?

The doors were closed, the engine purred into life. An ambulance man watching over him, the only thing that was different was that Judy was here this time. Thank God, it might have been Suzy.

The chest pains were gone along with the laughter. Out here it was all right, it was in there that the evil had lurked to take him. He tried to sit up but firm hands pushed him back.

'You lie back, pal. You'll be okay.'

But he knew he wouldn't. Because whatever it was that possessed him, had dragged him back from the grave that night, was still with him, no matter how he tried to convince himself that it was gone. This was just a reminder of how it had been that night and how it would be from now on.

CHAPTER EIGHT

Norma Pringle kept her curtains closed that Sunday morning when the city Festival opened. This was its third year and it angered her almost to the point of a tantrum. Whatever were the bishop, the dean and chapter and the city council thinking of, had they taken leave of their senses? They had lowered the dignity of the close almost to a level of blasphemy! Crowds were picnicking, scattering unsightly litter, young couples necking on the lawns, perhaps even going *further*; next thing the Whit fair would be setting up on these sacred grounds. Poor Peter was surely seething in his secluded grave at the far end beneath the horse chestnut trees with louts sitting on his tombstone!

She was trembling, her freckled face suffused with blood. How *dare* they! Well, she might not be able to stop this garish carnival but at least she could forbid people to sprawl all over her husband's grave. She peered from behind the curtains. Her view was obstructed by heads and shoulders, elbows propped on the sill. The crowd was three deep on the pavement, leaning up against *her* house.

'*Get away*!' She screamed hysterically, enforced her demand with a fierce tap on the window which threatened to crack the glass. '*Get away from my house, you scum!*'

Heads turned, a man wearing a green eye-shade grinned. But nobody moved.

Norma made a rush for the door, almost tripped over Pretty but for once she ignored the cat. As she pulled the door open a youth in jeans and a T-shirt almost fell inside, just managed to grab the post. She pushed him hard, sent him reeling into the throng which blocked her doorway.

'*Move away, the lot of you. Clear off!*'

'Gettin' yer knickers in a twist, ain't yuh?' A man with his bare stomach over-spilling baggy jeans laughed, cascading cigarette ash down his chest. 'Yer'll 'ave a bleedin' 'eart attack in a minute, missus!'

Guffaws from those around him, an angry retort from the youth who had been pushed. Surprised expressions, some of them backing off, stepping into the road. This woman was bloody crazy, swinging her arms, clenching her fists as if she was about to punch somebody. Her bosom heaved inside the frayed cardigan she had taken to wearing round the house and her ankle socks had slipped down to her scuffed slippers. Her face contorted with the rage that boiled inside her, momentarily deprived her of the power of speech.

'Damn you!' It was meant to be a shriek, came out as a shaky whisper. 'How . . . dare . . . you!'

A movement caught her eye, had her turning her head. A glimpse, no more, of a cat, one that was normally sluggish and contented but was now gifted with the speed and agility to slip through the forest of human legs which stretched right down to the close and into the road at the bottom.

'*Pretty*!' A despairing scream, Norma charged the

crowd, began to claw a path through it, fighting it with panic and hatred. 'Get out of my way! *Pretty, come back at once*!'

But Pretty did not come back; the huddled bodies swallowed her up. She might have gone on down towards the city centre or have headed east in the direction of the cathedral. Norma pushed, lowered her head, used it as a battering ram in her frenzy. A foot hooked around her own, caused her to stumble, and the crush miraculously parted so that she was able to fall to the ground. A solid thump that winded her, she tasted blood in her mouth, heard the mocking laughter. 'The old bat's fallen over!'

Scrambling up, heedless of her grazed and bleeding cheek and forehead, ignoring the jibes. Because all that mattered was Pretty's safety. Mouthing curses, moving sideways in a comical shoulder charge. 'My cat, give me my cat back, you rabble!'

'Stand back, please. Let the ambulance through!' A uniformed constable barred her path, she saw the masses parting. 'Madam, there's an ambulance trying to get past.'

Norma squeezed to one side then surged back behind the slow moving vehicle, let it cut the swathe she needed. She was stumbling, shook off the well-intended strong arm of the law. 'I'm . . . all right . . . my cat!'

She lost the ambulance, struggling with bodies that surged back on to the gravel track leading to the west doors of the cathedral. Wrestling with them once more, her hopelessness turning to panic as she seemed to be adrift in a human sea, becalmed and abandoned to drown. Finally she came upon the ambulance again.

It was backed right up to the cathedral's main doors and its crew were bearing a stretcher upon which a pallid-faced man stared at those who crowded round to watch. His glazed eyes came to rest on hers, and she started, forgot even Pretty for a second. The bank manager. Again! A moment of sadistic delight, staring. God never intended you to live in the close, Mister Cain. A money-lender defiling the Lord's temple. I hope you die this time!

'Move back, please!' The stretcher bearer bumped into her, which might have been intentional, and then the ambulance doors were closed and its engine was started up, the exhaust pumping out acrid fumes as a final deliberate insult to the woman who had impeded this mission of mercy.

Norma was wandering on in a daze. Her face smarted, her shoulder was hurting and she had twisted her ankle when she had stepped on an empty coke can. The crowds had dispersed now that the service was finished, just the day-trippers left to sunbathe on the trodden and littered spacious lawns. One couple were lying full-length, a youth stretched out in between a teenage girl's spread legs. Norma thought about kicking them, driving her slippered foot into this obscene simulation of the greatest gift bestowed upon mankind by God; except that her injured foot would not bear her weight and neither was it fit to kick with. Other couples were kissing unashamedly in public, one chap had his hand up his girlfriend's skirt.

Norma snorted, hurried on. The devil had, indeed, sent his minions to defile these sacred grounds. Pretty, where on earth was Pretty?

She saw the line of giant trees that marked the last resting place of Prebendary Peter Pringle. A cursory glance, there was nobody smooching on his grave; no, just litter left to remind her that it had not escaped this invasion by the ungodly. She would return later and clear it up. Pretty's safe return was her priority.

But nowhere was Pretty to be seen. Norma staggered on, exhausted, completed her perimeter tour of the cathedral close, dried bloody lips miming the cat's name. Over and over again until finally she arrived back at her own house.

The front door was wide open, those riff-raff might have rampaged through her rooms, ransacking them, stealing. But even that was of no consequence in comparison with her cat's safe return.

Norma's injuries were smarting, aching, she experienced an urge to burst into a flood of tears, crying her sorrow and anger together. But that would not help Pretty, she had to do something positive, like phoning the police. She phoned the police regularly, mostly to report motorists who had parked illegally in the close, or residents' children who sneaked the odd game of football on the lawns when they thought nobody was watching. She had reported the Reverend Williams' sons for building an igloo during that heavy snowfall in February. The constable who had called in answer to her complaint had seemed more irate with herself than with those abominable children.

All kinds of terrible things might have befallen poor Pretty. That ambulance might have run over her; rather that the bank manager had died because they had been held up for a few seconds. *Much* rather. And there were rumours that the Chinese restaurant were stealing cats to serve up in curries; the Indians might be doing the same. She hated coloureds, Peter had too, had once had a blazing row with the bishop over the appointment of a West Indian curate. Norma had admired her husband that day, more than at any other time, even if he did not fully understand politics the way she did.

Then she heard a faint mewing coming from the adjoining kitchen.

'Oh, my Pretty, darling!' Norma rushed forward, oblivious of her pain, the way her swollen ankle went over again; dropping to her hands and knees, scooping up the cat, clutching it to her, a sudden fear that it might be a mirage come to taunt her.

Pretty was real enough, a snarl as she tried to escape, dug her claws into Norma, raking her hand.

'Pretty!' It would have been a screech of anguish had not her voice been little more than a husky whisper. Holding the struggling feline, seeing the way its back leg hung limply, the fur matted with blood. 'Oh, my darling, you're *hurt*!'

With difficulty she managed to examine the injured limb. She did not think it was broken, just cut and bruised. 'Let Mummy put some TCP on it, my love, and then I think we'll have to call the vet. What happened?'

Pretty spat, tried to claw her mistress again as the liquid burned and smarted.

'There, there, darling.' Norma carried the cat over to its basket, laid it down gently. 'Did that ambulance run over you?' Peering as close as she dared. 'No, the leg would have been broken if that had happened. I think . . . yes, it's a . . . *bite*!'

A bite. The skin was lacerated where strong teeth had closed and held, crunched. Norma saw in her mind Pretty fleeing in terror pursued by . . . the bank manager's dog!

'That's it!' She straightened up, felt a little dizzy as her earlier rage flooded back to her tired brain and weakened body. 'It *couldn't* be any other dog. Well, I'm going to fix it. And *him*!' Except that she might be too late where Ed Cain was concerned; he had looked very ill on that stretcher. A heart-attack, without any doubt. 'I hope he's already dead!' She found some volume in her strained voice box. 'But that dog's going to be in trouble, rest assured of that, my pet. Now, let's ring the vet first . . . '

Simon Vine, the vet, was not prepared to make a 'purpose call' on a Sunday except in a case of dire emergency, so his wife informed Norma Pringle over the phone. Simon was down at the surgery right now, by coincidence, and if Norma took her cat there straight away then he would most certainly treat it. Otherwise there was the usual weekend surgery from 4 till 5.

Norma fumed, her voice became high-pitched and just when her anger was nearing its peak the line went dead and the dialling tone returned. Petra Vine was not prepared to be insulted when she was doing her utmost to be helpful.

Norma made a cradle out of her wicker shopping basket, wrapped Pretty in an old towel, and set out on the quarter of a mile walk to the vet's surgery, her ankle socks now grubby and steadily rumpling their way down under the soles of her feet. Her hair was awry and there were dried bloodstains on her face. Flushed with anger she ignored the curious stares of Festival revellers. That bank manager and his uncontrollable dog had a lot to answer for!

Vine was young and efficient, had only recently bought the practice from Archibald, the long-established city vet who had been a legend amongst animal lovers here since the war. Polite but non-communicative, it was not his way to discuss the intricacies of animal surgery with his clients. He ignored Norma's repeated questions, bathed the wound and applied a dressing.

'She'll be all right in a day or two.' He placed the cat back in the basket. 'That'll be two pounds fifty, please.'

Norma banged three coins loudly on the operating table. 'It's a bite, isn't it?' As if she was accusing the vet of having inflicted the wound with his own teeth.

'Yes,' he dropped the money into his pocket.

'A *labrador*'s bite!'

'I wouldn't swear to the breed,' Vine turned away, swilled his hands under a tap over the old stone sink. 'Too small for a lab, I'd say. More like a terrier, they have a reputation for chasing cats.'

'It's a labrador!' Norma Pringle picked up Pretty, strode to the door, slammed it as she went out.

She would telephone the Cain household first, she savoured her decision on the return walk. At least she would have the satisfaction of giving that stuck-up woman a piece of her mind, particularly if the banker had just passed away, which he surely had, judging by the look of him this morning. After that she would ring Canon Holland. If he didn't do something about having that dog removed from the close then she would go directly to the bishop. Failing that, his holiness, the Archbishop of Canterbury.

Damnation, Cain wasn't in the telephone directory. Her fingers shook as she dialled 192. Which town, please? A pause. Ed Cain was ex-directory, there was no way she was going to get through to him on the telephone. She thought about changing out of her comfortable old cardigan and slippers, decided against it. She wasn't dressing up for the likes of the Cains.

Somehow she resisted the temptation to kick the shiny new Volvo in the drive, scuffed up some gravel dust with her feet as she passed it, hoped it made a dirty film on the gleaming metalwork. Even as she rang the doorbell she heard a dog bark somewhere in the depths of number nineteen. Well, he wouldn't be barking for much longer!

'Can I help you?' The door opened silently, unexpectedly, and Norma recoiled at the sight of the bank manager standing there, wearing a blue short-sleeved shirt and drill trousers. He looked pale and tired but otherwise more or less normal. It was a set-back.

'I've come about that dog,' she snapped, feeling her skin goosepimple. 'It's time something was done about it!'

'Oh?' Ed Cain raised an eyebrow quizzically. Secretly he found himself agreeing with this ill-tempered old cow but he wasn't conceding any ground to *her*. Apparently she complained about everything and everybody. He heard Cling growling in the hallway behind him, presumed it was at himself.

'Your dog has bitten my cat!' Norma's bloodied face was scarlet, her fury mounting.

'When was that?' Ed stood there, hands in his pockets, eyes narrowing.

'This morning.'

'Then you've got the wrong dog. Cling has been in the garden all day, hasn't been out at the front at all and he can't get out of the rear garden because it has a fence all the way round.' (Not to mention the hedge.)

'*Your dog has bitten my cat*!' Her head was thrust forward, she was dribbling from her trembling lower lip.

'You're sick.' His voice was a low, barely audible hiss. 'You need psychiatric treatment.'

Norma sensed a further rush of adrenalin, a tightening around her chest that suddenly made breathing difficult. A wave of dizziness; she found herself clutching at the porch pillar for support. A moment in which she might have had a massive coronary. Or a stroke. Or just fainted. But she survived and was left standing there. When the crimson mist cleared away from in front of her eyes the door was closed and Ed Cain was gone back into the house. Alive.

Cling barked just once and then he was silent.

Canon Holland did not feel at all well. Today, the Festival Service, had all been too much for him. He was glad to be back in his widower's abode with the curtains drawn to keep out the hot sunshine. But even here there was no peace of mind for him.

Overweight and fleshy-faced, the heat did not suit him. The service this morning had been a nightmare, it was a miracle he had survived it. But it wasn't just the weather, nor the tension. God was punishing him for his wickedness and foolishness.

The canon had succumbed to the temptations of the flesh. He had prayed for forgiveness but it was too late. He tried to tell himself that it had all come about since dear Edith's death six years ago. But, in effect, it went back much further than that, to his days at theological college when a relationship which he had enjoyed with a young choir boy had been discovered. The principal had administered a severe warning, had taken it no further. Then Cecil Holland had met and married Edith and his physical needs had been fulfilled. He had erred just once during nearly half a century of marriage and he had not been found out. Except by God.

Then, just over a year ago, he had been approached by a young prostitute late one night just as he arrived back at the city station on the midnight inter-city from London. Such a pretty young girl; of course, if Edith had still been alive there was no way he would have gone back to Suzy's flat.

Her slim body was like a drug to which he became addicted. He returned to her the following week, and the week after that. A regular client who sneaked into that disreputable part of the city with a trilby hat pulled low over his face and wearing an ill-fitting suit that was a left over from the last jumble sale in aid of the cathedral restoration fund. Trembling in anticipation on the outward journey, overcome by guilt on the homeward one, asking the Lord to forgive him and he would promise to *try* not to fornicate again. Except that Cecil Holland knew only too well that he could never stop visiting Suzy.

Her death came as both a relief and a terrible shock. A drug addict suddenly deprived of his supply of cocaine, suffering the torments of his craving yet consoling himself that in time that need would no longer exist. Then came the most terrible, frightening guilt of all, one that allowed him no respite from his anguish, night or day, waking or sleeping.

Suzy had been murdered, strangled by a manic sex-killer. The police had launched a massive hunt for the murderer, a special headquarters had been set-up in the city police station, house-to-house enquiries were taking place. Of course, the detectives had not been to the close. Yet. But they were asking for Suzy's former clients to come forward. In confidence, naturally. They wanted to establish a list of the men who visited her, a process of elimination. And suppose, by some quirk of fate, they chanced upon information which led them to Canon Cecil Holland . . .

It was a terrifying thought, one that haunted him constantly. Then, this morning, he had suffered the most terrible ordeal during the opening service. He had attempted to purge himself in his address, he had warned against the temptations of evil and how none, whatever their status, were exempt from the guile of Satan. And as he spoke a strange and powerful sensation had engulfed him. It had begun with a persistent erection; his thoughts had strayed as he read from the typewritten sheet on the lectern in front of him. Erotic thoughts that refused to be dismissed; Judy Cain lying nude on the lawn next door. He had glimpsed her once, a gap in the lap fencing which was adjacent to a hole through the foliage of the hedge on the other side. A cramped position from which he peeped, could not discern the detail he craved but he saw enough to excite him, to make him do things to himself whilst he peeped. From then onwards he had done everything possible to try to make Ed Cain cut that hedge; a couple of feet off the top and the canon would have been able to observe the delectable lady sunbathing from the comfort of his bedroom, seated on a chair and watching from behind the curtain. A train of thought which led to . . .

Suzy.

He saw her in his mind as clearly as if she had been beside him in the flesh. Her supple body as she shed her clothing, teased him as she stripped, finally rolling back on to that soiled bedsheet, thighs wide and letting him feast his eyes upon that part of her body which he desired above all others. Touch it, Cecil; feel it, kiss it, do *anything* you like to it.

He could smell her body odours, her peppermint-flavoured breath, feel her slender fingers stroking his arousement, guiding it where he wanted it most. He closed his eyes, succumbed to her warm softness as he penetrated her, felt the beginning of his orgasm.

Suzy was here, in this holy place, she had come back to him from beyond the grave. And God would surely strike him down for his fornication.

Instead he struck down Ed Cain. Canon Holland was dimly aware of a commotion, a disturbance somewhere down the main aisle, screened from his blurred vision by obstructing pillars. Somehow he had managed to continue with his address, had read words that were meaningless, seemed to slur them. And only afterwards had he learned that it was the bank manager who had collapsed; a suspected heart-attack but it had turned out to be nothing more than a faint.

Now Cecil Holland was back in his house, plagued by guilt over what had happened to him and fear that a detective would turn up on his doorstep.

When the front doorbell rang his heart seemed to stop, then juddered back to an erratic fast beat which had the sweat streaming down his pallid rotund face. It took two more chimes to drag him from his arm-chair, his short legs quivering with every faltering step down the long hallway; cowering before the door, thick fingers almost incapable of securing a grip on the Yale knob.

I swear to God Almight that I never even knew the girl called Suzy, officer. Pulling the door open, leaning on it because without its support he would surely have fallen. Cringing, taking the name of his God in vain once more.

Then came overwhelming relief because it was Norma Pringle who stood there, wild-eyed and blood-smeared, her ankle socks now almost totally disappeared into her carpet slippers.

The Lord be praised! Holland's short legs threatened to buckle, he held on to the door whilst his strength returned, heard himself say, 'Norma, this is a most pleasant surprise. Do, please, come inside.'

Aware that he was standing back to let her pass, motioning to her to go on through into the library. Following her, his eyes centered on that bulky body and even in this moment of sheer relief he thought how positively attractive she was. Old Peter must have enjoyed himself, maybe that was what had killed him!

'Do sit down, Norma.' He gestured to one of the leather-covered armchairs, sank into the other himself. 'To what do I owe the pleasure of this visit which has brightened up a tired old man's dreary and lonely day?'

She regarded him fixedly, her eyes seemed to glaze over, then cleared; blazed with an anger that was almost frightening. Cecil Holland had known Norma and Peter ever since they had moved to the cathedral close, she could be fiery, threw tantrums which had become worse since her husband's death. In effect, she had made a recluse of herself in her grief, had never got over his death. She shut herself away and brooded, and that was dangerous. What she needed was another man, not a husband, that would be a traumatic experience for both of them, just a . . . boyfriend. A chap who dropped in occasionally and . . . no, he had promised God that from now on he would resist the temptations of the flesh.

'I've come to complain.' Her voice was terse, her lips were a thin bloodless line, her features darkly flushed around the bloodstains.

'Oh, dear!' He sensed a sinking feeling in the pit of his stomach, a twinge of guilt. 'I hope that I haven't . . . '

'It's *him*!' She jerked a thumb in the direction of the house next door. 'That bank manager and his bloody dog! Excuse my language, Cecil, but I've had about enough of both of them. I cannot for the life of me understand why the dean and chapter allow . . . *outsiders* to reside in cathedral dwellings when there is a shortage of clergy here.'

'I did raise an objection at the time.' That was a lie

and he hoped that God would overlook just a small indiscretion but it was necessary to placate the lady. 'Mine is only a small insignificant voice in the close hierarchy. I take your point and I agree entirely with you. I've been trying to get him to cut that dratted hedge, it's darkening these rooms, but the chap is stubborn and downright rude as well.'

'He collapsed in the cathedral this morning, but I see he's back home and apparently as right as rain.' There was no mistaking the disappointment in her voice.

'I think it must just have been a faint.'

'His dog chased and bit Pretty. I've only just got back from the vet's with her. And, in case you aren't aware, Cecil, it messes on the cathedral lawns. *And* on my doorstep!'

'I think the culprit for both offences is probably the Reverend Tate's Jack Russell terrier.' Holland found himself trying to imagine what Norma Pringle looked like without her clothes. 'They have been letting it run a bit too freely lately, I noticed it was loose in the crowd during the procession this morning which was probably when it chased your cat. Leave it to me, I'll have a quiet word in young Brian's ear. It's thoughtlessness, nothing more. I'm sure if I mention it to him he'll keep it shut up and . . .'

'It was the labrador!' Her head jutted forward, there was a wild, almost frightening glint in her protruding blue eyes.

'Oh . . . well . . . if you say so.' He found himself swallowing.

'I do! I saw it with my own eyes!' Almost a shout, gesticulating towards the Cains' house again. 'And I damned well want something done about it. Otherwise I shall confront the dean, the bishop if that doesn't work. And if he won't do anything then I shall send a letter to the Archbishop of Canterbury. Recorded delivery!'

'I'll see if I can get something done about it.' His mouth was very dry and he had to force another swallow before he could speak again. 'I'll tell you what, I'm going to ask the dean to write to Cain about the hedge and I'll get him to include a request that they keep that dog shut up.'

'And how long will it be before the letter is sent?'

'Oh . . . oh, sometime next week, I expect. It might have to wait until after the Festival is over . . . '

'I . . . want . . . it . . . sent . . . *right away*!'

Cecil Holland nodded puppet-like. 'Leave it to me, Norma. I'll . . . speak to him about it, remind him of the condition of his tenancy.' But it isn't the Cain's dog so it won't make any difference. They keep the animal shut up, anyway, so Norma will never know whether I've approached them or not. And, frankly, I don't care about the hedge any more, they can let it grow as high as they like. Because I've promised God I won't succumb to temptation again. He relaxed because he had side-stepped his responsibilities.

'I can hear that blasted dog barking now!' She inclined her head. 'Listen!'

'I can't hear anything, Norma. But I am a little deaf, you know.'

'It's stopped now.' She sat up straight and her expression softened a little. 'Cecil . . . ' her voice had dropped to a hoarse whisper. 'Don't you . . . don't you think there's something a bit strange about the bank manager?'

The canon hesitated before replying. 'I suppose it's because he's an outsider, come from the south, not one of us, if you see what I mean.'

'No, it isn't that.' It was the first time he had seen Norma Pringle nervous, whispering now so that he could barely hear her, as if she was afraid of being overheard by Ed Cain. And he had never known this fiery woman to be frightened of anybody. 'I read a lot, as you know,' she went on, 'and lately I've been studying alternative religion. Purely out of interest, I assure you. I have no intention of becoming *involved* in witchcraft or ancient rites.'

'Oh!' He started, felt suddenly embarrassed. No, more than that. Afraid! 'I always thought it was a load of mumbo-jumbo.'

'Well, I'm not so sure,' she leaned forward, wagged a finger. 'Cecil, I wouldn't say this to anyone else but . . . I'm sure in my own mind of one thing. That man is positively . . . *evil*!'

CHAPTER NINE

Ed Cain stood inside the closed front door, felt the adrenalin starting to pump, a raging torrent inside his own body that rushed and roared, pounded relentlessly at his senses. Deafened, he could not be sure whether there was laughter amidst the noise. Tensing, grinding his teeth, clenching his fists, swaying unsteadily because the hall was tilting from side to side, starting to gyrate. An instant uncontrollable rage, a boiling fury that would have been vented on the woman standing outside had he been capable of movement.

Norma Pringle. In his mind he saw every detail of her, that bloodied screwed-up face with its pouting venomous lips, the way she shouted irrationally. The old bag! The close boot, a ragbag asking to be screwed. Ed sensed his arousement, began flexing his fingers. Now he saw her naked, stomach wrinkled like a winter apple, the rolls of surplus fat, her crinkly thighs trembling. And that fleshy freckled neck with moles growing on the pressure points. Eyes blazing with lust and insanity, bulging as he squeezed; they would either pop out like corks or else burst. The flushed complexion now purple, swollen tongue strangling the screams, then her body limp and lifeless; himself a conqueror standing on that belly so that it ballooned like a faulty water-bed. A loud squelch as the stretched abdomen burst; he leaped away to avoid a rush of intestines that wriggled and squirmed like a nest of scarlet snakes. He was mouthing obscenities, a wild animal proclaiming its kill.

'Ed! Whatever's the matter?'

His racing pulses slowed, he turned slowly, saw Judy standing in the lounge doorway, hand clasped to her mouth. He was aware of Becky and Richard at the top of the stairs. And Cling growling throatily in the kitchen. Fuck you, dog, this is all your fault. He exhaled slowly.

'That bloody old bat!' A hiss through clenched teeth. 'She's complaining about . . . that dog!'

'Mrs Pringle complains about everybody and everything.' Judy approached her husband cautiously, rested her hand on his arm, felt how he shook. 'No point in getting yourself worked up over *her*, darling. Not after today.'

Today! The terror came back, stark and real. Lying there in the ambulance trying to plead with them not to put him on the life-support machine again. Just let me die! But he couldn't get the words out, they were fluttering frenziedly in his throat like a moth corked up in a bottle.

The journey to the hospital took an eternity. Traffic queues where there was nowhere for the cars to pull over to let the ambulance with its flashing blue light and wailing siren through. A bottleneck on the big island, that was predictable, a policeman on traffic control adding to the chaos.

'He seems . . . *all right*!' There was disbelief in the ambulance man's expression and voice as he checked Ed again. Judy joined him, scarcely daring even to hope.

Then the words escaped from Ed in a rush, 'I'm

okay, I tell you!' He felt almost normal, just sweaty and dishevelled, exhausted. Whatever had taken him during the service had gone. 'Look, I'm not going on that bloody life-support contraption and that's an order. Get it?'

'I don't think you'll need to, sir.' The uniformed attendant smiled weakly. 'But we'll have to get a doctor to check you over.'

'Just a faint, probably caused by the heat,' the young duty doctor examined Ed, turned to Judy. 'Call a taxi and take him home. He needs to rest, that's all.'

And Ed had still been resting when Norma Pringle had called. Now it had begun all over again.

'Ed, come and lie down on the sofa, please!' Judy was insistent, trying to pull him away from the door. 'That woman's sick, you don't want to end up like her.'

'The slag!' He grunted, allowed himself to be led back down the hall. Suddenly he looked up, saw the children staring down at him; Becky was close to tears. 'Whatever's the matter with you?'

Becky turned, ran for her room. They heard her starting to sob even before the door slammed shut.

'Ed, they're *concerned* about you. Don't you understand that?' Judy was fighting back her own tears.

But Ed did not understand. And just at that moment Cling showed himself in the kitchen doorway, low on his stomach, snarling; vicious. At bay but ready to flee if the occasion demanded.

Ed tensed, Judy felt his grip tightening over her hand with an intensity that almost made her cry out aloud; her husband's strength was unbelievable considering that he had been taken to hospital too weak to move only a matter of seven or eight hours ago. 'It's . . . all right, Ed. Relax.'

'It bloody isn't all right!' His reply was tinged with hate and fury, his eyes fixed on Cling who decided to back away to the safety of the kitchen, still growling. 'I'm pissed off with that dog. I'm going to phone the vet, have him put down!'

'No, Dad. Please!' Richard was gripping the stair rail, his features white.

'You can't do that, Ed.' Judy steered him towards the lounge. 'You're over-tired, weak from your ordeal. Come on, lie down and rest.' She kicked the door shut behind them. 'And I've got something to tell you.'

'What now?' He sat down on the sofa, unbuttoned his shirt. His chest was shiny with sweat. 'What have you got to tell me?'

'Richard has got a girlfriend,' Judy smiled. 'A really nice girl at school, Tracey Lee. She's sixteen but you know how mature Richard is. He's going back to her home tomorrow after school.'

'What!' Ed had seemed to be relaxing but suddenly he was sitting upright, his whole body taut, his expression almost frightening. 'No way, he's far too young. And, anyway, he's coming up to his GCSEs, he can't afford the distraction of some flighty little tart!'

'She isn't a tart!' Now it was Judy's turn to be angry. 'I've met her, she's very nice.'

'Sounds like it!' He sneered. 'A bloody sixteen-year-old cradle-snatching. She's just out to seduce him and the next thing she'll be wailing that she's in the bloody club!'

Judy checked an urge to slap his face. It might have sparked off a violent response. She had not forgotten that rape back in the spring, her terror because she thought he was going to strangle her. She never would forget it, at best she could push it to the back of her mind. Ed's expression was frightening, staring eyes that appeared to glaze over as if with cataracts, the veins on his neck and forehead corded. It wasn't doing him any good but there were times when a stand had to be made, and this was one of them.

'Richard's going to the Lees' tomorrow,' she spoke softly, firmly, 'whether *you* like it or not. And when Tracey comes here I don't want you making a scene. Got it?'

A moment of confrontation and then, much to Judy's relief and surprise, Ed nodded. 'Have it your own way and on your head be it. But don't get crying on my shoulder when that wench has a swelling in her belly!'

Judy turned her head away, didn't want him to see the way her eyes were glistening. Just when everything seemed to be getting back to normal they were now back to square one. Perhaps she could persuade Doctor Lawson to call and check him over because whatever anybody said this wasn't the man she had known prior to March.

'You'd better not go into work tomorrow,' she said, tried to change the subject. Not that I want you sitting around the house all day like a potential human time-bomb.

'I wasn't intending to,' Ed's voice was almost normal again. He had stretched back on the settee, picked up the newspaper, rustling through the pages as if trying to find where he had read to before this latest interruption. 'But we've got problems, that Pringle slag and that fat hypocrite next door.'

'For goodness sake don't start worrying about them.' Judy was at the door, wanted to go and comfort Becky. 'All we have to do is to ignore them and carry on with our own lives. Now, just you rest for a while, I've got things to do.'

But Ed's relaxed posture had been a sham, the

moment Judy was out of the room and the door had clicked softly shut, he was on his feet, staring out of the window across the close, tight-lipped and shaking. 'That poxy bitch,' he spoke under his breath, his eyes scanning the remnants of the Festival revellers in case she was out there. 'What she needs is a good fucking! And then . . . ' He laughed silently, and his gaze switched to the tall hedge that bordered the lawn. 'And bloody Canon Holland's got it coming to him, too!'

Controlled fury, and had it not been for the roaring in his ears he would have heard the labrador still growling in the kitchen.

Monday morning. Ed had slept late, he had not been disturbed by Judy rising at seven to get the children ready for school; he had not even heard them leave the house at 8.30 am. Clad in only his pyjama trousers he stood looking out of the bedroom window. The Volvo was gone which meant that Judy was going somewhere after she had dropped Richard and Becky off. Probably shopping; or visiting one of her gossiping friends, he smiled cynically. Bloody women's small talk!

Jesus, his head ached this morning. He drew his hand across his forehead, felt the dampness. Almost like he had a fever. Judy had no need to escort Becky to school. Richard was quite capable of chaperoning her. Her latest excuse was that there was a killer loose in the city, the police were warning mothers not to let their children out of their sight because the murderer might not stop at whores. Ed shuddered, found himself peering till his eyes ached with the strain, trying to see Norma Pringle's house through the foliage of the acacia tree at the end of the drive. Come and ring my doorbell again, you cow!

He sat on the edge of the bed, found himself visualizing Norma Pringle unclothed. He could hear her bitching and whining but she would do that whatever. Rolls of flab trembling, thick thighs shaking, the flesh beneath that mound of wiry hair soft and slippery. Touching it, stroking it. He pulled his damp garment down, kicked it away. And then he was totally out of control.

Sometime later when he showered he was still thinking of Norma, almost convinced himself that she was lying there in the bedroom motionless, her head twisted at an unnatural angle, that wingeing mouth gagged with a swollen tongue. He looked down at himself; it had been good. *Very* good.

He dressed in a red summer shirt, pulled on a pair of maroon shorts. It was going to be very hot today. He thought about phoning the bank, decided against it. He was the boss, he didn't have to account for his movements. If they needed him, Houghton would ring.

Ed's headache had receded, he felt refreshed now. He went downstairs, into the kitchen. There was no sign of Cling, the dog was probably skulking in the garden. Ed tipped some cereal into a bowl, reached a carton of milk out of the fridge.

10.15 am and there was still no sign of Judy. Which meant she would not be returning until later; she was almost certainly drinking coffee somewhere, probably glad to be out of her husband's way. Ed laughed; you stop where you are, sweetheart, I've got things to do and I don't want you around.

He went outside, stood scrutinizing the garden. A woodpigeon was cooing contentedly in the fir tree at the bottom, bees were buzzing as they searched for pollen in the flower borders. And faraway he could hear the raucous music of the fair down on the playing fields.

Now where the hell had that bloody dog got to?

There was no sign of Cling either in the house or in the garden. Not so much as a warning growl. Maybe he had sneaked out, gone hunting Norma Pringle's cat or else just shitting on her doorstep. Come on over and complain, you old bag!

He detected the clatter of a manual typewriter somewhere close by. That would be Canon Holland upstairs in his study typing out his next hypocritical address. Tough shit, you old bastard, Judy's out and I'm at home, you won't get a peek at her tits today! Ed tensed, looking towards the adjoining residence but the hedge obstructed his view. Your turn will come, Canon. You're on my list!

Ed wondered if Judy had taken Cling in the car with her, was afraid lest her husband's threat last night was no idle one. Which it wasn't. No, it was unlikely that she had taken him. Then where the fuck was he?

It was as he wandered through into the garage that Ed heard that familiar canine warning, a sound which was music to his ears, started his adrenalin pumping again. So that's where you are, hiding in the bloody garage. As if the labrador guessed what his master had in mind; but that was impossible.

The garage was, in effect, a store place for anything that was too good to throw out, an untidy lumber shed that still had a patch of treacly oil in the centre from when the previous owners had used it for its intended purpose. The Cains kept their Volvo in the drive, summer and winter, because they needed the storage space.

A jumble of impedimenta; the chest freezer, an old washing machine that might be useful as a spare if the new model broke down, a heavy Qualcast mower, empty cartons, piles of rubbish. And the gardening tools occupying the far corner.

Cling was standing by the freezer, and now there was no trace of fear in his posture; hairs upright, teeth bared and slavering, muscles tensed as if he had decided that possibly attack was the best form of defence after all. Keep your distance, you've pushed me this far and I'm not running from you any more.

'It's just you and me now, you sod,' Ed laughed, heard it start to echo in his brain, growing in momentum, 'and there's nobody around to protect you. You've had it too easy for too long.'

The dog barked, lowered its head in a threatening gesture. It was still uncertain of itself, it had never attacked anybody before.

'I *could* phone the vet, make it easy for myself,' Ed spoke his thoughts aloud, 'but this is something I've been looking forward to!' He glanced about him, looking for a weapon. The gardening tools were a couple of yards away, he began to edge slowly towards them, never once taking his eyes off the dog.

Cling was growling now, sensed what his master had in mind but he made no move to intercept him. Ed's hand stretched out; a rusted three-spined fork clinked against a spade as he began to drag it towards him. Just the job! He held it in both hands, swung it upwards above his head as if it was a club. And struck downwards with every ounce of the strength that hummed through his quivering body.

Cling moved instinctively, a sideways leap that was swift in spite of his age. Just swift enough. The head of the fork struck the freezer with numbing, vibrating force. Ed cried out, almost dropped this giant tuning fork, his arms conductors as the power sought an earth like an electric current. Metal on metal, sparks and chipped enamel showering as the steel casing of the freezer dented. By which time the labrador was safely behind the rectangular chest.

'Fuck you, dog!' Ed grunted, leaned his weight on the fork, saw how the prongs were bent. He was breathing heavly, waited for the numbing sensation in his hands to subside. Then he moved forward, crouched like a stalking hunter from the iron age. Caution now, treading on the balls of his feet, stealth replacing brute force. The bastard couldn't escape, he'd get him in the end.

A sudden lunge, he caught Cling's rump with one of the spines as the dog bolted from cover; swung again and missed. Now the animal was over on the opposite side, disappearing behind that ancient Bendix, toppling empty cartons as he burrowed beneath a pile of rubbish.

'All right, if that's the way you want it.' Ed was reluctant to approach too close, he had no idea exactly where his adversary was. Using the fork again, this time to hook cardboard boxes out of the way, drag down an old sheet. Like a huntsman digging out a fox that had gone to earth.

He saw an exposed patch of yellowish fur and speared downwards. A shriek of canine pain, an avalanche of lumber, and Cling was in the open, dragging a badly bleeding leg. The labrador was starting to panic; places of refuge were now few. A howl, turning one way, then another. But the only escape was via the side door which Ed barred.

'Come on, big feller, I want to *hurt* you!' Ed Cain dribbled saliva, lisped his words, and inside him the manic laughter was urging him to close in for the kill.

A raking sweep took the dog by surprise, gouged its flanks, rolled it over. Threshing in that congealed oil, head turned; snapping. Another thrust and this time the bent spines found the eyes, punctured them; burst and bleeding orbs that brought excruciating agony and instant blindness.

Ed took his time, Cling was at his mercy now. A blow felled the dog, had it twitching and whimpering. And then he moved in for the *coup de grâce.*

A frenzied onslaught, a crazed bludgeoning and spearing, hacking and tearing; jaws wide in a last snarl but the spines gouged the throat and released a flood of crimson blood. Ed was cursing, laughing in time with the hysterical peals inside his brain that drove him on. Depraved and malevolent, triumphant when he almost severed the head, then standing on his victim, just as in his fantasies he had trodden the ballooning stomach of Norma Pringle, grinding it with his feet until the walls burst and spewed out the wriggling, slimy entrails.

Only when the stail of the garden fork snapped did he stop.

He stood there, bowed and spent, closed his eyes whilst his body regained its strength. But when the killing lust was past its zenith he had no regrets. Just a sense of urgency.

He threw the broken fork behind some cartons, grabbed up the rusty spade and hurried down to the bottom of the rear garden with it. Here there was an empty space in the border, a place where Judy had planted out geraniums too early in the year and a sharp frost had taken them. Only their rotting stalks remained.

He began to dig, a rough rectangle, piling up the excavated soil, cursing when some of it cascaded back into the deepening hole. Periodically he stopped to listen; just the distant fairground music, the bees contintuing their relentless hunt for pollen and the *tap-tap* of an old typewriter as two ageing fingers worked its keyboard. No cars in the close, no Volvo changing down to negotiate the ramp then gliding majestically down the driveway and crunching gravel beneath its tyres.

Half a meter was deep enough. He laid down the spade, walked back to the garage and returned dragging the mutilated canine corpse, threw it into the hole. Filling in the grave was a work of minutes, smoothing it over, scraping the stones off the edge of the lawn.

He wasn't finished yet. A bucket of water and a stiff broom, washing the bloodstains off the concrete garage floor; piling back the fallen debris and restoring its former untidiness.

Only then did he go indoors and, having dropped his clothes into the washing machine, he showered for the second time that morning. The gushing water seemed to relax him and as he dried off he succumbed to a feeling of elation, what his banking colleagues referred to as 'job satisfaction'.

It was 12.15 when Judy returned and he was stretched out on the settee in the lounge as she entered, stirring drowsily, smiling and nodding when she enquired after his health.

He had never felt better.

CHAPTER TEN

'Where the hell's that dog got to?'

It was the question Ed had been anticipating ever since Judy had arrived home shortly before one o'clock. She had been to the Lees' for coffee, stayed gossiping with Mrs Lee, two mothers sharing their concern over a first romance.

Judy had rushed in, busied herself preparing lunch, pitta bread filled with coleslaw and a tin of fresh fruit salad which they had eaten on trays on the patio. Then she had washed up and only now was she aware that Cling wasn't to be seen.

'In the garden, I expect.' Ed was back on the settee in the lounge. 'I presume that's where he's been all morning because he hasn't been in the house growling at me!'

'I'd better check.' She dropped her teatowel on the working surface, went outside. Ed tensed, this was it, the moment of truth. He spread out his newspaper in a kind of defensive sceen. Well, there had to be an inquiry, he must show indifference.

'He's not in the garden,' Judy was back, her features flushed with concern, 'and the garage door's open. He could have wandered out into the close!'

'Then I expect that's what he's done.' He glanced

back down at his paper. 'He's probably doing right now what he was unjustly accused of yesterday, shitting on Norma Pringle's doorstep and chasing her cat!'

'You're hopeless,' she turned away, he heard her heading for the front door. 'I'd better go and find him, and when I do *you* can explain to that bloody woman how he got out!'

Ed smiled to himself. The hunt was on, later perhaps he would join the family search party. It gave him a feeling of smug satisfaction.

It was twenty minutes before Judy returned, and her earlier concern was bordering on panic. 'Ed, will you please get up off your backside and go and look for that dog! Cling is not in the close, there isn't a sign of him anywhere. He could have wandered on into town. Or anywhere. I'm going to phone the vet, that's where a lot of people hand in stray dogs, the police, too. The children will be frantic. Please do *something*.'

'All right,' he folded his newspaper, rose to his feet. 'I'll go and have a walk round, see if I can spot him.'

'And if you don't, then when the children come home you can explain that it was you who left the garage door open. Whatever were you doing in the garage, anyway?'

'I was thinking of tidying it up,' Ed replied glibly. 'I was going to do it this afternoon but it seems now that I'm going to spend the rest of the day hunting for that bloody dog.'

'Ed?' There was a tremor in Judy's voice, a hesitation.

'What now?' Irritable, the way a convalescing husband should sound when requested to interrupt his afternoon rest and undertake some chore.

'Ed . . . you haven't . . . ' She was eyeing him

carefully, almost afraid to put her thoughts, her accusation, into words. 'Ed . . . you threatened to take Cling to the vet's . . . to have him put down. You . . . '

'Don't be bloody silly,' he gave a reassuring laugh. 'You know very well I wouldn't actually *do* anything like that, no matter how much the dog was pissing me off.'

'Thank you, Ed.' She let out a long sigh of relief. 'Well, that doesn't alter the fact that Cling is missing.'

'I'll find him,' he kissed her on the cheek. 'In the meantime you ring the police and the vet, narrow the search, so to speak.' He went out of the front door, closed it behind him.

Ed walked down the side of the close, slowed his step as he passed Norma Pringle's house; a sideways glance, he thought he detected a movement of the curtains. Pausing provocatively but the door did not open. In his mind he glimpsed her again, sprawled grotesquely across a soiled blanket, her protruding swollen tongue choking her orgasmic shrieks. Then he moved on; right now he had other matters to attend to.

A circular route, down into the city centre and back up the by-pass, returning to the close from the opposite direction.

'Any luck?' Judy came down the drive to meet him, forlorn hope in her expression.

'No,' he smiled, 'not at the moment. But I'll bet he hasn't gone far.'

'Oh, dear!' Despair, then, 'I'm going round next-door to ask Canon Holland if by any chance Cling has got through into his garden.'

'No, don't do that!'

'Why ever not?' Her eyebrows raised. 'If Cling's

there then it's the first time he's ever got through and . . . '

'He won't be there!' A sudden insistence that bordered on anger.

'Why won't he?' Suspicious was back in her dark eyes.

'One: he can't get through. Two: if he had then he would've barked. Or else the canon would have brought him back.'

'Well, I'm going to check. I'm not leaving any possibility unexplored.'

Judy thought for a moment that her husband was going to grab hold of her, prevent her physically from disobeying his wishes. Instead he turned, went back into the house.

'Do come in, Mrs Cain,' Canon Holland's usually stoic expression transformed into pleasurable surprise as he opened the front door and recognized the dark-haired girl in the yellow summer dress.

'I won't if you don't mind,' she replied. 'You see, we've lost our dog and we're rather concerned. I was just checking on the off-chance that he might somehow have got through into your garden.'

'Well, we'd better go and look, hadn't we?' He stood aside, held the door open. 'I'm afraid I haven't been into the garden today.'

She felt strangely ill-at-ease as he walked behind her down the long passageway that led to the back door. Friendly, obliging, but her woman's intuition warned her that the portly clergyman's helplessness was merely a cloak for something else. Fantasy voyeurism; she felt his eyes on her, sensed a lust in the deep resonant voice. I'm watching you, Judy. Wiggle your tight little bum. And Ed's scathing angry tones echoing in the recesses of her mind, 'he wants to see your tits and cunt.'

She shivered in the cool of the house and it was a relief to be outside in the hot sunshine again. Her skin had pimpled, it was as though cold podgy fingers had groped her.

'Now, let's have a look,' she thought that Holland might take her hand, stepped smartly to one side. 'We'd better search the bushes.'

He was just going through the motions, he wasn't in the slightest bit interested whether or not they found the missing dog, except that he might have used its safe return as a means to strike up a friendship. Ugh, he disgusted her and there was no logical reason why he should. Just that awareness that bothered her almost as much as Cling's disappearance.

'I'm afraid it doesn't seem as if your dog's in my garden,' Holland was taking his time tapping along the lupin border with a stick. 'Would you like a cup of tea?'

'No, thank you,' Judy did her best to smile. 'Thank you for your time, Canon, but I really must be getting back. I want to find Cling before the children come home from school.'

'Of course, I understand perfectly,' he would have squeezed her arm except that she moved beyond his reach, hurried on ahead of him down that gloomy passage to the front door. 'I'll watch out for him, Mrs Cain, and if I find him I'll hold him here until you come to collect him.'

At least Ed was right about the canon, she quickened her pace back towards their own drive. You wanted to feel sorry for Holland, ageing and widowed, he had feelings the same as any other man. But her acute female senses had detected the lust and that was what revolted her. Go and get yourself a date with Norma Pringle, you dirty old man, she thought.

It was four o'clock by the kitchen clock; two hours

of panic and mental anguish that might stretch on into the evening. Another half hour and Richard and Becky would be home. Please God, let us find Cling by then.

A box of bedding-out plants were on the table; she lifted them off, carried them out to the patio. On impulse she had bought them in town, to replace those geraniums which the frost had killed in the bottom border. Sweet Williams, they needed watering but right now she did not care whether they lived or died. They might get put in, they might not. It all depended upon Cling.

Ed was in the garden, relaxing on the sun-lounger. It made her angry. Suspicious. No, he wouldn't have taken Cling to be put to sleep, or if he had then he wouldn't have lied. Whatever else, her husband never lied to her.

'No phone calls?' The question was sharp, angry.

'Calls?'

'The police. The vet. Or anybody else who might've found Cling.'

'Oh! No, no calls.'

Judy turned on her heels. Her next task was trying to play down the dog's disappearance when the children arrived home. I expect he's wandered off, gone for his own walkies. You'd better go and see if you can find him. No, don't do that, there's a murderer at large!

They would all go and look for Cling, walk the city streets until fatigue overcame them, with the exception of Ed.

'I'm going into the office in the morning,' Ed announced. It was after eleven, the children had only just gone up to bed, had been out searching for Cling with Judy until 10.30.

'Please yourself, go if you want. Because I'm not going to try to stop you.' She was angry, not because he had not joined the family search party but because he had not even enquired after their success or otherwise on their return home. He didn't care, he was secretly glad that the dog was gone; Cling's disappearance had let him off the hook, a threat which he had not had to enforce. Providence had done it for him.

She glanced across the room at him; he was still immersed in that bloody paper, he must have read it ten times over today! Anger laced with fear. Because just when everything seemed to be improving, it had all collapsed about her. The Festival opening service had been a retrograde step for the Cains.

And she recalled that rape and thought about sleeping in the spare bedroom.

It was raining when Ed threw back the bedroom curtains on Tuesday morning. The weather forecast had been right for once, an overnight downpour turning to a fast drizzle; an area of low pressure drifting eastwards, clearing the country by afternoon and then another high would dominate. Just an interlude to make one appreciate a fine summer.

Judy had not brought him his customary early morning mug of tea; he had not expected it. Damn it, he hadn't kept up the act, had been off-hand, upset the children, too, so that they were not speaking to him either. He should have consoled them with all kinds of possibilities as to Cling's whereabouts, led the late-night search, even gone out early this morning in the rain. You fucked it up, Ed Cain. But they'll never be able to prove anything even if they suspect it.

He decided to take the car. That meant Judy would

have to walk to school with the kids. And that was her bloody lookout, she should have let them go on their own; Richard was quite capable of looking after Becky. Still, if she wanted to get soaked, that was up to her. He did not breakfast, a mere glance into the kitchen where the other three were eating bowls of muesli and Judy was nagging them to hurry up. He took his coat out of the cupboard, heard the rattle of the car keys in the pocket, and then he was slamming the front door behind him.

This was only the second time that Ed had driven the replacement Volvo. It did not seem any different from the old one, might have been the same car except for the fact that it smelled new; nowadays one could buy an aerosol spray that gave an identical odour. Another yuppy gimmick like John Cutler's dummy car phones.

The facia clock showed 8.15 am., too early to arrive at the office. For a manager, anway. Managerial hours were late arrivals and early departures. Ed had left the house early just to spite Judy and the kids, now he had time on his hands. Time to kill.

The drizzle formed an opaque mist on the windscreen; the wipers cleared a swathe, squeaked back across the toughened glass. He put them on intermittent, wished it would either rain hard or else clear up. The roads were greasy, you could see oil streaks that had lain from the start of the dry spell, had not washed away; greasy and dangerous.

Five minutes to the office, ten at the most if there was a queue at the big island and the main traffic lights were stuck on red. Half-past eight at the bank was far too early. Ed decided to go for a drive; a spin just for the hell of it. He wished that it had been a sunny morning.

At the island he moved over into the right-hand

lane, headed south. The traffic was sparse; he overtook a dumper truck and a Range Rover, hugged the outside lane of the dual carriageway. A glance at the speedometer showed him that he was doing 70 mph.

He had not spotted the Mini in his rear mirror, was unaware of it until it drew alongside him and the blare of a musical horn made him start. The stupid bastard was overtaking on the inside, doing eighty, maybe more. Swerving erratically, signalling that he was going to move into the fast lane; cutting up the Volvo. Because it was a snob car, no other reason. High speed class warfare.

Ed felt his adrenalin begin to pump. A glimpse of the driver in profile as the small car forced its way in front of him. Long and matted hair, pallid features that were stamped with resentment towards society in general, the kind who started a fight in pubs or on football terraces. Oily overalls, probably a garage mechanic on his way to work; cars were the extent of his knowledge, he had re-built this one from a write-off, a souped-up engine and rally tyres, behind its wheel he was God and wanted everyone to know it. Aggro on the roads, pick out the Jags and the BMWs, a Volvo if there was nothing else going, cut the fucker up and teach him a lesson. Shower him with liquid shit and then lose him.

You stupid little prick, Ed thought, and had to brake as the yellow Mini slowed momentarily, on purpose, and then accelerated. Filth showered the windscreen, Ed flicked the wipers on to high, had to use the washer to clear his vision.

The Mini was pulling ahead. Maybe it was capable of a ton, even a T-registration. Momentarily Ed's eyesight was blurred, the spray coming at him from the wheels of the car in front seemed to be crimson tinted, there was a constriction in his chest that checked his breathing and speeded up his pulses. Like he was an extension of the Volvo, surging up to full speed and angry with it. A fury that took him over, was driving him just as he drove his car. Cutler, Suzy, Norma Pringle, Canon Holland, Cling whimpering in his own bloodbath; rapid flashbacks all strung together and merging into that stupid bastard in the yellow Mini. The peak of Cain's hatred, the scapegoat. He began to close in on him.

The carriageway was empty except for the two of them, Ed checked his mirrors just to make sure. The tipper and the Range Rover were not in sight, they were probably half a mile behind. Up ahead the outgoing and the incoming lanes were screened from each other by a narrow wood. His foot went hard down on the throttle pedal.

The Mini driver unaware that he was being pursued, was cutting back into the nearside lane, easing down his speed. Smug, self-satisfied, a blow had been struck for the cause of the lower classes.

The Volvo's engine purred effortlessly, a thoroughbred given its head. The speedometer registered 95 mph as it began to draw level with the smaller car, outpacing it.

Ed saw the silhouetted head turn, become a blur of white through the greasy spray. Shock and anger, hunching forward but that high-powered engine had met its master. Calling on all its reserves was not good enough.

Ed began to ease to the left, braced himself in case he accidentally nudged the other vehicle. But the Mini was pulling away from him, already had its nearside wheels in the slip lane. *And a couple of hundred yards up ahead the shoulder ended, merged into a thick verge of verdant summer grass and flowery headed hedge parsley.*

The driver panicked. Now the Mini was off the

carriageway, the Volvo edging still closer, and on the left the sheer grassy bank dropped down to a field of dazzling yellow oil-seed rape.

Ed eased his foot off the accelerator in case he overtook and allowed the other space to cut back in behind him. Out of the corner of his eye he saw that face, a mask of sheer terror, the mouth wide in a scream of fear. He heard the squeal of brakes, the screech of heavy duty tyres, thought he caught a whiff of scorched rubber. The Mini skidded on locked wheels, threatened to slew but held its course. The verge loomed up, its thick vegetation masking the concrete kerb that marked the termination of the hard shoulder.

The Mini was airborne, a squat wingless plane attempting stunt aerobatics. Shooting up, spinning, half-promising a loop and then it tilted over; an optical illusion, it seemed to be suspended, Ed thought for one moment that it might float gracefully earthwards then it plummeted.

Ed Cain followed its downward progress in his rear-view mirror. The Mini hit the bank, bounced outwards, and even as it began to roll and gather speed it exploded into a ball of fire.

A spectacular fireworks display on a damp, depressing morning, illuminating the greyness, singeing the wet grass as it embarked upon a downward course. Ed heard the explosion, seemed to feel its force inside the Volvo, an electrification of his own body that excited him, elated him.

Driving on, the road ahead and behind still empty, nostrils flared as he tried to smell again that stench of burning instant death. Exhilarated, angry but heady, re-living those last few glorious moments.

A mile or so further on he spied the flashing blue light of an approaching police patrol car in the opposite carriageway and even as he began to laugh that laughter inside his head began. It vibrated, hurt him, but he didn't mind because it had all been worth it. An unknown driver had angered him and had paid the supreme penalty for his foolishness.

At the next inter-section Ed turned off, circled and drove down on to the city carriageway. With luck he would catch another glimpse of the blazing Mini. And he was still too early for the office.

CHAPTER ELEVEN

'Dad isn't like he used to be any more,' Becky pushed her half-eaten bowl of muesli to one side, sobbed. 'He's like a . . . a stranger. Somebody . . . *nasty*!'

'He's not well,' Judy tried to sound convincing. 'It's going to take a long time for him to get right again.'

'How long?'

'I don't know. Months, maybe.'

'I don't want to go to the Lees' tonight,' Richard said. 'I'm going to come straight home and carry on looking for Cling.'

'No,' Judy was close to tears herself. 'We all have to carry on, Richard. You go and see Tracey, try and forget all this.'

'I can't. Cling *has* to be somewhere, he can't just have vanished. Do you think . . . ' he hesitated, 'that . . . somebody has kidnapped him? I read a book once about a gang who stole dogs, sold them for a fortune.'

'Definitely not,' Judy forced a smile. 'Cling is old, he wouldn't be worth anything to anybody. Except us. Look, Richard, please go and see Tracey tonight and I promise I'll carry on looking for Cling. Please, I want you to.'

'All right,' he stood up. 'We'd best get going. I don't want to be late for school, I've got an exam this morning.'

Judy did not know why her husband had taken the car, perhaps he had to go and see a customer out of town. That was fine, but the fact that he had not mentioned it, had not even spoken to them this morning, was a sure sign of the rift that was widening between them.

It was drizzling, fast fine rain that saturated you as much as a downpour. She was not going to linger in town, she would hurry home; the breakfast TV weather forecast promised a return to summer this afternoon. In which case she would plant out those Sweet Williams which she had bought yesterday; the soil would be just right after this rain.

On the walk back home she heard police cars and an ambulance heading south along the by-pass. Those sirens frightened her, reminded her of . . . no, she must try to forget that March evening. It wouldn't be anything to do with Ed this time because he didn't have to go that way, he would be safely in his office making life hell for the bank staff just as he did for his own family at home.

Judy did not go straight home after seeing Becky and Richard to their respective schools; Richard could have gone on ahead on his own, might have preferred to rather than have his friends see him being delivered to school by his mother, but this morning he was morose, stayed with Judy. On impulse she headed for the health centre where Doctor Lawson had his surgery, prayed that he would be on duty this morning. He was, according to the board in the porch, and she took a seat in the waiting room. She would wait until everybody else had gone because she needed to talk in confidence to the doctor and it might take some time.

'You've come to tell me all about it,' Lawson

closed the door of his consulting room, ushered Judy to a chair. 'In fact, I've been expecting you for some time.'

'There's something terribly wrong with Ed,' this was the time and place to let the tears come, Judy decided. 'Oh, it's awful. The children have started to hate him, the dog, too, except that Cling has gone missing. There just *has* to be some brain damage, doctor!'

'No,' Graham Lawson stroked his chin, shook his head. 'I can assure you that there is no brain damage. Ed has had several scans during the course of his treatment. One might have expected some kind of change in him for a few weeks after the accident but it shouldn't be affecting him months later. Physically, he's made a miraculous recovery, almost back to normal. Maybe it's depression and I should refer him to a psychiatrist.'

'He would refuse to go. You've no idea what he's like.'

'Hmm,' Graham Lawson was pensive. Judy looked ill, the strain was taking its toll on her. He contemplated prescribing some Valium for her, changed his mind. He was a rare breed of medic, one who believed in the old-fashioned cures; even now there was a jar of honey on his desk from where he had smeared some on a nasty cut on a patient. Drugs were a last resort. 'Tell you what,' he took Judy's arm, squeezed it. 'I'll call by after evening surgery, just a social visit. After all, Ed and I are more than doctor and patient, we've fished together on odd occasions in the past. I'll have a chat to him, see if I can spot anything. But if you need me at any time, night or day, just call me. Understand?'

Judy nodded and the tears started to flow again She was remembering how Cutler had died; that in itself was bad enough. But worse was Ed's attitude. Neither shock nor remorse, rather a carefree acceptance of a terrible tragedy that would have had most men on tranquillizers for weeks afterwards.

It was all very frightening.

It had stopped raining by midday. Judy finished cleaning the house and then noticed that box of plants out on the patio, fresh and dripping after the downpour, almost begging her to plant them out. Well, you had to do something; she had given up working out where Cling might have got to and it was pointless to wander the streets aimlessly in the hope of spotting him. If he turned up then either the police, the vet or the RSPCA would call her. From now on it was a waiting game. She might as well occupy herself with some gardening.

She went into the garage, found a trowel. What a mess the place was, one of these days she would tidy it out. One of these days. Gardening wasn't one of her favourite hobbies, either, but the dean and chapter had written a clause into the tenancy agreement of number nineteen that the garden had to be maintained in good order, which meant mowing the lawns and a bit of weeding in the borders which were mostly shrubs anyway. The Sweet Williams would make a colourful show when they flowered.

Judy carried the box of plants down to the bottom of the garden. Doubtless the border would need some preparation, she ought to have brought a fork. She was on the point of going back for one when she noticed the patch of newly-turned earth, the fine tilth where there should have been weedy soil; there were traces of mud on the lawn as if it had been swept clean in that spot . . .

Maybe Ed had decided to spend some of his time

gardening whilst she had been up at the Lees' . . . No, that didn't figure, he wouldn't do anything in the garden unless he was nagged. Puzzled, trying to push away an awful nagging thought. No, it couldn't be, Ed wouldn't do anything like *that*!

There was a sinking feeling in her stomach, she felt slightly sick. Rising anger but she checked it because it might not be true, probably wasn't. And there was only one way to find out!

She returned to the garage, found the heavy spade, and began to dig with it. The going was easy, the soil was soft and quickly scooped out of the rectangle which was fast forming. Afraid of what she might find down there but she had to know, one way or the other.

She was sweating in the heat, throwing the soil up into a heap, some of it spilling on to the lawn. The hole was deep, soon she had to reach the hard bottom, rock and stones, and there would be nothing else down there. She was already beginning to apologize mentally to her husband, had almost decided to fill the oblong crater in because she didn't want to know; and then the spade struck something solid, gouged into whatever lay beneath the moist earth.

As she freed the tool some soil shot up with it, and that was when she saw the dog's head. Yellow fur matted with blood and earth, eyeless sockets staring pitifully up at her, the mouth agape in a silent yelp of terror. The muzzle was lacerated with spiked holes, some teeth were snapped off, a barely recognizable animal lying mutilated in its grave.

Oh, my God! She smoothed some of the soil back, covered the protruding head but she knew she would see it until her dying day. She felt faint, wondered if she was going to be sick, and held on to an overhead laburnum branch in case she fell. It was true then, Ed had killed Cling, *brutally murdered him*, and buried the corpse. Then he had lied, deceived his wife and children.

With an effort Judy pulled herself together. Becky and Richard must never know and not just for their father's sake. Cling must never be found, as far as they were concerned, the children must always believe that he had strayed far afield, found a good home and eventually died peacefully of old age. She had to deceive them just as Ed had deceived his family but for a different reason.

She knew that she would never rest until she had confronted Ed with this terrible deed, whatever the consequences.

Once she had regained her composure she began to fill in the hole and then planted the Sweet Williams on top of it. For Cling. Oh, God, *why* had Ed done this, there had to be a deeper reason than just that the animal had taken a dislike to him?

She finished, left the lawn unswept and hurried back to the house but she did not make it indoors before she began to sob uncontrollably.

It was not until they were nearly home that Judy was aware that there was something wrong with Becky. At first she had put it down to grief over Cling's disappearance; not speaking, head bowed, dragging her feet.

'Becky,' Judy stopped, bent to peer into the child's pallid face, 'what's wrong?'

'Mummy,' there was definitely something amiss when 'Mummy' was used, 'I've had a pain in my back since lunchtime.'

'Oh, dear,' Judy took her daughter's hand, 'you've got an asthma attack coming on, haven't you?'

'Yes,' the first noticeable wheeze, a tiny hand

drawn across a sweating brow, 'and I've got a bad headache, too.'

'I was hoping you were out-growing your asthma.' She slipped an arm around her daughter and moved on. 'You haven't had an attack for nearly a year now. In fact, I'd almost forgotten about them. Well, I think the sooner you're in bed, the better. And you'd better take your Nebuhaler.'

Blast you, Ed, it's all your fault, you despicable bastard! And the last thing I want to happen is for Becky to find out the truth about Cling. Becky would be going straight to bed, she would sleep deeply with a bit of luck. And when Graham Lawson called he could have a look at her. And in the meantime Judy had some harsh words in store for her husband. It all had to be brought to a head. Thank goodness she had persuaded Richard to go and see his new girlfriend; that kept him out of the way for the evening.

Becky was asleep by 5.15 pm, her wheezing wasn't as bad as Judy had feared. With luck the attack would pass off. Judy went back downstairs, sat on the settee in the lounge. She wasn't preparing a meal tonight, no way! She wasn't hungry herself, the last thing she wanted was food, and if Ed needed to eat then he could bloody well get his own tea!

At five minutes to six she tensed as she heard the Volvo pull into the drive, crunching the gravel, stopping outside the garage. A door slammed, through the window she caught a glimpse of Ed; he seemed to be hurrying.

She opened up as the lounge door opened. Ed, an expression of boyish enthusiasm on his face, crossed to the television, switched it on, found the regional channel.

'Just in time for the news!' He seemed excited, obsessed, it was rather scary. Especially when one had dug down in the flower border and found the body of the family pet bludgeoned and gashed out of all recognition.

'What's the excitement?' Her tone was surly, resentful.

'Just want to catch up on the news,' he was staring fixedly at the screen, impatient as if mentally hurrying the adverts, now oblivious to herself and his surroundings.

'This is the Six O'clock News.' The presenter wore an expression of professional mourning; the news was bad, brace yourselves for it. 'Early this morning a car left a busy dual carriageway and exploded into flames. Police are still trying to identify the driver's charred body. Fire crews fought to put out the blaze, then had to cut the man's body free.'

There were pictures of a blackened, blazing wreck, foam being sprayed upon it. Firemen cutting through the charred and twisted metal, eventually bearing an unrecognizable shape on a stretcher, a blanket draped over it, towards a waiting ambulance.

Judy heard her husband's sharp intake of breath, saw how he was leaning forward in his seat, engrossed in the gory television pictures. Gloating, there was no other word to describe it, she felt a loathing, a contempt for him that had begun with the discovery of Cling's body.

'Why so interested?' Her voice quavered. She recalled his casual attitude the afternoon John Cutler had died. This was worse, he was drooling over an unknown corpse, delighting in violent death. As he might have found pleasure in the sadistic killing of a gentle dog . . .

'I heard the fire-engines and police cars as I got to the office,' the reply was too glib to be convincing, 'and I heard talk there had been an accident on the by-pass. I just wanted to . . . see it.'

'I'd rather not know about it,' she felt nauseated, was trembling. This was the moment of truth. She found herself listening but there was no movement elsewhere in the house. Becky was asleep. This was the moment of truth.

'What's to eat?' His eyes seemed to clear, it was as if now that he had viewed the gruesome accident he was returning to . . . *normal.*

'There isn't anything to eat,' she tried to speak firmly but there was no way she could stop her voice shaking. 'And furthermore, there won't be.'

'Oh?' A quizzical expression, he was watching her carefully. 'Why's that?'

'Because,' she took a deep breath, was aware how her pulses raced, '*I found Cling's body in the flower border today!*'

Her words struck him as if she had slapped his face. He started, paled, swallowed and dropped his eyes on to the carpet. At length he said, 'Oh, dear, I was hoping he wouldn't be found.'

'You bastard!' Now her voice trembled with rising fury. 'You bludgeoned that dog to death and doubtless enjoyed every second of it. You . . .'

'*I* killed Cling?' An expression of shocked innocence. 'Good God, Judy, you're not accusing *me* of killing him, are you?'

'I am,' sudden doubt, uncertainty, the fear of a wrongful accusation. But it couldn't be anything other than a frenzied killing carried out by Ed. She shifted uncomfortably in her seat.

'I suppose it must look that way,' he laughed weakly. 'I suppose I should have come clean yesterday but at the time it seemed the best thing to do. I suppose, indirectly, I am to blame.'

'Indirectly?' Doubts were crowding in on her now.

'Let me explain,' his head was in his hands, she thought he might be about to sob out his terrible confession. 'I'd gone into the garage primarily with the intention of tidying the place out but I didn't feel up to it. Thoughtlessly, accidentally, I left the door going through to the close open. I was back in the house when suddenly I heard a screech of brakes and a bang in the close. I went running out and there was . . . ' his voice faltered, 'poor old Cling lying under the wheels. I won't go into details but he was in a pretty awful mess. And then I had this idea that if I buried him before you got back, told you and the kids that he must've wandered off, then nobody would be any the wiser. Far better not to know than to see . . . '

'I saw,' she closed her eyes briefly. 'Oh, God, Ed, what a bloody stupid trick to do. Why didn't you tell *me*, at least?'

'Because I wanted to spare you the gruesome details,' he edged towards her, his hand found hers and squeezed gently. 'I'm . . . I'm sorry, darling.'

Her brain was in a whirl, apologies welled up in her throat but she couldn't get them out. Starting to cry; for Cling, for Ed. For the kids.

And finally she said, 'I guess I'd better go and make us both something to eat.'

CHAPTER TWELVE

Judy ought to have breathed a huge sigh of relief, relaxed, but she didn't. Her earlier tension was still there, a tautness in her slim body, a dryness in her mouth and a hint of a headache behind her eyes. Because even if Ed was telling the truth there was no getting away from the fact that he had attempted to deceive them and she had no option but to collaborate with his story for the sake of Becky and Richard.

She began to prepare a salad; they seemed to be living on salad these days. She would go through the motions of eating but the last thing she wanted right now was food. She felt physically and mentally sick, not just because of her discovery in the flower border but from the way her husband had watched that news item with undisguised relish. He had savoured every camera shot, had strained forward in an attempt to obtain a glimpse of that incinerated corpse on the stretcher. He was sick.

'There are some right bloody idiots on the roads these days!' She started, whirled around, almost cried out.

'Ed, you made me jump, creeping in here like that!' A kitchen knife slipped from her trembling hand, bounced and skated across the floor.

'No!' His arm stretched out, obstructed her as she

bent to pick it up. 'Don't you know it's bad luck to pick up a knife if you drop it?' He reached down, retrieved it, made no attempt to hand it back to her.

'Just an old wives' tale,' she eyed the knife with its serrated blade in his hand nervously. 'I don't suppose it really matters a toss who picks it up.'

'Better to play safe,' a half-smile twitched the corners of his mouth and even as she watched his eyes began to film over. 'Like I said, there're bloody lunatics loose on the roads and every one that kills himself without hurting anybody else is a bonus for the careful motorist.'

'You've been watching too much of *The Liquidator*.' It was meant as a joke but it came out terse, almost an accusation.

'It's a thought,' those glazed eyes narrowed.

'Becky's got an asthma attack,' she wanted to change the subject, refrained from adding *and it's because Cling has gone missing*. 'If I can have my knife back to finish slicing the tomatoes supper will be ready in about five minutes.'

'What did that cement-mixer guy get when his case came up?' It was no idle question, there was a frightening intensity about it.

'Grindle Construction were fined a thousand pounds for having an unsafe vehicle on the road,' she spoke cautiously, 'and the driver had a two hundred pound fine and an endorsement.'

'A pittance for . . . ' the veins stood out on his neck and forehead, the knife was held threateningly in his hand. 'That driver should be . . . *dead*!'

She gasped, would have backed away had she not already been up against the sink unit.

'*Ed*!' It was a half-scream, the blade was moving towards her, it was as if her husband was in some kind of frenzied trance, did not recognize her.

At that instant the front doorbell chimed.

Ed Cain started, groped blindly as though he was lost in a thick fog, and his eyes began to clear.

'Who's that?' he asked huskily.

'We won't know until we answer it, will we?' She began to circle him, heading for the hallway.

'If it's that bloody Pringle woman . . . '

'I doubt it very much,' Judy untied her apron, draped it over a chair. Through the frosted glass pane of the door she could see a pear-shaped silhouette and breathed her own prayer of thanks.

'Doctor Lawson, what a surprise! Do come inside, please.'

'I was just passing by, thought I'd drop in.' The GP's grey eyes flicked from Judy, saw Ed in the kitchen, that salad knife still clasped dagger-fashion in his extended hand. Lawson saw and understood that something was wrong. 'How are you shaping up, Ed?'

'I'm fine,' the knife-hand dropped to his side, he forced a smile. 'Glad to see you, Graham.'

'We're just about to have a bite to eat,' Judy followed the doctor through to the kitchen. 'Would you care to join us?' *Please.*

'To tell the truth I was feeling a trifle peckish,' the doctor watched as Ed dropped the knife on to the working surface.

'Whilst you're here,' Judy busied herself with the salad again, 'Becky's had an asthma attack, she's upstairs in bed, asleep. I was hoping that she had outgrown them. Anyway, she's had her Nebuhaler.'

'I'll go up and have a look at her,' Lawson made for the stairs and the hand in his pocket rustled paper. He always kept a supply of dolly-mixtures for child patients; it was important that they regarded doctors as friends. 'Won't be a tick.'

A few minutes later they heard his heavy footsteps coming back downstairs. 'She isn't wheezing now,' he seated himself at the table where Judy had laid three places. 'She'll be okay, Judy. Keep her off school tomorrow and if you have any doubts give me a bell and I'll be right over.'

Judy was relieved to see that her husband ate normally, joined in the small talk, even shared one of the doc's dry jokes; they would miss Graham Lawson when he retired.

'Where's Richard?' Lawson asked. 'Having a night out with the birds?'

'Apparently, yes!' Ed's voice was suddenly abrupt, terse. 'And not with *my* blessing, I can assure you. If he's not in by ten-thirty there's going to be ructions!'

Lawson's eyes narrowed and he said, 'I doubt whether he'll come to much harm. Boys generally don't start getting adventurous until they're around sixteen.' Trying to defuse the situation, sensing the rising tension.

'There was an accident on the by-pass this morning,' Ed appeared not to have heard the other. 'A bloody idiot got burning the road up and ended up burning himself up.'

'I know, I was called out.' Lawson had seen how those eyes blazed anger and something else which he could not quite determine. 'The Mini just went off the road, exploded. Doubtless the inquest will come up with something.'

'Just another stupid bastard who's better off in the graveyard!'

Lawson licked his lips, sipped his coffee. Judy was right about her husband, all was not well. 'D'you think it was wise going back to work so soon? After Sunday, I mean.'

'I'm fine and I'll do as I please. And don't suggest

another check-up!' Ed's teeth were clenched, grinding, and there was a threat in his tone.

'It never even occurred to me,' Lawson smiled, unruffled. 'I did think, though, that it was about time you and I found time for half a day's fishing. I haven't had my rod out since last summer.'

Ed was silent, it was as if his brain was taking its time adjusting to another trend of conversation. Nodding, struggling to comprehend why he was in agreement with their visitor. Finally he said, 'Yes, that's a great idea, Graham. I'll check my appointments diary at the office, give you a ring and we'll fix up an outing.'

'Fine,' the doctor scraped his chair back, stood up. 'Now, if you good people will excuse me, I've one more patient to call on before bedtime.' Which typified the dedication of the man.

Judy saw him to the door, and as he squeezed her hand goodnight she read the message in his eyes; I'm only at the other end of a telephone if you need me, night or day.

Which was both reassuring and disconcerting.

'Where the bloody hell's that boy got to?' Ed came out of the armchair with such suddenness that Judy recoiled. A sleeping tiger that had awakened into ferociousness. A human time-bomb. Her nerves were shot, she couldn't take much more.

'Steady on, Ed, it's only twenty-five to eleven!'

'I said *ten-thirty*! He heard me and so did you!'

'What's five minutes? We know he's safe and in all probability Mr Lee will bring him back home. And I told Richard that if he wanted fetching then he'd only got to ring us.'

'You did, did you?' There was mounting fury in his voice, his fist clenched as though to thump the table.

'The little bugger's up to no good, and don't try to convince me otherwise. Whilst we sit up waiting for him he's got that tart's knickers down. And next thing we know she'll be wailing that . . . '

'Oh, for goodness sake, Ed!'

They heard the back door click open, close; movements in the kitchen. And before Judy could stop him, Ed was rushing through to the hall. She heard her husband shouting, 'What time d'you call this, then? I said ten-thirty and not a minute after. What the hell have you been up to?'

Judy stumbled out of the room, her shaking legs threatening to throw her to the floor. And through the kitchen doorway she glimpsed Richard, no longer the fourth-year schoolboy in uniform but an adolescent in trendy shirt and jeans, suddenly grown-up both mentally and physically, towering a couple of inches above his father, anger and defiance on his youthful features.

'Pack it in, will you, Dad?'

'*Answer me!*'

Richard backed away a step, checked. Shocked surprise and then he recovered himself. His features flushed with anger and his fists clenched. He said in a low voice, 'Don't you bloody talk to me like that!'

'I'll talk to you how I like and you'll do what I say!' Ed was shaking with fury, his arm shot out, his hand grasped Richard's shirt, dragged the boy forward; two snarling faces within inches of each other, a confrontation of escalating rage.

'*Let . . . go . . . of . . . me*!' Buttons popped, bounced and skittered across the floor. Silence except for loud intakes and expellations of breath from father and son.

'Ed . . . Richard . . . stop it. At once!' Judy was inside the kitchen, a helpless frightened spectator.

Her husband was like he was that day when his hands had closed over her own throat, a raging wild beast that lusted to kill.

Richard's arm moved; went back, the fist balled. It shot forward, sank into his father's stomach inches above the waistline of his trousers. A gasp, a grunt of strangled pain, and Ed Cain released his hold, doubled up. Almost fell.

'*Stop it, the pair of you*!' Judy leaped forward, somehow squeezed herself in between them, her back to Richard, her face brushing Ed's as he straightened up. Eyeball to eyeball, she nearly screamed at what she saw in those burning orbs. The expression of a crazed killer but she did not flinch, her maternal instinct was stronger than that of self-preservation. She would die for her children if necessary. Oh, God, Becky was upstairs; Judy prayed that the shouting had not awoken her.

'Damn you!' Ed hissed. 'Damn you! As a father it's my duty to . . . '

'Richard is only doing what thousands of boys his age do.' Judy was surprised how calmly she spoke. 'He's dated a girl for the first time. You were sixteen. I was fourteen when we went on our first date. Or have you forgotten? We courted, married young. Can you deny your own children that or have you become a hypocrite?'

She glanced behind her, glimpsed Richard holding on to the table. He was trembling, he looked as if he was on the verge of bursting into tears. Don't, please, Richard, this is one occasion when we both have to be strong.

Ed stared and then his eyes began to clear. His hands went up to his ears, clutched at them as if he was trying to shut out some deafening sound. A momentary expression of anguish, the fluorescent light glinted on his sweat-streaked face. He looked down at the floor, shuddered, and when he raised his head again his look was one of bewilderment.

'I . . . I'm sorry,' he had to force the words out. 'I . . . I think I'll go to bed.' He turned, made for the stairs, did not look back. Mother and son stood there, listened to his footsteps across the landing, heard the bathroom door slam shut. The toilet was flushed, a rush of water that just failed to drown the sound of retching and vomiting.

'I think this is something we shall have to try to forget,' Judy took Richard's hand but could not bring herself to meet his eyes. She was remembering what she had found when she had dug down in the flower border. That time it had been just a dog. Next time . . .

'I think we'd better go to bed,' she said.

CHAPTER THIRTEEN

In spite of his eccentricities Doctor Graham Lawson followed a conventional routine during the evenings. After evening surgery, which usually dragged on until around seven o'clock, he made a few late calls on patients. Unscheduled visits, they were often both surprised and delighted to see him, more of a social occasion than a GP's home visit. It was his way of relaxing after a long tiring day, he did not regard it as a duty. Except in rare cases, like the Cains, he always declined supper. That was reserved for his return home, often the only time that he and his wife, Cicely, spent any time together.

Cicely Lawson was in her mid-sixties, tall and elegant, only her grey hair gave away her age; a visit to the hairdresser's, a perm and a dye, and strangers would have put her at about fifty-two. But she had no need to deceive, had no wish to. And secretly she was very proud of her husband, the way he had become a kind of institution, almost a legend in his own time in the cathedral city.

They had married a few months after he had qualified, and for the first few years he had worked in London hospitals, submerging his identity whilst he gained the necessary experience to take on what was then almost a rural practice. Taciturn, abrupt where obvious malingerers were concerned, he had not endeared himself to some of his patients in those early days. Cicely still smiled wryly when she recalled how Graham had once told an overweight canon to 'get his fat arse up on the couch' so that he could examine the holy man's piles. The matter had been reported indignantly to Bishop Westbury who himself had that same dry sense of humour and had telephoned the surgery to convey a complaint on behalf of the ruffled canon.

'Don't tell me you've got piles, too, Bishop,' Graham had grunted, and the matter had ended there.

Nowadays, with two additional doctors in the practice, it had become almost an embarrassment to Graham Lawson when his partners were sitting in empty consulting rooms whilst the waiting room was packed with patients prepared to wait for an hour if necessary to see himself rather than go to either of the younger men.

Flattering as it was, Cicely reflected, it did put an additional strain on her husband in his declining years. Thank goodness seventy was a compulsory retirement age in the medical profession for without any doubt Graham would have worked on until the bitter end. Tonight he looked particularly tired but she well knew the futility of suggesting an early night; he would read until midnight and almost on the stroke of twelve he would give one of his meaningful coughs. That meant he was ready for his mug of cocoa. At twenty past twelve he would shuffle off on a tour of inspection around the rambling house which also comprised the health centre, checking that doors and windows were locked. 12.30 and he would undress for bed, read for another half hour before settling down to sleep. There was no way that she would change his routine, it was far too late in life even to attempt it.

He wasn't reading tonight, although he occupied his usual chair and had a well-worn novel open on his lap. He was even staring at the pages but she knew that his thoughts were elsewhere. She glanced at him surreptitiously, saw how his brow was furrowed, his lips pursed. Deep in thought. Worried.

'You're worried about Ed Cain,' Cicely spoke at last, anticipated an answering grunt. Mind your own business, dear. In the nicest possible way, of course. They had built up an understanding over the years, a deep affection that was based upon not intruding into the other's thoughts. Tonight she was breaking the rules.

'Yes,' he did not look up, continued to stare at browning pages on which the faded print was a meaningless blur. 'I'm worried because it's got me beat.'

'Why not refer him to a neuro-surgeon? Philip Craddock. It has to be brain damage, doesn't it?'

'No,' he shook his head slowly. 'He's had enough scans and they haven't shown up anything. That's why I'm worried.' He glanced at the grandfather clock in the corner; in precisely three minutes, and it had maintained an unrivalled accuracy over the last thirty years, it would strike midnight. 'I think it's coming up to cocoa time, dear.'

Which meant that the discussion on Ed Cain was terminated. Graham Lawson would continue to ponder over the problem until bedtime. Then, as always, he would sleep soundly. Cicely had never known him to lie awake worrying. A form of rigid self-discipline, he would postpone his worries, without fail, until his next working day began at 6.30 am. Unless, of course, he got a call-out in the night. She got up, went through to the kitchen to boil a saucepan of milk.

Doctor Lawson's thoughts had returned to that March evening. He remembered the dreariness, the cold drizzle as spring reminded one that winter was not fully gone. A Friday. A raw chill in the atmosphere that had a foreboding about it even earlier in the day before those terrible events came about. Cold clammy invisible fingers touching you, stroking you; the hand of evil reaching out to warn you. He was not an imaginative person. Sensitive, yes, beneath that gruff exterior, but Graham had a premonition after morning surgery that death was in the air. It always was, as a medical practitioner you accepted death whether it was an elderly person who had lived out their lifespan or an horrific pile-up on the bypass because the bloody fools were driving too fast and too close to one another. But today the feeling was different. Almost . . . frightening.

On a 'normal' day there was every chance that he would have gone out to the Cain accident himself, administered a morphine injection through the mangled bodywork of the Volvo whilst he waited for the fire crew to cut the victim free. But the doctor had been called out just after three o'clock and he had not heard about Ed's accident until he returned to the surgery shortly after six.

Lawson had heard the police sirens in the distance around 2.30. A road accident or maybe a fire; if he was needed they would call him. The call had come through at 3.10; there was an armed siege taking place on the Meadows Estate on the outskirts of the city. The police inspector had requested a doctor in attendance, there was every likelihood that somebody would get shot. Because the man holding a family hostage was . . .

Blake Barrett.

That was when Doctor Graham Lawson knew that

his earlier premonition had not just been his imagination playing tricks on a day that had reeked of death and evil. Because there was none more dangerous than the psychopathic Blake Barrett.

Lawson had first treated Barrett in 1980. A court had asked for a doctor's report before sentencing for rape and assault. Graham would never forget the face of the young man who sat defiantly in the police cell, had to be restrained by two constables. Gaunt and hollowed features, eyes that blazed malevolently one minute, filmed over the next. Lucid speech that became maniacal ravings.

The doctor had advised that Barrett be put away indefinitely and only released subject to mental evidence that confirmed without any doubt that the man was no longer a danger to the public. Which, Graham was certain, would never come about because there was no psychiatric treatment possible which would retore that twisted mind to any degree of normality. Barrett had been committed to a mental hospital for an indefinite period but some do-gooder of a doctor had recommended his release on parole in 1986.

Barrett returned to the city, was convicted of burglary in 1987 and was sentenced to twelve months' imprisonment without any reference to his mental condition.

Barrett was walking the streets again the following February. And on that fateful Friday afternoon in March he had carried out a single-handed armed raid on the Meadows Estate post office.

The mini supermarket and post office was crowded at 2.15 when Blake Barrett entered, armed with a stolen pump-action shotgun. By some miracle nobody had been killed; women and children screamed as the raider fired a shot that raked a shelf of groceries and smashed the fluorescent light above it. Screaming obscenities, he demanded the day's takings, was handed a cloth bag containing cash ready to be banked.

He backed outside where a crowd had gathered. People dived for any available cover as a charge of shot patterned on a parked Metro. And then the gunman panicked, ran blindly for the housing estate, gun held pistol-fashion in one hand, his loot in the other. Possibly it was his intention to try to lose himself in the woods bordering the estate; whatever his crazed ill-planned getaway might have been, it was altered by the sight of a police patrol car coming down River View towards him.

Another shot. The police car slewed to a halt, the officers dived for cover. Barrett ran into the nearest semi-detached council house where the Turley family were watching television. Within ten minutes the siege had begun.

Neighbouring families were escorted to safety as police marksmen took up their positions. An ambulance was already on stand-by when Doctor Lawson arrived and Blake Barrett was visible at a broken upstairs window, screaming that nobody would take him alive and that if the police attempted to storm the house the Turleys would be shot. He was taken at his word and the police settled down for what they presumed would be a long wait.

It was all over by 5.45 pm.

Lawson watched from the safety of a police car, permitted himself one of his rare pipes of tobacco, a treat as opposed to a habit these days, saw a figure appear at that bedroom window again. Barrett was yelling, cursing; a policeman answered through a loud hailer, tried to defuse the situation. We'll send in food and drink, cigarettes if you want them. Let us know.

Seconds later they heard a dull report, the gunshot muffled by the interior of the house, at first difficult to recognize as a shotgun explosion. Everybody waited. And waited.

The chief superintendent spoke into his radio, received a reply from one of the marksmen on the roof opposite. It *was* a shot, we'll have to rush him if nobody shows inside a minute . . .

The front door was flung wide open, a woman stumbled out, screaming hysterically and that was when the special task force went in, bent low and running. Mr Turley was sitting dazed in front of a television screen that had the sound on mute. Two young children were clinging to him sobbing.

The three police officers went up the stairs, would have smashed the bedroom door in if it had not already been wide open, curtains flapping in the draught through the broken pane.

'Armed police!'

Blake Barrett was inside the room, all right. He lay on the floor in a pool of his own blood, the gun still clutched in his hands, face downwards. An officer kicked the pump-action away, pushed the muzzle of his own weapon against the prone man's neck. That was when Blake Barrett groaned and moved slightly.

Graham Lawson knelt to carry out a cursory examination, the ambulance men with their stretcher standing behind him. The charge had blown away Barrett's chin, he was bleeding profusely, would not last the hour.

A shot of morphine, begrudging every drop of it. The bastard should suffer until he died; they should bring back hanging. Angry, straightening up and motioning to the men to load the dying gunman on to the stretcher.

'I'd better come with you,' Lawson spoke as a

trained and dedicated doctor. He had to do everything in his power to save life, no matter whose.

Barrett bled heavily all the way to hospital but he had not lost consciousness. Those pale eyes roved the interior of the ambulance, settled on Graham Lawson. Manic, there was no other word for it, the way they blazed and hated, mocked. You have to save me, doctor, shirk your duty and you're in trouble.

Craddock was waiting in the theatre, a Ku-Klux-Klan figure in his white overalls and mask, just his eyes visible. There was no need for Graham Lawson to stay, they would not need an ordinary GP. From now on it was the specialist's job to try to save a life that would be a blight on the human race and a burden on the tax payer.

Lawson heard the rest from Philip Craddock a few evenings later when he and Cicely dined with the neuro-surgeon and his wife.

'The bugger should have made a proper job of it and saved us all time and trouble,' Craddock said. 'There was nothing on this earth that was going to save him but we still had to put him on that life-support machine. For just half an hour. And I'll let you into a little secret seeing as we four have shared a few in the past,' it was the cognac that was talking now. 'We could perhaps have kept him alive for four or five hours at the most but then they brought that bank manager fellow in. Sometimes it falls upon us surgeons to play God and that was one of the times. And I can tell you I didn't hesitate! Which was more important, a banker's life or a killer's? You don't have to answer, you'd have done exactly the same. We switched off, *executed* Barrett, if you like, and saved the banker. Cain made a miraculous recovery against all odds and my conscience is clear.'

'Here's your cocoa, dear, and I do think you ought to come to bed. You look drained.'

'Oh . . . thanks,' Graham Lawson started, his rugged features managed a smile. 'You go on up, I won't be long. I'll just drink this and then check the house.'

Reliving that night wasn't good and it wasn't the first time, either. Except that tonight had been the worst. He had seen in his mind Barrett's eyes again, felt the malign force that emanated from them, something that transcended madness. *Sheer evil.*

Most terrifying of all was the fact that they existed not just in his memory, that would have been bad enough. Tonight he had seen them again in the flesh, orbs that burned and filmed over, cleared again. The hatred, the evil was still there, alive when it should have been dead and finished.

For the dying gunman's eyes were reborn in Ed Cain. And the contorted expression on the bank manager's face had been that of a dangerous psychopath.

Graham Lawson knew that he must not delay that invitation to a fishing expedition for he had to learn what it was that festered inside Ed Cain's rebuilt body. There must be no delay for if his suspicions were correct then Judy and the children were in terrible danger.

CHAPTER FOURTEEN

The idea of a half day's fishing appealed to Ed Cain more now than it would have done a year or so ago. Or before last March.

He was finding enthusiasm for things which previously had been boring, a social function connected with customer relations. Like golf. His body tingled with the memory of that drive; the swing, the physical force, the direction. The satisfying *thwack* as he found his target. His breathing quickened, his pulses raced, he was back there in the rough savouring every second. He laughed. Golf was really a *blood sport* if you played it right.

He thought about taking up shooting for the coming winter. The only time he had ever handled a firearm was on the rifle range when he was in the cadet force. He had won a marksman's badge so he surely had a flair for guns. They took on an exciting prospect, a matter of life and death. One gentle squeeze of the trigger . . . much the same as driving a golf ball where you wanted it.

The morning following his row with Richard he had not breakfasted with the family. The atmosphere he had created would take time to disperse in spite of his apology. Funny thing, he really *was* sorry. He tried to tell himself that he was being protective towards his son but he knew he lied. It wasn't that at all, it was . . . *jealousy*. Because Richard might have been out screwing with some comely wench and that was an electrifying erotic thought. An idea that began to arouse him, tell the boy he can invite the Lee girl round one evening . . .

It was mid-morning when Graham Lawson phoned, as taciturn as ever. 'How about a spot of fishing this afternoon, you young bugger? And don't tell me you're too busy else I'll write you out a sick note now and keep you off work for a fortnight!'

'Sounds a great idea,' Ed glanced out of the window, saw a cloudless blue sky. It was hot out there, it would be lovely and cool down by the river. 'I'll see you down by the Fiddler's Bend around three.'

'And don't come pissed,' Lawson's dry sense of humour might have been misinterpreted by any who did not know him well. 'I'm too old for life-saving acts now and I don't fancy giving an ugly bugger like you mouth-to-mouth resusitation!'

Graham Lawson as he always was and always would be. But Ed was suspicious; that visit last night was just too much of a coincidence. The doctor was shrewd, too bloody clever for his own good. He *might* just suspect something. And even as he pondered Ed thought he heard that laughter inside his own head but it faded like a distant echo.

Ed cleared his desk shortly after one o'clock, did not fail to note the look of relief on Houghton's face when he informed the accountant that he would not be returning to the office today as he had a business appointment. And it's nobody's business what, where or with whom. Then he took a quick bar lunch in the

Green Dragon and drove home to collect his fishing gear.

There was no sign of Judy or Becky. Ed could not remember whether or not the latter had been up when he left this morning. If his daughter was not at school then in all probability Judy had taken her to the park for some fresh air.

He drove out of town, turned off the bypass on to a winding country lane, and after a mile or so he pulled into a farm gateway. Tatton's Farm, a hundred acres or so of meadowland bright yellow with buttercups that ran down to the river. Cattle grazed peacefully, did not even bother to look up as he walked through them; so peaceful, it was almost impossible to realize that three miles away the city was a hub-bub of carnival-like atmosphere, that industrial estates were gradually swallowing up Nature's kingdom as they sprawled their way across the landscape. He almost felt at peace with the world. Almost.

Lawson had not arrived yet, perhaps the doctor had had an urgent call-out. An emergency; a cement-mixer rolled back and crushed the car behind or a Mini gone off the dual carriageway and exploded into a fireball. Or some hapless golfer with a golf ball smashed through his skull right into his brain.

The laughter came back, just a couple of peals, enough to make him clasp his hands to his head, groan aloud. Then it receded, left him sweating in the hot sunshine. *Oh, God, what has happened to me?*

Again he attempted to reason it out. Not brain damage, a series of scans had proved beyond any doubt that his brain was uninjured. What then? It had begun with his accident, there was no doubt about that. Unbelievably he could remember being transported to hospital, the closeness of death. He should have died but he had not. The life-support machine had saved him, modern technology preserving that tiny spark of life.

Ed sat down on the river bank, leaned back in the shade of an overhanging willow tree. He closed his eyes. Oh, Christ, it was like being back on that machine! All in the mind, he tried to tell himself. Everything was in the mind. He could see his own body, remembered it as clearly as he had on that awful night; the fight to stay alive, exerting every vestige of willpower to prevent his astral from slipping away into the unknown. Then gently floating down to rejoin his physical form. The agony of that re-entry, it was like being mortal again and yet having *something* desperately trying to enter his body, a kind of obscene rape. Attempting to close every orifice against it but in the end it found a way in, claimed him like some filthy virus seeking a host to spawn and breed its fever.

That was when his terror, his manic fits, had begun. Whatever it was that had claimed him like a demented soul in search of a human body now controlled him. He was a human robot at its bidding, a slave to lust and violence.

'What's this, napping when you ought to be fishing?'

Ed started, opened his eyes as he straightened up and in any other circumstances he would have had to conceal his mirth at the sight of Graham Lawson in fishing attire. The latter wore a tweed deerstalker hat which was a couple of sizes too small, pushed back so that it perched precariously on the crown of his head. A shirt that was unbuttoning itself under the strain of a protruding waistline and rumpling up out of his trousers, part of the tail already flapping free. A misshapen sports jacket and the trousers of a discarded suit tucked untidily into wellington boots.

'Oh, I was just relaxing whilst I waited for you,

Graham.' Scrambling up, reaching for his rod like a young boy disturbed in the midst of some nefarious deed.

'Are you sure you're feeling okay, Ed?' The doctor's jocular tone was gone, he was staring fixedly at his companion's pale and haggard features, the way those haunted eyes roamed around as though Ed Cain expected to find some nameless monstrosity lurking in the bushes around him.

'I'm fine!' Abrupt, defiant almost. 'It's bloody hot, the heat has never suited me. Well, we'd better get set up. Where do you want to go, Graham?'

'I'll fish from that clump of hawthorns,' the GP indicated some straggling bushes fifteen yards or so downstream. 'No point in being half a mile apart, after all it is something of a social occasion.' I want to keep an eye on you, boy, you look absolutely ghastly. 'I'll go and set my stall up.'

This part of the river was merely a tributary of the wide fast-flowing one which it joined a quarter of a mile further down river beneath a monstrosity of a viaduct. From then onwards the sluggish current became a foaming torrent, boiled its way down to the wide weir, eventually cutting back towards the city itself.

Ed cast his hook, heard it plop into the water three or four yards from the opposite bank, watched the bobbing float. Hypnotic, in a way, his pulses speeded up. The killing game again. Like golf. That hook would embed itself in the jaws of an unsuspecting fish and . . . the float bobbed, he felt a tug on his line. Oh, sweet Jesus, I've caught one already!

He began to wind his line in and seconds later a threshing, flapping fish was dragged clear of the water. A grayling, perhaps a three-pounder, it swung upwards, gyrating, fighting him all the way.

I want you to suffer, you slippery, slimy bastard! Words inside his head before he had even thought them. Frightening, but exciting. Taking his time, savouring every second of the fish's tortured struggles until finally he had it wriggling in his grasp. Forcing the jaws wide, seeing how the hook had buried itself deeply, easing it free like a sadistic dentist intent on hurting his patient, inflicting a maximum of pain.

'Bloody beginner's luck!' Lawson was watching, his headgear at an even more ridiculous angle.

Cain did not reply, tossed the flapping grayling into his keep-net, thrilled at the sight of its torn mouth and its slowing movements. Bulging fish eyes inflated with pain and terror. Take your time dying, you fucker!

He cast again, this time into mid-stream. His hands were trembling; the killing lust was taking hold of him. Come on, I want another. And another.

The doctor hooked a small trout, tossed it back into the river. A pause whilst he unscrewed his thermos and poured some dark brown tea, took his time filling and lighting his pipe. The midges were becoming troublesome now that late afternoon was approaching, the rank tobacco smoke would help to keep them at bay. Even doctors had to satisfy their conscience when the craving became too strong to resist.

Lawson glanced towards his companion from time to time. Ed was ill, there was no doubt about that but the treatment did not fall into an ordinary GP's field of capabilities. It went further than that, Ed Cain needed to see a psychiatrist, it was definitely no physical problem. Maybe he could be persuaded, the doctor did not relish the prospect but his concern was for Judy and the children.

Six-thirty pm and the fish were not biting even though conditions were ideal. Lawson secured his rod between his battered wicker fishing basket and a convenient low bough, stood up and stretched his bulky frame. Cain was still intent on watching his float, the man's intensity was disturbing, like that of a primeval fisherman whose family depended upon his catches to survive.

Pipe in mouth the doctor sauntered along the top of the steep bank. Ed Cain was not aware of his approach until Lawson was within a couple of yards of him. Again the surprised start, those wide eyes taking time to filter through their opaque glaze.

'Getting bored?' A reprimand rather than a casual enquiry. I'm busy, I have to *kill.* Fuck off and leave me alone!

'I don't think we'll do much good today,' Lawson lowered himself down on to the springy grass. 'If you ask me there's pollution seeping into this river, that's why the fish are scarce. There's a nice little pub in the village about a mile from here, I could just sink a pint of ice-cold lager and lime.'

Ed Cain did not reply, he was concentrating on his float again, oblivious of all else.

'I'm worried about you, Ed. You haven't made the progress I'd hoped you might after such a marvellous recovery in the early stages.'

'Got one!' A shout that transcended a fisherman's euphoria, was throaty with bloodlust. 'Come on, you bugger, I want you!'

Lawson watched, saw a small brown trout break the surface, a tiddler no more than four inches long, threshing madly as it was hauled in. Ed's hand clamped over its slippery body, fingers cruelly wrenching at the jaws; pushing the hook in deeper, gouging, laughing to himself as fish blood welled up in the tiny mouth. A sudden wrench that freed the bloody hook, then using the needle sharp point to pierce the eyes, popping them like bubbles. He flung the trout on to the grass, watched its death throes.

Doctor Lawson thought he might vomit as nausea flooded over him, the sharp taste of bile scorched the back of his throat. He opened his mouth to speak but the words of revulsion would not come. He tried to avert his gaze but his neck seemed to have temporarily lost its power of movement. Oh, my God, what's he going to do now!

Cain had his fishing knife in his hand, holding it by the blade, the stout bone handle a miniature cudgel. Raising it, pausing as he delighted in the act he was about to perpetrate, then bringing it sharply down on the bloody trout's head. A frenzied attack, bludgeoning mercilessly until the fish was a bloody mulch, battering the pulp until it squelched in all directions, laughing his obscene glee aloud throughout. And only when the fish was obliterated did he stop.

Lawson's vision swam, he was on his feet, having to hold on to a willow branch because he felt faint. And once again his thoughts turned to Judy, to Richard and Becky. They were in terrible danger.

'Ed, let's go and have that pint,' he thought he spoke reasonably calmly, as if he had noticed nothing untoward in the despatching of a tiny fish that any angler would have returned to the river.

'I want to catch another!' Churlish childish behaviour, a small boy on his first fishing trip refusing to pack up at his father's suggestion.

'Ed . . . you're sick, man!'

Doctor Graham Lawson recoiled as the other's head turned and those eyes were uplifted to meet his own. Filming, then clearing like a stage curtain revealing the finale of some gruesome play. Blazing hatred that was directed towards himself. 'Like I said, I want to kill another!'

Lawson backed away a step instinctively. There was no mistaking that expression, he would never forget the maniacal fury that had burned in those orbs that terrible March evening. *He was seeing again the living dead eyes of Blake Barrett!*

'Ed, you're ill. You need treatment urgently.'

It was a damnfool thing to say, the words just seemed to slip out. Too late, he should have known better; you never tell a madman he's ill, basic training at medical college.

'So you think I'm mad, do you?' Ed Cain straightened up, a supple movement that defied those horrific injuries which his body had fought to repair over the past months. A tensing of his frame, head thrust forward, arms extended, fingers flexing. The mouth was fixed in a mirthless smile but again it was the protruding eyes that brought a sharp stab of fear to Lawson's chest as his heart missed a beat.

'Come on, Ed, let's go and have a drink and . . . '

'You've guessed, doc, I feared as much,' the words were a lisp, not the voice belonging to the city bank manager. 'You didn't come here to fish with me, you came deliberately to spy on me. And now you're going to do your best to get me put away. Aren't you?'

'No, Ed, I . . . '

'Don't lie to me,' edging a step closer, the hands reaching out. 'You're going to end up like Cutler. And that whore, Suzy. *And God, how I'm going to enjoy every second of it!*'

Lawson panicked, turned to flee, felt the other's fingers clutching at his jacket but somehow tore himself free. Laboured breathing, his body was not used to sudden movement, his heavy rubber boots clumsy. A shriek of fury behind him had him lurching forward and even as he tried to run he felt the sheer bank beneath him starting to collapse.

He screamed as he fell, his flailing arms brushing against those of his pursuer as he plunged dizzily downwards. A fall of no more than five feet, he saw the dark murky waters coming up at him, would have taken a deep breath and held it had there been time and his lungs had been capable. Instead he splashed down into the sluggish depths, was swallowing water and threshing helplessly even as he disappeared below the surface.

Ed Cain ran along the river bank; stopped, waited. His gaze searched every ripple, anticipating that at any second that capacious form in bedraggled tweeds would float into view, that he would be able to reach out and drag the doctor to the side. *So that he could vent his escalating fury upon the old man, pulp him like he had pulped that fish, squeeze his neck until the swollen tongue protruded between the purple lips and the eyes swelled to bursting.*

A euphoric cry escaped Ed's lips as he saw the deer-stalker hat bob up, then he screeched his anger and frustration as no head followed it. The sodden garment floated, waterlogged, a yard or so from the bank and then began to drift downstream.

Ten minutes later there was still no sign of the body, for surely the doctor had to be drowned by now. Ed walked a hundred yards or so along the bank, came back slowly, his eyes scanning every clump of water weed and rushes. But there was nothing, apart from the fishing basket with the rod wedged up against it beneath those hawthorn bushes, it was as if Doctor Lawson had not been here this afternoon.

Ed squatted on his haunches, braced himself for the insane laughter which was beginning somewhere deep inside him, this time laced with rage and frustration, chiding him for allowing his prey to escape his clutches. Doctor Graham Lawson was dead, there was no doubt about that, but for Ed Cain the other might as well have lived for he had been deprived of the pleasure of killing. A wasted death, the only consolation being that Lawson had taken his suspicions to his watery grave with him.

The evening shadows were beginning to stretch out across the slow-moving river when Ed finally straightened up, shook his head in an attempt to clear the muzziness left by that enraged screaming inside his skull. Trembling, weakened by the sheer mental effort which he had undergone, trying to think logically.

An accident. Like John Cutler's, nobody could dispute it. Cain the Jonah; shun his company else you might die, too. He saw the fishing tackle, left it where it was and began the long walk back to the parked car through the buttercups.

Remorse now, almost having to force it because his mind and body still ached from the craving to kill. That fish had been but a passing pleasure, an aperitif but the main course had not been served.

He reached the Volvo, looked back once, shaded his eyes against the evening sunlight as he followed the black ribbon of the river down to the ugly viaduct. The corpse would be out there somewhere, maybe already being rushed by the raging torrent of the mother river down towards the weir, beyond his reach.

Ed pulled up by the phone box on the edge of the village and made a 999 call to report the drowning.

CHAPTER FIFTEEN

Pretty was dying.

Norma Pringle gave way to a shriek of hysteria when Simon Vine broke the news with about as much sublety as a television weather forecaster informing his viewers that tomorrow would be warm and dry. No emotion, just an unequivocal statement of fact.

'I don't think she'll make it beyond tomorrow,' he turned away to swill his hands under the tap.

'*What*!' Norma recoiled, hand clasped to her mouth. 'But you can't . . . let her *die*!'

'I've no choice, I'm afraid,' the vet reached down a towel.

'But . . . but the bite is healing nicely,' Norma panicked, looking for a scapegoat. '*You* treated her and you said . . . '

'The bite has got nothing to do with it, directly,' Vine's patience was becoming rapidly exhausted. 'It healed well, better than I dared hope for a cat her age.'

'She's not old.'

'She's a good fifteen, you can tell by her teeth. When was she born?'

'I don't know,' Norma's usually florid complexion had turned an off-white. 'She was a stray, just arrived one day. Whilst my husband was alive.'

'There you are then. Possibly the shock hastened her end, it's difficult to say.'

'I refuse to pay you.'

'You've paid up-to-date. There's no charge for this visit, I didn't do anything. Now, if you'll excuse me, there are people outside in the waiting room.'

Norma sobbed her way back home, carrying Pretty wrapped in an old cardigan in the wicker shopping basket as though she bore a priceless Wedgwood dinner service. Heads turned in amazement as she pushed her way through the crowded Festival streets, hindered by a throng spilling out of the civil theatre where a matinée performance of the *Life of Samuel Johnson* had just finished. Norma hated people more than ever now, they were laughing and joking in a time of crisis. They didn't understand.

Back home, with Pretty still sleeping in her basket in the corner of the kitchen, Norma sought solace in a bottle of Black Label. Whisky, she admitted privately, was her only vice and right now she needed it.

Three glasses later her thoughts returned vengefully to Ed Cain and his abominable dog. She had not seen the brute for a day or two which meant that the Cains admitted its guilt and were keeping it shut up. Well, it was going to pay for what it had done!

She made no attempt to hold back her tears as she went out to the garden shed; this had been Peter's abode where he spent most of his leisure hours messing about with seeds that seldom germinated or potting cuttings that died. Bless him! She had a vague memory of that time when he had been nearly frantic because he had seen a rat in the garden. Norma remembered him going out and buying some rodent poison; she had been a trifle unfair to him, shrieked at him to 'keep that awful stuff well away from the house'. It *might* just still be around somewhere. It was, on a ledge amongst some piles of plant pots, the faded label just legible. POISON. KEEP WELL AWAY FROM CHILDREN AND PETS. Well, that spoke volumes, it was just what she was looking for.

Norma worked with enthusiasm; two slices of wholemeal bread and the remains of a tin of Whiskas which Pretty wouldn't be needing any more; Norma wasn't going to get another cat, none could replace Pretty. Still crying, she smeared cat food on the bread, sprinkled it liberally with the greyish-green powder out of the rusty tin once she had managed to prise the lid off. A lethal sandwich, she wrapped it carefully in a freezer bag. Now all that was necessary was to feed it to the Cain dog. She paused; that wasn't easy, if she just threw it into their drive anything might get it, probably half the jackdaws that fouled the stonework of the cathedral would drop dead. Which wasn't a bad idea except that it would not help Pretty's cause.

And then she had an idea, almost smiled to herself. Canon Holland would help her, she was sure of that.

Ed Cain was exhausted. He had spent over two hours being questioned at the police station. Damn it, they were getting suspicious, there was no doubt about that.

The lean-faced Detective Sergeant Biddle reminded Ed of a ferret, a predator which never relinquished the faintest of scents, prepared to hunt down its prey until it dropped. He was surprised that the policeman showed no signs of embarrassment; Biddle was a customer of the bank and was always in financial difficulties. Lived beyond his means, there was always a pleading phone call towards the end of the month. 'Is it all right if I go overdrawn for about a week until my pay cheque comes through? Fifty quid should see me all right.'

Every month without fail, and getting a day earlier each time. Eventually Biddle would be a month in arrears. Ed let him overdraw, at least he had a regular income, and it was peanuts really. Likewise it was prudent to keep in with the law, you never knew when you might need them. Right now, though, it had all blown up in Ed's face, the detective was treating him like a stranger. No concessions, no favouritism.

'You were involved in a fatal accident a few weeks ago, I believe, sir?' Keen grey eyes watching every movement the banker made, noting each twitch of a facial muscle; trained to detect guilt.

'Yes.' Don't elaborate, just answer the questions.

'A man was killed then. A Mr . . . ' consulting a file although he doubtless knew the name. 'Cutler. John Cutler.'

Ed nodded.

'And now on another sporting outing your companion slips into the river and drowns. We recovered Doctor Lawson's body beyond the weir, by the way.'

Ed nodded again. Play it deadpan, don't give anything away. His greatest fear was that they might suddenly throw Suzy's name at him. Or the Mini driver's. Even Cling. Now you are getting shit scared.

'I guess I'm a kind of Jonah,' he made an unfunny joke of it which the policeman appeared to ignore.

It was 11.30 that night when Ed finally arrived home. He knew that there would be a second interrogation from Judy, it was going to be difficult.

Only Judy and the children weren't at home, he sensed the emptiness of the house even as he parked the Volvo in the drive. No lights showed at the windows, everybody could have been in bed. He tried to deceive himself, only accepted that number nineteen, The Close, was empty when he had checked every room.

And then the phone rang. And his premonition was correct, it was Judy.

'I'm at Mother's,' she sounded tired, strained. 'Becky and Richard are with me. Mother's not too well . . . '

Mother was never well, Ed reflected cynically, if it wasn't varicose veins or arthritis then it was suspected angina. 'Oh, I see.' You're keeping out of the way in case I drive a golf ball at you or push you in the river.

'I'll be back tomorrow evening, all being well,' which contradicted his suspicions. Judy's mother only lived on the other side of the city, she could have commuted to tend the sick. Maybe she just needed a break from the tension. 'Is everything all right with you?'

So she had not heard the news yet, had probably left earlier in the day when Richard and Becky came out of school. 'More or less,' he tried to sound casual, 'a bit of news but I'll tell you tomorrow.'

He replaced the handset before she could ask further. It had been quite a day.

'Why, Norma!' There was surprised relief on Canon Holland's fleshy features as he edged the door open and recognized his caller in the shadows of a late summer evening. 'Do come inside.'

She followed him down that same gloomy passage and into the library where a reading lamp on the mahogany roll-top desk shone on reams of typewritten sheets. He shuffled across to the bow window, drew the curtains. Norma's nostrils wrinkled, the atmosphere was thick with tobacco smoke; smoking should be banned by law, it was another form of drug addiction. But right now she had more urgent matters on her mind than to launch into a tirade on the evils of 'the weed'. Besides, she needed Cecil's co-operation.

'My dear, is something the matter?' His thick neck was thrust forward, gave the impression that his cleric's collar was attempting to strangle him. 'You've been crying.'

'I have,' she didn't attempt to check her sobs, let a tear roll down her cheek. 'That blasted dog of the Cains' has killed my Pretty!'

'Oh, dear, I'm most terribly sorry. Please accept my sympathies.' He smelled whisky fumes on her breath. 'When . . . when did poor Pretty die?'

'She's not dead yet but she will be before morning,' Norma placed a polythene-wrapped package on the desk, covered her face with her hands. She began to shake uncontrollably.

'Sit down, sit down,' he took her arm, steered her over to an armchair. 'Let me get you a drink. What would you like? Whisky?'

After some minutes Norma regained her composure; she would keep on the whisky for a week or two at least, she decided, to get her over her bereavement. It had helped when Peter died.

'I want you to do me a very big favour, Cecil,' Norma lowered her voice to a rasping whisper.

'Anything, my dear. Just anything,' there was an eagerness about him now. 'Nothing is too much trouble where you are concerned. What is it you want me to do?'

'There's a . . . a *sandwich* in that bag,' she gestured towards the desk. 'When it's properly dark I want you to slip it through the hedge into the Cains' garden.'

'Oh!' He stiffened.

'There's rat poison in it. I want to kill that brute of a dog!'

Cecil Holland tensed and his entwined fingers began to shake. 'I . . . I haven't seen that dog for some days. I think they might have got rid of it.'

'In which case there'll be no harm done, will there? If it's dead, it's dead. I just have to be sure for my own peace of mind.'

'Vengeance is mine, sayeth the Lord,' he quoted in a nervous voice.

'Yes but sometimes we have to help Him with it,' she smiled cynically, dabbed at her eyes with a tissue. 'You will do it, won't you, Cecil?'

'Suppose they have got rid of the dog and one of the children picks it up,' he had paled in the half-light cast by the lamp on the other side of the room.

Then serve 'em bloody well right, she thought. She said, 'They're too old to eat food they find lying about.'

'Have you heard the terrible news?' The canon glanced round the room as though he feared an eaves-dropper might be hiding in the shadows.

'No.' Norma wasn't interested in anything other than Pretty's pending death and her vengeance on that labrador which, without a shadow of doubt and no matter what that stupid vet said, had bitten her cat.

'Doctor Lawson has been drowned in the river!'

'My God!'

'Yes, and he had gone fishing with Mr Cain!' There was no mistaking the innuendo. 'I hear that the police had him down at the police station for some time but they let him go without charging him. A detective came to see me this evening, asked an awful lot of questions. They're as suspicious as you and I, particularly after that . . . er, *accident* on the golf course a few weeks ago. They've got no proof and until they have . . . '

'Like we said the last time we talked.' Her face was deathly white in the semi-darkness. 'He's *evil*, Cecil. As evil as his dog. It's as though anybody who crosses him, and that other poor man and the doctor must surely have offended him, get *murdered.* You will put that poison through the hedge for me, won't you?'

'I . . . I . . . ' the canon was trembling, searching for a valid reason why he should not become a poisoner. *It's as though anybody who crosses him gets murdered.*

'Please, Cecil!'

'All right,' nodding, aware that his ill-fitting dentures clicked like distant castanets. 'For you, Norma. I wouldn't do it for anybody else.'

'Thank you, Cecil,' she stood up. 'Now, I must get back to Pretty, every second with her is precious now.'

He followed her to the front door, stood watching her shapeless, shuffling silhouette until the darkness swallowed it up. Then he returned to the library, picked up that lethal package, and waddled through to the back door and out into the rear garden.

Cecil Holland stood there in the sultry summer darkness, his sweat chilling on his body and causing him to shiver. Vengeance is mine, sayeth the Lord. He glanced heavenwards, muttered, 'Forgive me, Lord, for my deceit.'

Moving as quickly as his overweight body would allow, he approached the battered dustbin, struggled to lift the dented lid, and dropped the wrapped sandwich inside.

He hoped that the Cains had got rid of their dog, it would save an awful lot of awkward questions if they had. He had taken the cowardly way out, he had lied and deceived and his sleep would be a fitful one tonight. *Anybody who crosses him gets murdered.* At least

Cecil Holland's conscience was clear in that respect, he had opted for the lesser of the two evils and God would surely understand.

'Oh, my Pretty, my darling!'

Norma's first thought was that the whisky was causing hallucinations as she entered the kitchen and switched on the light. There, standing by the table, back arched and stretching, was her cat who was doomed not to awake from her last slumber, stretching and mewing plaintively.

'And you're asking Mummy for a drink of milk! Oh, my sweet, I'd buy you a tanker full!'

Hurrying, trembling with relief and excitement, Norma went to the fridge. A single milk bottle, a quarter full, its contents partially solidified due to the hot weather, was jammed in the door basket. Her shaking fingers grasped at it, tugged feverishly. Blast that holder, it was too small, a bad design; it always gave trouble, she frequently slopped milk on to the salad box or spilled it on the floor wrestling to free the bottle!

This time it seemed well and truly stuck. Pretty purred, rubbed herself around Norma's ankle socks. 'Hang on, my sweetie. I've a damned good mind to write to the manufacturers about this!'

She grasped the neck with both hands, swayed unsteadily for a second or two, felt dizzy. She really ought not to have accepted that whisky from dear Cecil, she had drunk more than was good for her earlier. But it didn't matter because Pretty appeared to have made a miraculous recovery. Thank you, God. Damn this bloody bottle, Pretty needs a drink of milk to give her strength.

Without warning the milk bottle came free. An upwards rush, Norma's hands still clutching it, grazing her knuckles, and then the neck shattered on the bottom of the egg-holder immediately above. A crashing and splintering of glass, cream that was fast turning to cheese splattering on her bare arms and face. Staring in dismay at the jagged bottle neck still grasped in her fingers, hearing glass tinkling and splintering on the quarry-tiled floor.

'Oh, Pretty, I've spilt the milk!'

Norma stared at her hands, the thick white fluid oozing over her flesh. A sudden desperate idea, she would hold out her hands, let the cat lick the milk off them.

Suddenly the white was turning pink, then claret. No longer thick and sluggish, it was bright scarlet and spurting with force.

Norma Pringle screamed, held up her hands, saw the gashed wrists, jagged gouges from which arterial blood sprayed like a lawn sprinkler, jetted over walls and ceiling.

Staring in terror and disbelief. It had to be a trick, an optical illusion, because there was no pain. She heard the swish of spouting blood, felt its warmth as it showered her face, tasted its bitterness on her lips. Her vision clouded, a kind of fog that was tinged with crimson; she had to hold on to the fridge door or else she would have fallen.

Terrible realization came slowly, slurred by alcohol. Pretty was licking up milk splashes off the floor. Mind you don't cut your tongue, darling, Mummy has to get help. Quickly.

The telephone was in the hallway. Norma staggered one step; two. Something furry moved between her legs and she lurched to one side, afraid in case she stepped on her resurrected cat. Mind, my love, I have to ring for the doctor. Doctor Lawson's dead, murdered by the bank manager. Never mind, one of the other doctors will do.

Then she was falling, pitching forward, Pretty leaping out of the way just in time to avoid being crushed as Norma hit the floor with stunning force, rolled over and lay still.

Pretty sat and watched as twin spouts of blood fountained, began to lose their impetus, slowed to a treacly trickle and formed a sticky pool in the centre of the kitchen floor.

The cat finished lapping the spilled cheesy milk, then curled up close to its inert mistress. And later that night Pretty passed peacefully away in her sleep.

CHAPTER SIXTEEN

'I suppose accidents *do* happen,' Judy seemed to have aged five years since Ed had seen her last, the day before yesterday. There were dark rings round her eyes; her hair was awry. 'But you do seem to be having more than your fair share lately, Ed.'

'It's the luck of the draw,' he watched her carefully for signs of disbelief, suspicion. 'The bloody police haven't exactly been sympathetic. Christ Almighty, they rang and asked me to go round to the station again this morning, went through the whole rigmarole again. Wasn't there any way you could have saved him, Mr Cain? It was over an hour before you reported it, according to the pathologist's finding of the time of death! Bloody hell, I walked half way to the viaduct trying to get a glimpse of him. Then they asked me all about Norma Pringle, they knew we'd had a barney or two with her but as she bled to death from a severed artery caused by accidentally cutting her wrists on a broken milk bottle, I don't see what that has to do with *me*!'

'It's all a routine procedure, I suppose.' Judy sank down on to the settee. 'They have to explore every possibility.'

'They've virtually accused me of murdering Lawson, Cutler *and* that bloody old cow!' He shouted, his eyes staring, protruding the way they had the other night when he had quarrelled with Richard.

Judy's mouth was dry, she was tense. She ought not to have returned home, would perhaps have stayed another couple of days with her mother if it had not been for these latest deaths. She was reproaching herself for bringing the children back. Becky was asleep upstairs, still drained from that migraine, Richard was out with Tracey. And, please God, don't let there be another row when he comes home. She had asked him specially to be in by ten-thirty, pandering to Ed in a way that she could not stand any more. If it had not been for finding Cling's body buried in the flower border she might just have passed everything off as a series of tragedies. Or at least tried to.

She heard the back door open, click softly shut and every nerve in her body went taut.

'Hi, Mum, Dad,' Richard pushed open the lounge door, looking in. 'I'm back. Think I'll get an early night.'

Ed nodded, did not say anything. She let out her pent-up breath; a minor hurdle crossed but she could not stand hurdles every night.

'Maybe we should move house,' she had been considering the idea for the last day or two.

'Why?' Abrupt, challenging.

'A place can get you down. Also there are such things as . . . jinxed houses.'

'Rubbish!' He laughed harshly. 'Anyway, I happen to like it here.'

'I don't, not any more. And all this isn't doing the children any good. They have to go to school and kids are cruel. Jimmy Cutler is in Richard's year, he's been making comments, keeps on that "your dad murdered my dad'' and so forth. Also Graham Lawson was a legend in this city, folks are going to bear a grudge, hold it against us.'

'Shit that!' His cheeks flushed. 'Anyway, we can't move, I'm tied here for the next three or four years and then I might get a top job at Regional Head Office. If I request a transfer it'll either be a sideways move or demotion.'

A sense of being trapped, claustrophobic terror. But this was neither the place nor the time to tell her husband that she was going to leave him. When she did that the kids would be with her in some nice safe place miles away from here and she would break the news by telephone or letter. She could not continue to live with a killer much longer, even if the deaths were not proved to be directly associated with Ed.

'Let's go to bed,' he straightened up, she noted the stiffness of his limbs where they had been re-built.

For Judy, Ed had died that night in the crushed Volvo beneath the cement-mixer.

Ed Cain was on his way to the hospital again. Semi-conscious he was aware of the moving ambulance, going round the big island, picking up speed. People with him, he sensed their presence, could neither see nor hear them. Frantic because it was terrifying even if it was only the recurring nightmare.

The short journey on the stretcher, the bright lights dazzling him through closed eyelids. Trying to force his lips to move, to throw out the words that were jammed in his throat.

'I don't want to go on that life-support machine again!'

But they would put him on it, attach the wires, start it up. And then the terror would return for real.

He felt the upward pull, was able to see now, look down on his own mutilated body. *But this time he wasn't going to fight to return to it. He would let himself drift upwards into the unknown. Let himself die because that was the only way he would ever escape this hellish torment.*

He reckoned he looked pretty mashed up, wondered to what extent the morticians would stitch him up in case his family requested the macabre experience of viewing him in the chapel of rest. Goodbye, Ed Cain, nice to know you.

He was aware that his astral body was up against the high emulsioned ceiling; he relaxed, waited to pass through it. Floated like a kid's balloon on a windless day.

Nothing was happening, he was just suspended there. *But I am not returning to my body. I don't want it any longer. Bury it, cremate it, do what the hell you like with it.*

The feeling of vertigo came gradually, a nauseating dizziness, a sense of falling. He was aware that he was drifting slowly downwards. He fought against it but he was powerless, a needle on a carpet being dragged towards a magnet. So gentle, it was far more frightening than being catapulted downwards. Despair, if he could have groaned aloud he would have done so.

Then he was back in his body, aware that he had limbs, fingers and toes that might have moved had he the strength. But this time it was different, an awareness that crept upon him. Everybody was gone, surgeons and nurses had abandoned him, left him here alone.

And within himself he began to scream his terror, his fear of that unknown evil entity which was lurking close by, awaiting its opportunity to enter his flesh and blood.

He heard it start to laugh, a chilling, taunting sound that was now so familiar; that same manic laughter which mocked him as it took control of him, brought with it an insatiable lust. An overture of death; Cutler's skull smashed by a golf ball, Suzy lewdly spread on a soiled bedsheet, Doctor Lawson flailing and screaming as he hit the water. He even saw in his mind how Norma Pringle might have looked with arterial blood spouting up out of her gashed wrists and making bright red crazy patterns on the walls and ceiling. He pulsed with excitement at the thought and then he felt that cold feathery touch on his body as the thing played with him, seeking a means of entry.

Screaming at it to go away, to leave him in peace. *Please let me die*!

The laughter was deafening, vibrating his skull, threatening to crack it; Ed writhed in agony and then he heard the voice. At first it was a whisper barely audible against the echoes of that crazed shrieking, insistent. Growing louder by the second.

Nasal tones that lisped, there was no mistaking the mocking, the taunting. A rush of speech, he heard words but failed to understand them. A tirade of ecstatic evil that was a thousand times more frightening than ever the laughter had been.

Listen to me.

Ed was listening, cowering.

I have now taken your body for my own, there is no way you can rid yourself of me. When I command, you will obey. They killed me but I live again so that I can have revenge upon them. You will kill, and kill again, and lust for blood and death. Because you are ME, and I am you.

Not understanding, only knowing that this vile astral being had obscenely forced its way into his own flesh and blood just as he, himself, had returned to his body when life was ebbing from it.

Oh, Merciful God, no! Drive this devil from me and let me die!

But God was not there for Ed's body now belonged to the dark powers, the ungodly. He had asked for life and this was Satan's price for living.

Suddenly he found that he could move again, that the attachments of the life-support machine had been removed. He stretched out his arms, his legs. Opened his eyes. The blinding light was gone, he was in pitch darkness, some ghastly hell pit to which he had been condemned. Writhing, convulsing, fighting the unseen in his panic.

He screamed, 'I want to die!'

Then he felt hands closing in on him, grasping his sweat lathered body. Striking out at them but they grabbed his wrists, held them with a puny strength. Somebody shouted 'Ed!' A voice which he knew yet could not identify at the peak of his terror. Still struggling because he was on that machine surely, even if he was not wired up. They had given him life, sacrificed him to unearthly powers in some satanic bargain. Take him, he is yours, we have no further use for him. Do what you will with him.

The blinding light came back, red hot irons to blind him into eternal darkness. This was the torment of hell, without a doubt.

'Ed, wake up!'

Slowly his vision returned and kneeling over him he saw Judy, naked as though she demanded a mating between human and inhuman. Maybe it was a trick, another of their tortures. He closed his eyes; perhaps when he looked again she would be gone and in her place . . .

Judy was still there, pinning him down, her features a mask of fear.

'No, keep away from me,' he grunted, 'or else they'll take you, too!'

'You've had another nightmare.' She relinquished

her grip as his struggles ceased. 'A bad one. Shall I make a drink?'

He nodded. Anything *normal* was acceptable right now.

He lay there in the lighted bedroom, listened to her going downstairs. God, it had never been as bad as this, not even that time when it had actually happened. Then it had been mercifully beyond his ken, he had been spared the awful knowledge. Now he *knew*!

He attempted to reason it out. First, his astral body had begun to leave his physical one because he was on the verge of death. Somehow it had managed to return . . . *or something had*! A lost astral searching for a body, his own had been there for the taking. *The possession*!

A being now lived within him, a soul that was steeped in evil, a thing that lusted for death and was using his body to satisfy its cravings. He was powerless to resist it, a robot at its command. A slave to evil, Satan's puppet. Kill and kill again.

But whose soul? *For Christ's sake, whose*?

'Here, drink this and take these aspirins.' Judy was back, setting a mug of tea down on the bedside table, two tablets in her extended hand.

He rested on his elbows, stared at the drink, accepted the aspirins. 'Judy, I think I need more than pills to cure me.'

Her relief showed, she had half-expected an outburst. At least now her husband was accepting that there was something wrong with him and that was a major step in the right direction.

'Maybe you should see a . . . ' she almost said 'shrink', 'a psychiatrist, Ed.'

'I think I need more than that.'

'What, then?'

'I . . . don't . . . know.' Tonight it had been more than a dream, more than a re-run of that awful night. Whatever it was that possessed him had shown its hand, left him in no doubt, whatsoever, that it had control over him. It was playing a subtle, terrible game; act normal and deceive everybody, Ed, I'll let you know when I need you. *When the blood lust gets out of hand.*

He popped the pills in his mouth, swigged tea. It tasted bitter. 'I think maybe I should go away for a whle. Instead of driving you and the kids away.'

She was close to tears. Oh, Ed, I *know* you killed cling and maybe Cutler and Doctor Lawson weren't accidents either. She spoke huskily, 'I want to help you. Please let me.'

'We'll talk about it tomorrow,' he finished his tea, lay back. 'I think, though, that we both need all the sleep we can get.'

There would be no more sleep for him tonight, he found himself forcibly staying awake. In case that malevolent force came again. *I want you to kill for me, Ed.* And Judy was by his side, the children just across the landing.

A sudden idea had him tensing with excitement, hope. Perhaps he should try an exorcism. People had had devils banished from them since the days of the bible, you read in the newspapers of modern day evil spirits being driven out of the possessed. Where did you find an exorcist? The bishop, the dean, Canon Holland would know, probably. Ed winced at the thought, the embarrassment. We always knew you were screwy, Mister Cain.

It was a possibility, though. But first he had to discover what exactly it was that had entered his dying body that night; *whose* soul had claimed him. *Somebody who had died in that hospital within a short time of his admittance to the theatre.* Somebody incredibly evil who had seized upon the opportunity to live on within himself.

Lawson might have known but the doctor was dead now. Deliberately silenced to preserve the secret? Would the hospital staff be able to help him? People were dying all the time and four months was a long time where nurses were concerned, they might not even remember who was on duty at the time. And then it came to him.

Philip Craddock, the neuro-surgeon.

Craddock must know, if he could not remember then there had to be records to refer to. Ed trembled; it was a frightening prospect, in some ways he would rather not find out, just accept that he was possessed. But in a way he was fighting a guerilla war within himself, he had to know who his adversary lurking in the darkest shadows of his mind was.

Tonight had been a night of terror but it had not been without its compensations. The enemy had shown his hand and now the battle was on, the loser's forfeit madness and eternal torment.

CHAPTER SEVENTEEN

Philip Craddock's large Edwardian country house was situated just outside the city limits, a miniature commuter belt where the residents were resisting the sprawl of industry. A hamlet of five dwellings, each one secluded in its own spacious grounds.

Ed Cain experienced a sense of nervousness that bordered on awe as he swung the Volvo into the gateway marked 'entrance'; on his left another gravelled track led round to the rear of the house and was signposted 'tradesmen'. Spacious closely mown lawns were dotted with croquet hoops and lined with mature shrubberies.

The house itself was an imposing red brick edifice, its windows seeming to frown down on visitors. Is your call really necessary? If so, please be as brief as possible.

Apart from his recent treatment, Ed had met Craddock on a couple of occasions at the golf club. A tall strikingly handsome man with greying hair, the neuro-surgeon was aloof to a point of rudeness. He played golf with his specialist associates, a clique that was a strictly closed shop and moved only in high circles. Ed had learned that Craddock did not bank in any of the city's High Street branches; he had seen one of his cheques once. Coutts, the Strand. And that relegated Ed to the status of a country bumpkin seeking audience with the great man. Nevertheless, he had to give it a try.

The front door was open, Ed thought he could hear muffled voices somewhere inside the house. He grasped the bell-pull, tugged it once and heard a resonant clang from the inner reaches.

'Can I help you, sir?' The girl was no more than nineteen, attractive, and but for her local accent Ed might have presumed her to be Craddock's daughter. The maid? They probably had a cook, housekeeper and a couple of gardeners on the staff. Perhaps even a part-time butler when they entertained lavishly.

'I'd like to see Mr Craddock, please.'

'Is he expecting you?' All part of the protective barrier, Ed wondered why the surgeon didn't padlock his gates or else have a guard dog patrolling the grounds.

'No, but it is rather important,' he held out one of his business cards; suddenly 'bank manager' seemed low down on the social scale. 'I won't keep him a minute.'

The girl glanced at the card, nodded. 'Wait here, please, and I'll find out if he can see you.' And don't you dare step into the hallway.

The minutes ticked away. All part of the process, Ed used it himself. If a customer asked to see him without a prior appointment then the manager kept him waiting. A ploy that put the caller at a disadvantage.

He could not hear the voices any longer, wondered what had happened to the maid. He found himself subconsciously counting the red quarry tiles on the wide doorstep. Fidgeting: it was an experience which he had almost forgotten.

Somebody was coming, shuffling dragging steps

from the rear of the house and then a tall stooped figure was shambling down the long hall. Ed scarcely recognized Craddock, the immaculate white-coated figure who had officially discharged him from further treatment. The grey hair was ruffled, the lean jaw was unshaved, baggy cord trousers which hung low on the waist and seemed to be sliding down with every step. Scuffed shoes that were unlaced. Craddock had possibly been gardening, an unlikely hobby for the man but there was no telling what turned people on, Ed thought.

'Yes?' The grey eyes narrowed, squinted as if they needed time to adjust to the evening sunlight flooding the porch. 'What do you want?'

Ed caught his breath, felt his mouth go dry. He hoped his lower lip didn't start to tremble or his voice quaver when he spoke. A second or two to prepare himself for this encounter, noting that the other did not have his calling card nor did he appear to recognize the man on whom he had performed a brilliant re-building job.

'I . . . ' Christ, it sounded bloody looney, 'I was wondering if you could tell me who was on the life-support machine immediately before myself on the night of my accident?'

'What night? What accident?' Staccato hostile questions fired back in answer. The handsome features were screwed up into an expression of irritation, head thrust forward.

Jeez, he doesn't even remember me! There was a tang of alcohol fumes on the surgeon's breath. Ed should have phoned to make an appointnemt but Craddock was ex-directory.

'I'm a local bank manager . . . ' seeking any form of status which might lift him above that of a time-wasting crank.

'So?'

'I have a very good reason for wanting to find out . . .'

'I'm sure you have,' a deprecating wave of those long sensitive fingers. 'But I only see patients by appointment and during consulting hours. But I am fully booked until mid-August and I cannot undertake anything of a frivolous nature.'

'Please,' there was a whine, a desperation in Ed Cain's voice now. 'It's very important and . . .'

'This is all very unethical,' Craddock's tone was sharp, reprimanding. 'Have you consulted me or received treatment from me at any time?'

Fucking hell, he doesn't even remember! 'Yes, you did an absolutely superb job on me after a road accident last March.'

'Then if you wish to have a further consultation, if you are experiencing problems, please make an appointment.'

'There's nothing wrong,' nothing that *you* would understand. 'It's just that I have to know who went on that machine before I did.'

'You're mad!' Another wave of the hand. 'Now, as I have already gone to great lengths to point out to you, Mr . . . Wain, I'm exceedingly busy. Good day to you!'

The door was swinging shut, one last glimpse of that angry stubbled face, and then Ed was standing alone on the step. And as he turned away, began to walk dejectedly back towards the Volvo, he heard that voice inside his head again. Not deafening peals of insane laughter this time, just a snigger that embodied contempt and smugness.

It was as he drove out of the 'exit' gateway that the idea came to Ed. So simple and yet so frightening that he tried to shrug it off. Breathtaking, in fact. It nagged him all the way home and by the time he was back in the close he knew that he was going to go through with it.

Tonight.

Judy was edgy when he arrived home. Richard was up at the Lees' house again and Becky was doing her homework. The latter's presence in the lounge saved Ed from the embarrassment of an interrogation. Where the hell have you been, Ed? You really must get some treatment, you said it yourself. Before there are any more . . . accidents.

'Richard's bringing Tracey home tonight,' Judy handed him a cup of tea.

'Afraid I've got to pop out. Shouldn't be long.'

'Oh?' Those lines on her face etched deeper. 'You really should take it easy, rest up until . . . '

'Just a loose end I've got to tie up,' he spoke calmly even though his pulses were hammering. 'A signature needed on a document.'

'Whose?'

He almost retorted, 'I never discuss confidential business outside the bank' but he smiled and replied 'a new customer, lives out of town. You wouldn't know him, I didn't until last week. His personal loan for a new car is ready but as he's a newcomer I think I'd better call and check him out. As I said, I shouldn't be gone long.'

'Oh, all right,' she turned back into the kitchen, 'but I was really hoping you would be here to meet Tracey, to see for yourself that she isn't the tart you seem to think she is. She's sweet, you'll really like her.'

'I might be back in time,' he made for the stairs. But that was unlikely because it didn't get dark until around ten o'clock and he wasn't sure how long the job he had in mind would take. Or even whether he would have the nerve to go through with it.

10.10 pm and it was barely dark, one of those long summer evenings with an even longer twilight. Ed had driven slowly past Philip Craddock's house, found a convenient grove of silver birch where there was room enough to pull the Volvo off the narrow road so that it was screened from passers-by. He was tense almost to the point of calling the whole thing off, even considered turning round and driving home. Except that he had to see it through, it was the only way.

The early signs were favourable, there were no lights showing in any of the house windows. That did not mean that the surgeon wasn't still out in his garden, enjoying the warm twilight, reluctant to go back inside four walls where the heat of the day still lingered. Or that the maid wasn't relaxing for half an hour, sprawled in a deck-chair on the terrace. It was unlikely that the house would be left completely unoccupied. Ed was regretting his hasty plans; perhaps tonight should be a reconnaissance, suss the joint out as they said in the movies. Except that time was running out for him, he had to know who had been on that life-support machine immediately prior to himself, whose astral it was that had entered his dying body.

And the only way to discover that was to burgle Philip Craddock's house and go through his files.

Doubts now. Suppose Craddock didn't keep files here, relied upon the hospital. No, he would surely keep his own methodical records, he was the type of man who trusted nobody and thought everybody was a fool. The files might not be accessible, locked away in steel cabinets. His hand strayed to the passenger seat, he heard the clink of his basic tools; a screwdriver, a chisel. He felt the latex softness of a pair of hairdressing gloves which he had found in one of Judy's drawers. Oh, Christ, I'm an amateur burglar about to bungle this first job!

The place might be wired up with burglar alarms, not the kind that gave off a piercing whine and sent you away on the run but a sophisticated model that alerted the police station without warning the intruder. And the first thing the criminal knew about it was when the police surrounded the house.

Five years for breaking and entering; anybody else would have got three, two with remissions for good behaviour but a bank manager had the book thrown at him because he had abused a position of trust. Disgraced. Sacked. Divorced. *And still a victim of this astral freak!*

Even if he discovered who it was who possessed him he was still no nearer banishing the evil entity. A step at a time, he forced himself back under control as he slid out of the car, closed the door softly behind him. First, find out *who* it is.

The house was still enshrouded in deep dusk as Ed crept along the edge of the grass close to the shrubbery, ready to dive into the laurels and rhododendrons at the first sign of anybody in the garden. But still nothing moved. No sound except the distant hum of traffic on the bypass two miles away. The stillness was frightening.

He was within a couple of yards of the front door. Make an appointment if you want to see me, Mr . . . *Wain.* You supercilious bastard, he thought.

The door was partially open! Ed recoiled into the shadows, glanced about him, suspecting a trap. Maybe Craddock had phoned the police! I've had a nutcase here, tonight, he might come back. No, it wasn't likely, he had to take chances in this desperate game. He was playing for high stakes. His freedom.

He edged forward, pushed the door open with a hand that was hot and sweaty inside the tightly-fitting latex glove. Well-oiled, the hinges did not even creak. The interior was dark, he had to wait whilst his eyes adjusted to the deep gloom and he was able to make out the wide oak staircase.

He moved inside treading on the balls of his feet, stopped every time his trainers squeaked on the stone floor. I'm sorry to disturb you again, Craddock, but I was wondering if you would make an exception in my case, as I'm a bank manager, and tell me what I want to know. My car's broken down, that's why I'm carrying these tools. Do you mind if I phone the AA? I'll pay for the cost of the call.

Doors led off at intervals from the hall, oak panelled and heavy. His trembling fingers gripped a brass knob, he held his breath as he turned it, pushed it open a few inches. The lounge. The adjoining room was some kind of library, two walls bookshelved from floor to ceiling, a desk at the far end. He was in the act of moving on when he stopped and his heart speeded up again. This *could* be the room he sought.

He knew it was when his outstretched hand touched a squat steel cabinet that was refreshingly cool to his overheated fingers. A consulting room, a medical reference library and up-market office.

And, oh, sweet Jesus, the cabinet wasn't locked either! And the interior was a systematic array of alphabetically-sorted index cards.

God, something had to go wrong soon, Ed thought as he switched on his small torch and shielded its beam with his free hand. What I'm searching for won't be here and then the police will arrive. I'm a pawn in a grotesque game. Go on, start laughing, you fucker! But there was silence except for the roaring and pounding of his rising blood pressure.

The cards were typewritten; obviously Craddock would have a receptionist-cum-secretary, as well as the maid. Codings Ed did not understand; files partitioned, then two sections. The living and the dead?

A feeling of faintness swept over him when he saw his own name typed in block capitals. Codings again. And a date. March 25.

Scrabbling now, looking for a corresponding date on another file, a bizarre game of whist in which he had to find the matching card.

Just when he was on the brink of despair he found it. Amongst the dead. Craddock's failures banded together, at least Ed presumed that was what they were. A name, just give me a name! His eyesight blurred, stung as the sweat ran down from his forehead as if trying to hide the truth from him. A name, that's all I want to know.

Blake Barrett.

Shocked but there was no logical reason why he should have been. Just a name, vaguely familiar but it meant nothing right now. Somebody who had died.

And lived again.

Sweating, trembling in the darkness of that stuffy room. With an effort he began replacing the files, pushing the cabinet drawers closed. He tip-toed to the door, eased it open and stood listening. Still there was no sound, an empty house from which he could leave as he had arrived, stealthily and unchallenged.

He tumbled back into the Volvo, peeled the thin gloves from his over-heated hands, sat there in the darkness, mentally and physically drained. By some miracle he had entered Philip Craddock's house and escaped; in all probability the surgeon would never know that his filing system had been rifled. Ed had found what he had been seeking.

'Barrett,' he spoke aloud in a cracked voice. 'I know you're Blake Barrett. *I'm* Blake Barrett. Well, what have you got to say for yourself? Why are you doing this to me? *Come on, answer me*!'

His hoarse whisper seemed to hang in the atmosphere, came back at him off upholstery and facia. But there was no reply, even that mocking laughter remained silent.

Finally Ed started the engine, reversed the car out on to the road and drove back in the direction of the city.

So far, so good. But who the hell was Blake Barrett?

CHAPTER EIGHTEEN

There was no mistaking the look of sheer relief on Judy's face when Ed walked back into the kitchen. It said 'Oh, thank God!' The wall clock, a free gift for holding a lingerie party a few years back, showed 11.15.

'I got delayed.' He was perspiring heavily, eyes shifting from one to the other of them as they sat drinking coffee and eating cheese biscuits at the table; Judy, Becky, Richard and . . . the girl had to be Tracey Lee. 'You know how it is where customers are concerned, you can't just dash away, can you?'

Tracey was tall and slim with long fair hair, a natural blonde. Finely moulded features, blue eyes smiled along with the full red lips. She was wearing a T-shirt and denim shorts that showed off her shapely figure to perfection. Almost fully matured, her bosom would fill out still more, Ed thought. She might still be sixteen but he would not have doubted her word had she claimed to be eighteen or nineteen.

'This is Tracey,' Judy's voice seemed to come from a long way away, maybe from down at the bottom of the garden. Ed felt his pulses begin to race again. So this was Tracey, he was glad he had made it back before she left.

'Hi!' He saw her unclothed, the flat stomach going down to a fluffy mound of fair hair, the thighs eased apart just enough to tease, her smile inviting him to look. 'Sorry I'm late.'

'I would have run her home an hour ago except that I didn't have the car,' there was a veiled reprimand in Judy's voice. 'I rang Mrs Lee, told her I'd bring Tracey home the moment you got back. We thought we might as well have some supper whilst we waited. I was just on the point of phoning for a taxi.'

'I'll run Tracy home,' Ed said, just a trifle too quickly.

There was a momentary silence. 'No, it's all right . . .'

'*I'll* take her,' Ed's words were clipped, his gaze meeting his wife's defiantly. 'I might as well get back in the car seeing as I've just got out of it.'

'I don't see that it matters who takes Tracey back,' Richard eased up out of his chair.

'I said *I'll* run her home,' Ed was tight-lipped. 'I want you in bed as soon as possible, you've got mocks again tomorrow.'

This time the silence was long and pregnant, everybody glancing at each other.

'OK.' Richard sat down again, he did not wish to spark off another confrontation.

Judy was gathering up plates and cups to hide her embarrassment. Becky made for the hall and the stairs.

'I'm ready when you are, Mr Cain.' Tracey moved towards the door; Richard clasped her hand, let it go again.

'There's some things on the seat,' Tracey Lee edged to one side, Ed heard a clink of metal. 'A screwdriver, I think, and a pair of rubber gloves.'

'Just drop them on the floor,' his heart seemed to

miss a beat. 'I've been tinkering with the car. The timing. I always wear gloves when I'm doing anything to the car, a bank manager can't go round with oily hands, can he?'

He pulled out into the close, slowed right down as they approached the raised ridge. 'And what are you going to do when you leave school?' A question any father might ask the first time he met his son's girl-friend. He stole a sideways glance at her. God, she was beautiful and in the glow of the dashboard lights he saw again the firmness of those teenage breasts.

'I start at sixth form college in the autumn,' a cultured voice, it was hard to believe that her folks lived up on that new estate. 'I want to go on to university, to get a degree in biology and maybe study medicine.'

Biology; it set him thinking about her body again, what lay beneath that flimsy clothing. He wondered if Richard's hand had strayed inside it. The boy was slow if it hadn't.

Ed drove slowly, chose the longest route; out on to the by-pass, take the second exit, a circuitous approach to the estate.

'You understand about Richard having to have an early night, don't you?' An attempt to excuse his earlier dictatorial manner. 'I only had his interests at heart, it's important that he gets his GCSEs.'

'That's all right,' she smiled demurely in the dim green light.

He clutched the steering wheel with sweaty hands, was glad that she was unable to see the protrusion in the front of his trousers. There was a roaring in his ears, he thought he heard that voice inside him but he could not make out what it was saying.

'Next road on the right,' his companion interrupted his thoughts. 'If you go on up to the end of the road you can turn round in the entrance to the playing fields.'

Ed's fingers rested on the edge of the passenger seat but her hand had moved from where it had been seconds earlier. His fingertips brushed against denim and he remembered again the smoothness of her thighs in the kitchen earlier.

'Here's the playing fields' entrance now,' she was pointing to her right.

He swung the Volvo in a half-circle, felt the tyres crunching on cinders, slowed to a halt instead of pulling back into the road. Out of the corner of his eye he saw her glance at him questioningly. What are you stopping here for, Mr Cain?

'I'm very glad you and Richard are together,' he spoke huskily, throatily, had to fight against the urge to slide his fingers on to her thigh.

'Thank you,' she was turned to face him, he saw those full lips smile. Sod Richard, you're out with me now. He started to lean towards her.

His hand was moving up towards her breasts, anticipating the first thrilling contact, the way he would stroke her through the material, feel her nipples harden. Their lips would brush, his tongue would demand entry into her mouth, a simulation of that which would follow. Both of them naked across the seats, her gasp of pain because she was a virgin – and then she would be clutching at him, writhing with him; head back, neck arched, stroking it like he had rubbed her . . .

'Hey, there's Dad backing the car out!' She fumbled for the door catch. 'I bet he's on his way to your house to collect me, thinks you haven't got back yet. Must rush. Thanks for bringing me home, Mr Cain.'

She was gone, running along the pavement,

waving and shouting at the pair of winking stop lights in the driveway to the next house along. Innocent, unaware, leaving Ed Cain groaning his mingled relief and frustration aloud and clutching his arousement.

His mouth was dry, the voice inside him was gone and he felt drained.

Oh, God Almighty, that beautiful girl had come within seconds of being Blake Barrett's next victim.

Judy was alone in the kitchen when Ed returned. She was at the sink washing the crockery which she had collected half an hour ago. Head bowed, she did not look up as he came in and closed the door.

'I'm sorry,' his tone was subdued.

'For what?' Churlish, reaching down a teacloth and starting to dry a mug meticulously.

'For behaving like I did,' he lowered himself into a chair. 'Oh, God!'

'Ed,' she turned to face him and he saw that she had been crying. 'Oh, Ed, *please* go and get some treatment. Before . . . '

'Before anything else happens?'

Their eyes met, anguished but there was still a barrier between them. He pursed his lips, considered telling her the truth. Not yet, though, he still needed to know . . .

'*Who was Blake Barrett*?' An urgent question that spilled out in a rush, had him gripping the edge of the table with intensity.

'Blake Barrett?' Her dark eyes widened, she stared blankly at him. 'The name's familiar but I can't quite place it. Somebody on telly? Why on earth do you want to know?'

'I have to,' tight-lipped, his cheeks hollowed and ashen. 'Somebody who used to live in the area for a guess. Judy, I have to know who he was!'

'*Was*? Is he dead?'

God Alive, how I wish he was, well and truly dead, his vile soul departed for hell never to return. 'He's dead, figuratively speaking. Never mind, I'll find out tomorrow. Now, as we were saying earlier, I think it's best if you and the kids go and stay with your mother for a while. Or else I'll move out.'

She licked her lips. Had her husband got another woman, a secret mistress holed up somewhere? No, it didn't fit. His reason for a temporary separation was simply that he knew that he was . . . dangerous! 'Suppose you get some treatment first. Go and see Doctor Law . . . Kyne in the morning. Please, Ed. Promise?'

'I'll do something positive tomorrow, I promise you that,' his lips stretched into what was supposed to be a reassuring smile.

She tossed the teatowel on the draining board, took his arm. Tonight they would sleep together and she prayed fervently that that nightmare did not return.

Ed had cleared his desk by ten o'clock the following morning, told Houghton that he might or might not be back today; if anybody wanted him it would have to wait until tomorrow. Then he left the office, walked through the cobbled square and down the old market place. Five minutes later and he was entering the public reading library, its tranquillity and silence broken only by the rustle of newspaper pages being turned by those regulars who preferred to browse here rather than spend a few pence at the newsagent's. Mostly pensioners with time on their hands. He stood inside the doorway momentarily bewildered, embarrassed. This dome of silence had a frightening austerity about it, an atmosphere that was laden with escalating tension. He almost turned and left.

'Can I help you, sir?' A whisper that was loud enough to echo, a pallid dark-haired girl with heavy-rimmed glasses smiled formally. Probably a student with aspirations towards becoming a librarian, he thought.

'Er . . . yes,' glancing at the half-dozen readers, the way their gnarled arthritic fingers fumbled the news sheets. 'I . . . do you have any back copies . . . local papers, preferably, around March 25?'

'Over there, that shelf in the corner.' She sounded relieved that his query was within her capabilities. '*Mercury, Herald, Trader,* they go back to January. If you want any earlier ones I can arrange with the chief librarian for you to see . . . '

'That'll be fine, thank you,' he checked the urge to rush towards those loosely-bound files, aware how he trembled, how dry and sour his palate had become.

And somewhere in the midst of his frightened confusion he heard a snigger.

Ed found Blake Barrett within two minutes of reaching down the first binder. The one who had haunted his waking and sleeping thoughts since he had left Philip Craddock's office, had his photograph on the front page of the March 29 issue of all three local newspapers.

The bank manager stared with revulsion, found himself recoiling from that full-face portrait as a child might have cringed in front of a glass cage containing some hideous snake in a glass cage in an eerie dimly-lit reptile house. A face that was the epitome of malevolence; small deep-set eyes that mirrored manic hatred even in black and white, a slightly deformed nose with flared nostrils and a slit of a mouth stretched in a leer.

Look at me, Ed Cain. This is how I was before I took your flesh and blood. Hear me when I speak to you. Obey me because you cannot fight me. Kill when the urge is upon you. For I am you and you are me. We are inseparable.

Other pictures showed the siege, a body on a stretcher with a blanket draped over it being carried towards a waiting ambulance.

Like they carried me to the ambulance that night.

A detailed account that spilled over on to pages two and three. Ed had to force himself to concentrate, will the printed words to register in his bemused and terrified mind.

Madness. The siege. The suicidal blast from a stolen pump-action shotgun.

' . . . Barrett died later in hospital.'

Oh, how bloody wrong they were! The shot-blasted flesh had died but that twisted soul had gone in search of another body, had been presented with one within minutes of Barrett's physical dying, a badly mutilated one but it had sufficed. Truly the living dead had risen up from the grave and stalked its unsuspecting prey again.

'Have you found what you were looking for, sir?'

Ed heard the girl's voice somewhere behind him. He nodded, turned and made for the exit, fought against a wave of dizziness as his terror peaked. For he was none other than Blake Barrett, murderer and rapist, and the voice inside him was screaming its insatiable lust at him.

CHAPTER NINETEEN

Judy had gone with the children to her mother's which was a relief for Ed. There was a note on the hall table when he arrived home in the early evening to the effect that she would be telephoning later. Mother wasn't well again; there had to be a basic mundane excuse for leaving home. You're sick and you're dangerous, Ed, was just too daunting a prospect. Get some treatment, see Doctor Kyne; Ed was going to get treatment, all right, but it wouldn't be anything as simple as a GP's diagnosis.

He made himself a sandwich, poured a glass of wine. It was too early in the evening to do what he had in mind; he dared not even think about it, pushed it from his mind because the last thing he wanted was to forewarn Blake Barrett.

A guy was only supposed to have one soul, he smiled cynically at the thought. If that had been the case then he would be either Blake Barrett or Ed Cain, no in-betweens, no compromises. Some kind of freak had taken place, like a split personality in a way, a modern-day Jekyll and Hyde. Barrett lurked in the shadows of his mind, emerged when the lust got too powerful for him. There could not be any other explanation.

I'm getting to like you, Blake, he lied. I ought to be

grateful for just being alive, no matter what. Guess you and me will have to learn to get on together.

Don't think about what you're going to do.

8.30. It was surely time enough now. Ed went out on to the patio, heard the rattle of that old typewriter from an open upstairs window next door. Holland was at home, certainly alone if he was working.

It was now or never.

Norma Pringle's funeral had taken place in the cathedral that morning. The bishop had not been keen on the idea, it should have been conducted in one of the city's churches, a stubbornness which was only swayed by the fact that Peter Pringle was buried in the Close. Norma was part of the Church, Canon Holland had pointed out, and it would be seen as uncharitable to refuse her a last resting place in her husband's grave. She wasn't going to take up any more ground, after all. Admittedly she had been a trouble-maker but her condition was brought on by grief from which she had never recovered. And, the canon, added, he was quite willing to take the service himself.

Reluctantly, the bishop had agreed. A short service, there were no mourners, no representative of the dean and chapter. A brief graveside ceremony and then it was all over. There was now a vacant house in the Close, it was already rumoured that the Reverend Tidlesley from St Jude's would move in so that the rectory could be sold to swell the Church's coffers.

Cecil Holland returned to his house, he had a relatively free day which would be usefully employed in compiling his addresses for the next two Sundays. A sense of sadness now that Norma was gone, his fantasies had come to nothing, he must forget them. Not that he would ever have indulged in anything like *that* with her, he almost convinced himself. Just titillating thoughts for one in the twilight of his life, nothing more.

He grunted his annoyance when the doorbell rang. It caught him in mid-sentence, he tried to complete it but the words had been chimed out of his thoughts. Better to see who the caller was, get rid of him and then concentrate again.

Canon Holland stared in almost disbelief at his visitor. His adam's apple bulged as he swallowed, he felt himself begin to tremble slightly. Ed Cain conjured up an instant feeling of guilt in the clerygman's mind; the plot to poison that dog, he had never been part of it, had only agreed in order to pacify Norma Pringle. Surely she had not been foolish enough to say anything. No, she had never conversed with anybody, had taken her wicked secret to the grave. I wasn't having any part of it, Mr Cain, I put the dreadful stuff in the dustbin. And, to be truthful, I'm not really bothered whether you cut that hedge or not. And the only reason I delivered your Festival Service tickets to the bank was because I happened to be passing.

'Good evening, Canon,' Ed smiled affably, edged a step nearer the half-open door.

'Why, Mister Cain, how nice to see you.'

An awkward silence lasted perhaps ten seconds. Holland was reluctant to invite his visitor inside, if there was going to be a row he wanted to be in a position to slam the door. Besides, there had been some terrible happenings recently concerned with his neighbour. Norma's last words to him seemed to echo as if she was whispering a warning from her coffin. *He's evil, Cecil!*

'I wondered if you could spare me a few minutes, Canon.'

Holland's mouth was suddenly dry. It did not bode well, why not say what had to be said here on the doorstep. 'I . . . I'm just in the middle of a rather difficult sermon. Writing it, that is,' he gave a nervous laugh.

'Then I won't keep you any longer than necessary, I'll be as brief as I can.'

Damn the cheek of the fellow, the canon had not meant to pull the door wide for him to enter, he had merely leaned on it accidentally in his nervousness. And now Cain was over the threshold, still smiling.

'Come this way, please,' there was no alternative now. Take him into the library, get rid of him as soon as possible. Come to think of it, I haven't seen that dog for days now.

'It's awfully good of you to see me, Canon,' Ed lowered himself into the vacant chair, the other sat at his desk.

'What can I do for you, Mister Cain?'

'You see, Canon, you're the only person I can think of who might help me,' Ed fidgeted with his hands, 'as you know I had a terrible accident last March and it was only due to modern medical technology that I'm here now. But I'm afraid it isn't quite as simple as that . . . '

It had to be the direct approach. The truth, the whole truth and nothing but the truth; with certain things omitted. Like Cutler and Doctor Lawson. And Suzy. Cards on the table, a last desperate throw. Fuck you, Blake Barrett, I'm going to finish you once and for all.

Cecil Holland stared wide-eyed. The man was crazy, of course. Humour him and afterwards he would call the bishop. We can't have a lunatic like this living in the close, bishop. The police should be informed, also, perhaps they could get Cain certified, put away. You were right, Norma, except that he's sick rather than evil. Hallucinations but they might be dangerous. Those accidents . . . The canon began to tremble visibly.

'I'm asking you, *begging* you, to carry out an exorcism, Canon.' Ed was sweating. Christ, Barrett was quiet, he had expected a battle before now. 'It's all that's left for me. My job, my marriage, my family, my life rest on it.'

'I think I shall have to consult the dean, even the bishop,' the other glanced in the direction of the telephone. 'I'm not qualified, or rather, *gifted* in that way. They might know an exorcist who could . . . '

'Have you ever tried one?' Terse, desperate now.

'No, I haven't.'

'Then give it a try!'

Canon Holland's eyes stung as the sweat rolled down from his wide forehead, distorted his vision. He remembered how that poor family had been held hostage by Blake Barrett. In a way this was a parallel. You only had to look at Cain's face, see the madness in his eyes, contorting his expression. Not that there could be any link between this man and that killer but it was a like situation. And Holland was the hostage, a prisoner in his own home.

'I could try,' stall for time, don't anger him. 'I do have a book on exorcisms . . . '

'*Do it!*'

'All right, just give me a moment to locate the book. It's here on the shelves somewhere, I remember seeing it only the other day.' He was trembling, he could hardly stand and his visitor was following him around the room. Don't try yelling for help, I'm right behind you.

Row upon row of leather-bound volumes, many with faded spines that had him peering closely.

Pulling books out, pushing them back. Cain was clicking his tongue in annoyance, he was obviously in a hurry. Because he was mad.

'Ah, this is the one!' A book with broken hinges, the front board coming free and bouncing off the floor. EXORCISING DEVILS. Holland did not know how authentic it was, he had picked it up in the second-hand bookshop in town a year or two ago out of interest. He wished he hadn't, he could have truthfully pleaded ignorance of the subject. He should not have mentioned it but it was too late now. His fleshy fingers were shaking so much that he could barely thumb through the pages. Chapter Six: Banishing evil spirits.

'Let's get on with it, Canon.'

'All right,' a whimper. 'I think you'd better lie on the settee, Mr Cain.'

So bizarre, Holland prayed that it was all a bad dream, that he would wake up and Cain would not be here. The room was stuffy and outside the light was failing fast. Dusk was turning to darkness and suddenly that was a terrifying prospect.

Cain was stretched out on the old settee, arms by his sides, a patient in a doctor's consulting room awaiting an examination. Or an operation. Holland shuddered. He switched on the reading lamp, strained his eyes to read the small print. Christ had banished evil spirits but that was different; this was a kind of blasphemy. Forgive me, Lord, it is not of my doing.

The faded print was difficult to read, did it really matter? The old book shook in his trembling hands, his voice was dry and husky. 'O God, unconquered Might, who keepeth all that are against Thee . . . who by his death has destroyed death and overcome the prince of death . . . ' pausing to glance at Cain, the man's eyes were closed, he appeared to be fighting against some kind of convulsion . . . '*beat down Satan* under our feet, and cause this evil force to depart and never more hold tyranny over your soul. And give place to Christ.'

The book fell from Canon Holland's fingers, thudded on to the floor as though cast down by some evil force. He stepped back, felt a rush of coldness in the room, his sweat icy on his brow. Wanting to flee, to rush from the house out into the close. Anywhere. But his feet were leaden and his legs jellified. Mouthing his terror with rasping incoherent words.

Ed had tried to relax initially, as if he was practising yoga the way Judy sometimes did on the rug in the lounge. His mind seemed to go blank; he let it. Then he heard the voice, venomous obscenities that came in a fetid, icy rush. He jerked, almost passed out, forced his eyes open.

Canon Holland was towering over him, fat and loathsome, his features distended so that they were no longer recognizable. A body that threatened to burst as it inflated and then began to shrink.

Gone were the jowls, the face aquiline, unshaven. Close-set, deep-sunken eyes that glowed with the fires of hatred, nostrils distended, mouth stretched in a leering, triumphant slit.

Blake Barrett!

Ed writhed, tried to edge away but there was nowhere to go. The monster who had lived within him was now standing before him in human form, a creature terrible to behold, stinking of decomposing matter and emanating a coldness that transcended death. Mocking him, the crazed laughter vibrated his skull. A thing of cunning, it had lured him into this trap, waited its chance. Doubtless Holland was lying dead in the shadows, his corpulent body still twitching from the seizure which had struck him down. The lamp had dimmed to a faint glow and the atmosphere was alive with an evil that had come from beyond human ken.

Cain tried to scream. Barrett, for it was undoubtedly him, stood motionless, watching and taunting.

You tried to trick me, Ed, but I saw through your infantile ploy.

Ed's terror escalated. Peaked. And then he sensed anger flooding over him. He had lost everything, the final trick had failed. He had nothing left to lose, not even his soul.

'You bastard!' He screamed, forced himself up. Cold hands were trying to push him back but in this final dreadful hour he found new strength, his fury which smouldered and burst into flame. With an insane shriek, he was on his feet. He no longer feared this entity, his days of astral slavery were over. And in that instant of unbelievable transformation he saw an expression of fear on his adversary's face.

'I'll kill you as I killed the others!' His arm shot out, secured a hold on that scrawny neck, held it as it squirmed and the eyes bulged in their deep sockets. The lips twisted into a snarl of fear, the flared nostrils bubbled mucus.

It was not possible but it was happening. Ed's fingers dug deeper. And deeper. Those eyes began to glaze. Slowly he forced the head back, exerting every vestige of strength that remained in his exhausted body, his lust for revenge the power that drove him on. Wrenching and squeezing that neck until the eyes dilated and the swollen tongue lolled over the wasted lips, he tightened his grip with numbed fingers.

Until finally there came a sharp crack and the head sagged on one side. Only when he felt the body go limp in his grasp did he relinquish his hold and let it slump to the floor, a huddled, lifeless heap at his feet.

'Oh, sweet Jesus, I got you, you fucker! I was too clever, too strong for you in the end!' He gave way to euphoria, laughed crazily. Sobbed his relief. Sobered up suddenly because something was wrong.

He was looking round the partially-lit room, searching for a second body. Blake Barrett was dead at his feet, the canon had to be somewhere around.

He wasn't, which was crazy. Barrett had killed Canon Holland, taken his place, so the latter had to be here somewhere. Ed's flesh chilled, icy trickles ran up his spine, spread up his neck and into his scalp. A sense of panic. Still searching with his eyes until his gaze returned to the crumpled form at his feet, the head twisted at an unnatural angle, looking up at him with dead eyes that still pleaded for mercy. No longer near-skeletal but puffed and fleshy, those jowls bruised where he had gouged into them.

'Oh, God, *please! No!*' Ed screamed.

His vision blurred as faintness came and went and he prayed that when he saw again clearly the dead face at his feet would be unmistakably that of the maniacal killer.

His focus returned. He was unable to check his cry of anguish, wanting to kneel and massage life back into that still form. Instead he backed away from it, sobbing.

For now there was no doubt in his numbed brain that the man who lay dead before him was Canon Holland!

And that was when Blake Barrett began to laugh uncontrollably, crazed peals of sadistic, triumphant mirth that sent Ed Cain staggering from the room, stumbling down the long corridor and out into the driveway. Arms aloft, he pleaded to the night sky, to the God who had deserted him, to spare him from the thing that was himself.

The laughter drove him mercilessly on, lurching

blindly back into his own drive, clutching his head in a futile attempt to stop the noise, battering his own skull in his despair. Trick and counter-trick, Barrett had made him hallucinate, murder the one who might have saved him.

Much later, in the awful stillness of his own empty house, Ed Cain realized that there was only one course of action left open to him if his own family was to be saved from the terrible beast which was both himself and Blake Barrett.

He knew what he had to do.

CHAPTER TWENTY

Alone in the house; really alone, not even Blake Barrett to drive him over the final brink with that insane laughter. Ed realized that he was sitting in the kitchen, the patio door still open, mosquitoes flitting and battering themselves against the fluorescent light strip. He glanced at the clock. 11.45 pm.

A few minutes later the telephone started to ring, went on and on. It was Judy, of course. He let it ring out because there was no point in answering it. Not now.

Are you all right, Ed? Oh, sure, I'm fine, I've just strangled Canon Holland. No, not a row over the hedge again, just that I thought he was someone else. Look, if you'd like to come over I'll explain. And maybe I'll kill you, too.

Stop away, darling. It won't be long now.

Thinking logically. They would find the canon sometime tomorrow, or it might stretch until the following day. It depended how soon they became suspicious at not seeing him around. This was one murder that could not be side-stepped, could not be passed off as another accident. The police would come here first, they were bound to, they were still suspicious of Ed after Doctor Lawson's drowning.

Which meant that he had come to the end of the

road. A failed exorcism, what else was there left? Oh, Jesus wept, there was only one solution, one way out that would leave Judy and the kids safe.

Suicide was not for cowards, Ed knew that as he sat there with his head in his hands. It was an act of bravery or madness, depending upon your state of mind. Unbalanced, a spontaneous decision without stopping to think, that was fine. But when the chips were down and you knew there was no alternative, that was when you needed courage.

Death *might* free him. Those split astrals would be released to go their own way into the dark unknown. All he was losing was his body, it wouldn't be any good to Barrett after he was dead.

Nothing painful or messy, something nice and quick that did not leave anybody a gut-wrenching cleaning-up job. Hanging was slow, not always successful. No wrist-slashing, nothing that gave you time to change your mind because Blake Barrett would fight for survival every inch of the way. Eight paracetamols were said to be lethal but they still left you time to phone for assistance. He found himself staring at the oven, the gas jets. The best way except that he would have to kneel in an uncomfortable position with his head inside the oven. The Volvo . . . .

His mind was made up, the longer he sat and thought about it, the less likely he was to go through with it. All he needed was a length of hose; there were six feet of heater hose hanging on a nail in the garage. Ed remembered buying it to fill watering cans through the kitchen window, but it needed an attachment to go over the tap, which was about the extent of his gardening knowledge. What a waste of a fiver and then Judy had gone out and bought a plastic garden hose on a roll – after all that they hadn't got round to watering the garden.

He laughed. He remembered trying to vindicate himself and telling Judy that the heater hose would come in for something one of these days. It had now.

Car keys in his hand, Ed went out to the garage. That length of pipe was where it should have been, suspended on the wall like a dead snake, a coating of dust on it. He reached it down, went out to the car.

No, not here, not in the drive. Judy might decide to come home in the morning before school. That's funny, children, Dad's car is still here and isn't that him in the driving seat. We'll just have time to say 'hi' before he goes off to work.

He started up the car, began reversing out into the close. A dead world, God's deserted garden. Ed slowed for the ridge at the bottom, glanced in the direction of Norma Pringle's house. I'll be seeing you before long, you old bat! Christ, just suppose she was the first person he saw on the other side! Complaining and wingeing about Cling because he was here, too. Maybe the dog would be waiting to get his own back. Cutler and Lawson, too. And Suzy. Was there any screwing in hell? You went there because you fornicated but did they let you carry on once you arrived? Don't be bloody stupid, there's nothing after life, it's all a myth. Jobs for the boys, Cecil Holland and all. Do away with religion and you would put thousands on the dole.

He found himself on the big island taking the south road. Force of habit, like that morning. Driving steadily because he had not got any particular destination in mind. A police patrol car overtook him, had him uneasy for a moment. Would you mind blowing into this, sir? A random check because it was the early hours of the morning and the cops were getting bored after an uneventful evening. But the police car did not slow, soon he saw its rear lights disappearing round the big bend up ahead.

The hard shoulder was as good a place as any because the police would find his body and they were hardened to that sort of thing. He slowed, eased over to the left, braked because fifty yards further on the tarmac ended in a high verge. And down below there was a steep bank dropping into a field of bright yellow oil-seed rape. Oh, Christ, what a bloody place to choose! It was as though violent death had attracted him.

A glance in his rear-view mirror. There were no headlights in sight. Good! He picked up the hose, opened the door and got out. Make it look like I'm changing a wheel if anybody comes.

Shitfire, the diameter of the hose was almost identical to that of the exhaust pipe! He cursed, struggled feverishly with it, using brute force. Somehow he got it over the stainless steel cylinder, checked that it held firmly. His shirt was wet with sweat, when they found him he would have a rash beneath his armpits. As if that mattered. What the fuck are you pissing about for, get on with it!

The length of rubber reached stiffly up to the rear window, he adjusted the latter to grip it, just enough hose poking into the car to emit the necessary carbon monoxide fumes. All set and ready to go.

Ed was trembling as he got back into the car and closed the door. No Blake Barrett, this is one you aren't going to win! There was no sound from the other, not so much as a hiss of anger. All I have to do is to turn on the ignition; his fingers gripped the key. Goodbye Judy, Becky, Richard. I'm sorry, but I'm doing this for you.

He turned the key.

Nothing. Not even a complaining whine from the engine.

Annoyance and, somewhere deep inside him, *relief*. A let-off, he had done his best, it wasn't his fault if the bloody battery was flat. Trying it again. And again. Frantic now, I want to get it over and done with!

He groaned his despair aloud. A reprieve, a stay of execution was no good because there was nothing left to go back to. He had to make that bloody engine fire!

He got out, jacked the bonnet up, found a torch in the glove-box. Fuck it, the battery was nearly gone in that, too, just enough glow to see by if you held it close. Ed was no mechanic, his only interest in cars was year and model. You filled the tank up with petrol, pressed the starter and they were supposed to go. If they didn't then you rang for a mechanic.

He explored the limits of his basic knowledge. The battery leads, the terminals, looked fine. Anyway, he had run the car enough to charge the battery up if it was flat. Except that he recalled his garage once telling him that modern batteries decharged without any prior warning. One moment they were fine, the next *kaput*!

Blinding headlights had him shielding his eyes, cowering behind the raised bonnet. A vehicle was approaching; slowing. Piss off, you bastard! No, hang on, I could do with some help starting this car.

'Trouble, sir?'

Ed saw that it was a bright yellow AA van which had pulled on to the hard shoulder behind the Volvo. A uniformed man was alighting, coming towards him.

'Afraid so. Just conked, not a bloody spark!'

'Let me have a look, sir. I see you're a member by your sticker. To save you a walk and a wait, I'll see what I can do.' The other returned to his vehicle for some spanners and a powerful torch. 'Hmm, the battery seems all right, I'm getting a spark. Could be the starter-motor . . . '

'Can you fix it?' Because I'm in a hurry to kill myself. Ed had sidled out of the patrolman's view, tugged the hose off the exhaust and threw it on to the back seat.

'Hmm,' the other's initial confidence was waning, maybe he wished he had not stopped after all. 'I'm afraid it is the starter-motor. It'll need a new one. Hang on whilst I just radio back to headquarters and I'll give you a tow. There's a Volvo garage about five miles from here, AA appointed, and they give a twenty-four hour service. If they've got a starter-motor we'll have you on your way within the hour.'

'I'm sorry, sir,' the bleary-eyed mechanic had been in the stores for almost a quarter of an hour, 'but it seems we're out of starter-motors just at this moment, otherwise I would have fitted it for you now. There's a delivery just after nine in the morning, we'll have one for sure then.'

'Isn't there *anything* you can do?' There was no mistaking the desperation in Ed's voice. 'Can you *hire me a car? It doesn't have to be a Volvo, anything will do.'* Just so long as it has an exhaust that pumps poisonous fumes.

'We do hire cars, sir, but only when the manager is here. He arrives about eight-thirty but, as I said, we'll surely have your own car fixed soon after nine.'

It was starting to rain, heavy droplets that splattered on the oily forecourt. In the distance Ed thought he detected a rumble of thunder that sounded eerily like Blake Barrett's crazed laughter. You're a sucker, Ed, I'm one step ahead of you, no matter what trick you try to pull.

'I could give you a lift back into town, sir,' the patrolman's exuberance had diminished somewhat. 'In fact, I'll drop you off at your house. It looks like there's going to be a thunderstorm before long.'

Ed nodded, climbed up into the passenger seat of the yellow van. You've won again, Blake, but if they put me away for twenty years I won't be much good to you.

'I tried to ring you several times last night,' there was suspicion in Judy Cain's expression as she eyed her dishevelled, pallid-faced husband in the kitchen. 'Christ, you look absolutely dreadful! And where's the car?'

He looked at the clock. 9.20 am; the Volvo might be ready for collection by now. He vaguely remembered the drive home in that van with its travelling workshop rattling all the way. He had intended to give the patrolman a fiver for his trouble but it had slipped his mind. Perhaps Ed had slept in the chair, he did not know, only that it was daylight and raining hard outside. That thunderstorm had broken the heatwave, it was damp and chilly.

'I broke down on the way home from the office,' he said. 'I was hoping that the car would be fixed last night but it wasn't. I have to fetch it this morning.'

'Oh,' she did not believe him. 'And what about this treatment you were supposed to arrange?'

'It didn't work.'

'All right, so you're not going to tell me what it was, but, whatever, you don't seem to have given it much chance.'

'I've got something else fixed up,' he averted his eyes. 'I think that will work.'

'And in the meantime I have to stay at Mother's?'

'Only until this evening. In fact, you don't have to go back there unless you want to. You . . . I should know by tonight, one way or the other.'

'All right,' she was puzzled. 'By the way, it's all over between Tracey and Richard.'

He stared at her blankly.

'I'm very sorry, but not half as sorry as Richard, he's very cut up. I hope it won't mess up his mocks. No explanation, she just rang him at Mother's and said she didn't want to see him any more. Ed . . . you didn't . . . say anything to her when you took her home the other night, did you?' An accusing look. You didn't *do* anything to her, did you, Ed?

'I just dropped her off,' he was still staring down at the kitchen floor. 'There's no understanding these kids today. Richard will find somebody else. Now, I'd better go ring and see if the Volvo's fixed.'

The Volvo was repaired and awaiting collection. Ed arrived at the garage at eleven, saw the car standing out on the forecourt.

An over-apologetic service manager had deducted a small discount from the bill. 'I'm terribly sorry about last night, sir. Apparently another agency had rung for starter-motors in an emergency and our stores assistant had parted with our last one. It won't happen again, I can promise you that.'

'I don't think I'll be needing another starter-motor,' Ed wrote out a cheque, walked out to the car. This time there would be no mistake. There could not possibly be.

A farm gateway, so familiar with its rolling meadowland of buttercups brightening the dullness of a cloudy day. It was starting to rain again but that didn't matter. Nothing mattered now because the engine did not even need to fire, it was ticking over sweetly and no way was Ed going to risk turning it off. Attach the hose to the exhaust, let it pump fumes in through the partly-open window even as he got back inside.

You're all washed-up this time, Blake Barrett. And

I hope you don't find another convenient body. You're on an express trip to hell where you can't harm anybody.

He got out of the car, moved to open the rear door. A brief glance down those fields to the river, apologizing to Graham Lawson. I'm sorry, Graham, what else can I say?

Ed reached inside, groped on the back seat for the piece of heater hose. It must have fallen off on to the floor. Looking, not seeing it. Maybe it had squirmed beneath the front seats like a furtive black snake trying to hide. It wasn't there, either . . .

Blast that bloody garage, they had shoved it somewhere, in the boot perhaps. They had no business touching it, their only concern was with the starter-motor.

Ed fought against rising panic, his hands shook as he opened up the boot. Scrabbling inside; his fishing tackle, he had not removed it since that fateful trip, an old rug. Cling's spare leash. Everything was joining forces to mock him. *And then Blake Barrett started to laugh.*

Shrill hysterical peals because the hose was gone, because Ed's means of gaining his astral freedom had been snatched from him.

Ed Cain sobbed his despair uncontrollably: there was no way he was going to die.

CHAPTER TWENTY-ONE

Ed Cain had had a dislike of crowds, rather than a fear of them, since childhood. It had started when he was seven, that November Saturday afternoon when his father had taken him to see a football match, a Welsh derby cup game between Cardiff and Newport. A capacity crowd jostled for places on the terraces and there was little chance of a small boy being able to see the pitch through a forest of adult bodies.

His father had spotted somebody he knew, possibly a colleague from work, down towards the front. 'Hey, Dai!' He had managed to make himself heard in the chanting. 'Do us a favour, have young Ed down there with you where he can see.'

Reluctantly Ed had allowed himself to be passed down the tiers of spectators, nervous because he did not even know the man who was going to look after him. Mounting fear because he despaired of ever seeing his father again and Dai was fully engrossed in the game. Ed cried throughout and he would never forget his relief when he was reunited with his father afterwards. He had not enjoyed the football, had never watched it since because it always brought back memories of being abandoned in a crowd which kept surging forward and threatening to trample him.

Now he was hemmed in by a crowd again. His mind seemed to have blanked out, he could not remember where he was or how he had got here, like waking disoriented from a deep slumber. Seeing that he was in some kind of underground place illuminated by artificial lighting, cold air gusting from somewhere close by. A crush of bodies stretched to the right and left of him, a dozen or so deep, shoulder to shoulder, jostling one another for places or the room in which to read a newspaper. Everybody waiting impatiently. For what?

Advertisement hoardings on a concave wall opposite, a diagram of some kind with a huge arrow pointing to THIS STATION. Temple. *Of course*, the fog that had enveloped his mind dispersed. A London Underground station. He was tired, exhausted. He had dozed even as he stood, those around him supporting him as they hemmed him in.

His memory returned to . . . this morning? Well, some time ago, hours that seemed like days. The Volvo parked in that gateway with its engine running. All set up, nothing could go wrong this time. Fuck you, Blake Barrett! Then the hunt for the missing heater-hose, rummaging everywhere in the car, cursing that garage and its mechanics. Bloody thieves, they'd nicked the pipe! And Barrett laughing again.

Ed had sunk down on to the wet grass in utter despair. He could have driven on, found a garage somewhere, bought another length of hosing. Even a hosepipe from a garden shop – ultimately it would not have made any difference. Because death was denied him whatever he did.

He could not return home. Judy was there, maybe the police as well. A man is wanted for questioning in connection with the murder of Canon Holland. Radio and television news, the papers, too. His photograph displayed as they had splashed Barrett's on the front pages after that siege. Ed glance furtively about him but nobody was looking at him. Yet.

He had climbed back into the Volvo, driven on to the by-pass, headed south. M6. M1. London. He had ditched the car, left it in a West Hampstead street, it might not be spotted or reported for days. On the run now, some money and the clothes he wore, nothing else. Just running blindly, himself and Blake Barrett.

A tube train approached deafeningly, drew to a halt. A recorded voice that sounded like Barrett talking said 'mind the gap'. Maybe it was Barrett speaking, Ed didn't really care if it was. Not now. You've won, Blake, I'm not going to fight you any more.

The carriages were packed with passengers, shoulder to shoulder, a few were fighting to disembark. The crowd on the platform pushed forward, elbowing one another in an attempt to squeeze into those overcrowded cars.

'Mind the gap.'

Nobody took any notice. The doors were sliding shut, unlucky travellers rejoined those on the platform and the train moved off. A breathing space, room to move, Ed sighed with relief.

And then he saw the girl.

She was standing immediately in front of him right on the edge of the platform. Tall and shapely but not fully matured, long fair hair; he could just see her features in profile and as he looked his heart flipped, his adrenalin began to pump. God above, it's *her*!

It could not possibly be, not *here*! It was. He looked again, could not be absolutely certain but the likeness was such that if it wasn't her then it was a twin sister. He almost spoke, checked his rising words just in time. He could not risk being recognized by . . . *Tracey Lee*!

Some quirk of fate, maybe even another trick of Blake Barrett's, Ed could barely come to terms with it. A million to one chance but it had happened. *You bitch, you little prick-teaser*!

His anger was almost instant, came on a wave of dizziness, nausea caused by exhaustion and lack of food. The sickness subsided, his fury escalated and with the reminder of the night when his hands had edged towards her as she sat seductively in the passenger seat of the Volvo, he sensed his arousement. I want to fuck you, Tracey.

She half-turned, gave him a glimpse in profile, it was her, he was almost certain of it. She caught his eye, half-smiled, turned away again. Daddy's waiting for me, Mr Cain.

Ed swayed slightly on his feet, the platform behind was filling up again as another wave of commuters arrived. Hustling for places; the girl was immediately in front of him now, he was pushed up against her. A waft of perfume, it made him heady, his erection pushed inside his trousers. Leaning on her, touching her.

They were back in the Volvo, he was dimly aware that she had spoken; it took time for her words to register with him. Something about turning at the end of the road in the entrance to the playing fields. He had done that, they were sitting there with the engine ticking over, Tracey so beautiful in the soft green glow of the dashboard lights.

His fingertips brushed against her denim shorts, travelled on down until they found the smooth flesh of a bare thigh. Stroking it, holding his breath and watching for a reaction. She tensed, he heard her intake of breath. But she did not push his hand away.

Her hair had fallen over her face so that he was unable to see her expression. His bosom was heaving, he could feel her trembling. When his hand began to fondle her breasts through her clothing she groaned softly.

Back down again, her thighs had parted in an unmistakable invitation to him to feel in between them. She shuddered, stretched as wide as she could in the cramped confinement of the passenger seat. They ought to clamber over into the back but there wasn't time; this was going to have to be a quick one.

She eased herself up off the upholstery, helped him to drag her shorts down. Her knickers were wet and warm, he poked his fingers up into them and she clutched at him so that he felt her fingernails gouging into his back through his shirt. Now she was naked from the waist downwards, and struggling to remove her top and bra. Oh, Richard, you lucky lad, I never had it so good in my day!

She wanted it badly, there was no doubt about that. Positioning herself beneath him across the seats, groping for him, guiding him where she wanted him. He wondered if she was a virgin, probably not, she knew the procedure too well. Inside her, his hands cupped over her small breasts, his lips crushed on hers, pushing his tongue into her. Then the car began to creak rhythmically.

His breathing was fast, it wouldn't be long now. You're a fast one, you are, Tracey, but you're going to pay for what you've done, seducing my son! His fingers moved off her breasts, crept upwards. Her head was back, her eyes closed, that neck milky white and inviting in the semi-darkness. He touched it, felt her flinch.

Then, just as his hands were about to close over it,

the grip to tighten, she moved. Fast. Somehow she came up from beneath him, slid free with the suppleness of a snake, disengaged from him in one movement and found the door catch. A click, a creak of hinges, and she was out of the car.

'Hey . . . ' He reached out for her but she was beyond him, staring at something out of his view.

'Daddy's here!' Her nakedness mocked him in the glow of the streetlamps. 'I must go. Good-bye, Mr Cain, and thank you again for bringing me home.'

He made to go after her but his trousers snagged on the handbrake. Moaning, lying there, clutching at himself as his orgasm began. You little tart!

His body was exploding, doubling him up with the force of his climax. A mist fogged his vision, he was aware of a deafening rushing sound, the ground beneath him shaking as though an earthquake was beginning.

Back on that underground platform, everybody starting to push forward. A train just emerging from the tunnel; Tracey was back, fully clothed, standing on the edge of the platform, turning to face him angrily.

'You filthy beast!' She yelled at him but the noise drowned her words. Her skirt was rumpled where his fingers had tried to explore, he was dimly aware of a sticky dampness inside his trousers.

Her beautiful features were contorted with anger and a hint of fear. Shouting at him again but nobody noticed because they were too intent on preparing to fight for places on an overcrowded train.

'You cow!' he yelled. 'You prick-teaser!'

Kill her, don't let her get away!

His arm began to move, there was no way he could have stopped it; like driving that golf club that afternoon, eye on the small white ball, knowing exactly what was going to happen, powerless to prevent it. One shove; too quick for an eye to follow had one been watching but everybody was staring fixedly at the approaching, slowing tube train. Contact. Just enough to tip the girl off balance.

Ed watched her totter on the edge of the platform, arms windmilling, legs bent as she fought for her balance. Then she was falling backwards, reminding him of a ballet dancer with her grace and poise, back arched; she screamed but nobody heard her.

Nobody saw her until it was too late and then everybody was screaming. A cartwheel, plunging down as the train squealed to a halt, thudding into a kneeling position with that lovely neck laid invitingly across the line. Not moving in that last second as though she had resigned herself to her fate and was determined to die gracefully as she had lived. The train was both executioner and guillotine, decapitated her with merciful swiftness, sent the head rolling, blood spraying and splattering the advertisement hoardings opposite, the body slumping down, hidden from view.

Ed felt himself being pushed as the watchers reacted, some fighting to get away, others jostling one another for a ghoulish view. He stood still, let them sort themselves out. A teenage girl had spewed all down herself, looked as though she was going to faint. Somebody was yelling for a doctor and an ambulance, mostly they were panicking.

Slowly he began to retrace his steps, shouldering his way unobtrusively along the crowded platform in the direction of the 'way out' sign. Not hurrying, the shouting and screaming music which he savoured.

Letting the escalator carry him upwards, fully aware now of the way his pants clung warm and wetly to his groin, delighting in the aftermath of his pleasure and its breath-taking climax. Tracey or no, she had served her purpose and Blake Barrett was satisfied. For the moment.

CHAPTER TWENTY-TWO

Judy had become concerned because Ed was not answering the telephone each time she rang. She resisted the temptation to return to the Close to check whether or not her husband was at home. He had talked of seeking treatment, she told herself that was where he had gone. A psychiatrist somewhere, she would ring again tonight and see if there was any news. In the meantime she had to appear unconcerned for the sake of her ailing mother and the children.

Then the police had rung, asked her to go down to the station. From that moment onwards she knew it was the end of the road for Ed.

'Have you absolutely *no* idea where your husband might be, Mrs Cain?' The Detective-Inspector had an abrasive, accusing manner. Overweight, but shrewd eyes were in total contrast to the bulky body, his slow movements were deceptive. You're hiding him, Mrs Cain!

'He's gone to . . . to seek treatment!' That sounded damning, she would have to ask to go to the toilet in a minute to be sick. Canon Holland murdered and this time there was not even a suggestion of an accident.

'Treatment! For *what*?' The policeman leaned

forward across the desk, thick eyebrows knitted, his penetrating stare unblinking.

'My husband's not well. It's all due to that accident he had . . . '

'What accident was that?'

Oh, God, start at the beginning. We know all about it, Mrs Cain, but we want you to tell us again. Looking for a slip, a contradiction. Hunched and waiting to pounce like a buzzard watching an unwary rabbit from an overhead bough. She was shaking visibly; a WPC brought her a cup of tea but Judy left it untouched in case she brought it all back.

A faltering account of events from that terrible March night. Missing out some, Cling and that time Ed had raped her, almost strangled her. Dropping her eyes in case the detective noticed. Cutler, Doctor Lawson; they *were* accidents, officer. Weren't they? She knew now that they weren't.

'There is evidence to suggest,' the officer took his time lighting a cigarette, let the smoke drift across towards her, 'that your husband was in Canon Holland's house at the time of the murder.' We know damned well he killed him, we can prove it but we just need to find him.

'Oh!' Feeling faint, looking at the door, knowing that they wouldn't let her go and be sick because this was all part of the breaking-down process. Throw up on the floor if you like, Mrs Cain, we don't mind. 'On the floor, by the body, was a book on *exorcism.* Was your husband in any way involved in occult practices? Black magic?'

'Oh . . . *no*!'

'How do you know he wasn't? He might not have told you, kept it a secret.' Maybe you're into it, too, stripped naked in the circle and the coven taking it in turns to screw you.

They let her go three hours later and shakily she headed back to the close. Because she was in no fit state to undergo another interrogation by her mother, maybe the kids, too. Something's wrong, we can tell, you look terrible.

There was no obvious evidence to suggest that the police had been in the house, she just knew that they had. They had searched it from top to bottom, pried into everything. Hey, look what's at the back of this drawer, his wife uses a vibrator so they have to be kinky. Both of them into black magic, doubtless.

Ed had finally snapped. It had to be some kind of brain damage that had gone undetected all along. Poor Ed, it wasn't his fault, it was *hers*. She could have instructed them to switch off the life-support machine that night; her husband had died on it, they had given her back an alien creature disguised in Ed's re-built body. *A psychopath.*

Judy decided to remain in the house rather than return to her mother's. With surprising calm she telephoned her mother, lied that Ed had gone to hospital, just a routine check-up, and she would hang on here. You can manage the children just for one night, can't you, Mother?

Judy didn't want him back, but she had to wait nevertheless. Afraid for him and what he might do to her if he returned. Oh, Ed, or whoever you are, I hope you're dead somewhere.

She didn't go upstairs to bed, remained in the lounge, sat on that same settee where . . .

It was sometime after midnight when the phone rang, jerked her out of an uneasy, exhausted doze. Stumbling out into the hall, grabbing up the receiver. It was her husband, all right, she could tell even though he did not speak. Just breathing at the other end like somebody making an anonymous dirty phone call. A click and the line went dead. I'm just checking on you, Judy.

She went back into the lounge and sobbed herself to sleep.

A nurse had come into the ante-room to ask her to come this way. Non-forthcoming, striding on ahead, not even turning to check that Judy was following. It's not my place to tell you there's no hope for your husband.

A stark grim theatre where the whiteness dazzled you, threatened to bring on a migraine. Masked figures in white, the tall one had to be Craddock. He turned towards her, said something unintelligible through his protective face mask. That's him, take a good look.

Judy looked. And screamed.

A bloody mulch, crushed arms and legs sticking out of it, twitching, writhing. The face was gone, it could have been *anybody*.

It's not Ed.

It is. It's up to you, Mrs Cain.

Standing there, all of them watching her, eyes that burned into her. *What do you want us to do, Mrs Cain. You're God now. Life or death*?

Back to the beginning, start all over again. Richard had asked her once, some years ago, 'Mummy, if you could be young again would you do anything different?' This was the moment of truth.

Her eyes misted, the white room tilted one way, then the other, threatened to gyrate crazily. She closed her eyes. And saw Cling's unearthed head, bloody jaws agape. John Cutler, standing looking at her with a monstrous third eye, white like these walls, splinters of bone peeping out all around it and starting to ooze crimson. Graham Lawson, floating down river, bloated like a fish that had died in polluted waters. Canon Holland; the policeman had said that the canon's neck was broken so that his head twisted right round.

You can save them all, it's up to *you*.

'Well?' The surgeon was impatient, shifting his weight from one foot to the other. Hurry up, I've got a meal waiting for me. I could do with a cigarette, too. Don't piss me about, please.

She moved closer, recoiled from that trembling heap of what had once been a human being. Not Ed, it couldn't be him, there had to be some mistake.

There isn't.

Craddock, she wasn't sure it was him but it probably was, he had a reputation for dealing with mangled bodies and playing about with that God machine, was talking. Jumbled meaningless words but the gist of them was not lost on her. We're playing God, Mrs Cain, or rather, *you* are. Which is it to be, life or death.

That body, whoever it was, was in indescribable agony, no matter what they tried to tell you about pain killers. *Something was happening to it, it was convulsing, trying to arch its back.*

The head flopped over to one side and Judy leaped back away from it, felt herself bump into one of the nurses. Fighting off a wave of dizziness. She knew what she had to do. But why me? It's not my Ed!

She could hear it screaming even though it was incapable of speech. Shrieking in anguish, the words jarred her brain. *Something's trying to get inside me!*

She closed her eyes, clutched the arm of the nurse standing alongside her, took a deep breath. It was *Cling*, that was what that abomination on the machine was, they had dug him up, were trying to bring him back to life in some obscene, blasphemous experiment. I can't let them do this to my dog!

'*Kill it*!' She screamed. And carried on screaming hysterically until she fainted.

Judy came out of the nightmare trembling and bathed in sweat, rushed in panic for the lounge door, was through it into the hall before she was fully awake. In many ways waking was worse than dreaming. Everything came back at her like a swollen river in full spate. Ed, or rather, the creature which passed for him, was wanted for murder, might kill again. But now she knew, without any doubt, where it had all begun; on that machine, life when there should have been death, a bizarre transformation that had given her back a monster when euthanasia could have spared them all this agony, saved the lives of others.

Oh, dear God, what have they done! She hung on to the door, sobbing uncontrollably. Please let them find him before . . .

The telephone in the hall started to ring, a staccato purring as if there was a line fault somewhere and it laboured under the strain.

Don't answer it.

She tried to turn back into the lounge, close the door on whoever was on the other end of that phone but in the end she stumbled across to it, lifted the receiver.

'Hallo, Ed.'

A crackling and buzzing made it difficult to hear but it did not obliterate that deep asthmatic wheezing. She held the handset away from her, afraid to listen, afraid to replace it. And then it went dead, just the dialling tone.

It was Ed, all right, she never doubted that. Or,

rather, the evil that had entered his mangled body that night and had taken it for its own.

And her greatest fear was that it would return here to complete its rampage of death. A thing that had been spawned in a dying body and had resurrected it, had hidden behind a screen of family love where it had plotted to kill. And kill. A sudden terrible thought, the intricate mechanism of the human brain repeating words that had long been forgotten. Ed's words.

'*Who was Blake Barrett?*'

Oh, merciful Jesus, it was just too impossible to believe. But in the stark terror of an empty house Judy Cain believed it.

CHAPTER TWENTY-THREE

Money was the biggest problem he faced right now, Ed Cain stared out of the drab hotel bedroom window at an adjoining blank wall. When one had a secure job and a reasonable salary one learned to live within those margins, occasionally exceeded them but never catastrophically. He had been advising other people for years, he smiled bitterly, and now for the first time he was unable to help himself.

His £50 credit card was trifling and dangerous. Doubtless the bank had already issued a nationwide warning on it; the first branch in which he attempted to draw cash the police would be called whilst he was purposely delayed until they arrived. A block would have been put on his code number in the cash dispensers.

In his wallet were three ten pound notes, not enough to pay the hotel bill in the morning. But he would be gone long before then. His Access would maybe work for a day or two, he would be able to buy meals in a restaurant, maybe another hotel stay. After that it was sleeping in the subways, joining the growing ranks of dropouts; scraps to eat, charity meals if he could discover where they were distributed. He needed money; without it he would not stay on the run long.

He should have planned ahead whilst he had the opportunity. Not that he had any sizeable amount in hard cash in his own account, bank managers' salaries were swallowed up in the lifestyle which they were forced to adopt. You earned good money and you spent it as you went along because there was always a pay cheque at the end of the month and the cushion of a pension on the distant horizon. If you played your cards right you might even get early retirement and a golden handshake, put your feet up before you were due. All of which wasn't any good to you when there was a manhunt on for you.

Fuck it, with a little forethought he could have fiddled a few grand which wouldn't have been missed until now when it was too late. Like Jacobs, one of the city's former managers had done and the bloody fool didn't even *need* the cash, he was just greedy. Cunning in the short term, Jacobs had opened half a dozen fictitious current accounts, sanctioned personal loans for non-existent customers and drawn it all out in cash. He got careless and the inspectors rumbled him. Ed pursed his lips, he could have worked it all within a month and he'd be a lot better off than he was now and it wouldn't matter a toss when they found out.

He could have gone abroad, Spain preferably. You really fucked it up for both of us, Blake.

'*Why don't you rob a bank*?' Blake Barrett said, and laughed.

Ed tensed, began to tremble. When you hadn't got any fiddles left, to hell with subtlety, go in and take what you want. At gunpoint. But I don't have a gun.

'*Then go get one, Ed.*'

It was a breath-taking thought, one that brought him out into a cold sweat. Go get a gun, Ed, and rob a bank. Just like that! His stomach started to cramp, he knew he would have to go to the toilet in a minute. I can't get involved in armed robbery. Why not? You've murdered, raped. In for a penny, in for a pound. Nothing to lose now, everything to gain.

Fuck you, Blake Barrett!

Ed thought about a gun. The basic equipment of a bank robber. Maybe a lifelike toy revolver would suffice, perhaps one of those replicas that collectors adorned their walls with. No, Ed, it has to be the *real* McCoy.

You could buy shotguns over the counter, Ed remembered all the fuss a year or two ago after the Hungerford massacre. Certain sections of the public wanted all guns banned, or at the very least certificated so that the police knew the whereabouts of every weapon in the country. It had all fizzled out, wasn't practicable. Tomorrow he would buy a sporting weapon, a small light one, just sufficient to scare the shit out of some unfortunate teller and any customers who happened to be in the bank at the time; nothing that needed the barrel sawing down or anything laborious like that.

He left the small hotel shortly after daybreak, crept furtively out into the dingy side street. Glancing about him as he walked, so conspicuous in these deserted streets. A refuse cart was embarking upon an early collection, one of the overall-clad figures glanced quizzically at him. Blimey, mate, we usually only see bloody dropouts at this hour and most of them are asleep!

He found a recreation park, the gate sagged on a broken hinge where night-time vandals had forced an entry. He squeezed through the gap, found himself a bench that was screened from the road by some straggling rhododendrons. The sky was grey and overcast, it might rain later but at the moment it was dry. He zipped up his anorak against the early morning chill. The breakfast bars would not be opening for another couple of hours yet. It was going to be a long wait.

The gunshop had an impressive look about it, prided itself in its long established name, the façade seeming to resent the security grill which protected its plate glass window. A row of shotguns chained together, a display board of antique ammunition in a variety of eye-catching colours so different from the modern-day plastic casings. Stuffed gamebirds with glittering glass eyes that stared malevolently as if they recalled the day half a century ago when a charge of well-directed shot, mayhap from one of those empty shells on the board, had terminated their freedom in some remote setting far from here.

Ed pushed open the door, heard a bell clang somewhere in the gloomy recesses. An odour of oil and polish assailed his nostrils; the walls were oak-panelled, his feet sank into a fitted carpet. His mouth was dry, he licked his lips to moisten them. A feeling of awe, akin to that in the cathedral back home. Another place of worship where one bowed humbly to the craftsmen of old.

'Can I help you, sir?' The man who came through from the back was tall and stooped, wore a frayed grey smock, peered intently, almost with hostility, at this stranger who had dared to enter this hallowed place.

'Er . . . yes,' Ed swallowed. 'I'm taking up shooting and I'm interested in seeing some guns.' Some ammunition, too. Just so that I can hold up a bank.

'Ah, yes, sir,' a wan smile, a sudden feeble enthusiasm. You didn't sell a gun every day of the week; just accessories, a cleaning mop, the odd box of cartridges. 'Now, let me see. A good English make undoubtedly, we don't stock imports. New or second-hand, sir?'

'Oh . . . I think I'll begin with a secondhand.' Christ, I think I've come to the wrong place! 'A lightweight, if you have one.'

'Ah, a twenty-bore!' The other unpadlocked one of the glass-fronted cabinets. 'A couple here I can recommend, sir. A lovely little Cogswell, and this one's a real beauty, a Watson.'

Exquisite examples of English gunmaking, the scroll engraving as perfect now as it was on the day it left the workshop. Ed sensed the balance, the art of the gunmaker, as he held it in his hands.

'They're both two thousand, sir. They're advertised in the sporting press for the weekend, they'll be snapped up, I can assure you of that.'

Two bloody grand, I sure have come to the wrong place!

'I don't think you'll find a better buy anywhere, sir,' there was a smugness about the other now, lean hands rubbing together. 'Oh, by the way, sir, you *have* brought your shotgun certificate with you, haven't you?'

Ed tensed. Shit, you needed a certificate to buy a shotgun, he thought that only applied to firearms, rifles and pistols. Bandit weapons. 'Er, no, it's back at home,' he tried to sound casual, an understandable oversight.

'I'm afraid I can't let you take the gun away until I see your certificate and record the number in our book, sir. But if you like to leave a deposit on whichever gun you choose then I'll hold it for you until you pop in with the certificate.'

'I'll go and get the certificate right now,' Ed

handed the gun back, smiled. 'I'll be back within the hour.'

'But there's always the chance somebody will pop in and buy it in the meantime.' A hard sell technique, almost a desperation. The guns had been in stock for nearly a year, capital chained to the wall.

'I'll be right back, don't worry,' Ed headed for the door, 'see you soon.'

Jesus Almighty! A set-back that even you hadn't thought of Blake. Even if I find a cheap import I'll still need a certificate. Maybe it was different in your day.

It wasn't. When I needed a gun I stole it.

It was after midnight when Ed Cain arrived back in the city, alighted from the train and kept his head down as he handed his ticket in at the barrier. Unshaven, a new set of casual wear, apart from extremes such as a false beard that might fall off it was the best disguise he could think of. The hunted fox had returned to its home territory hoping that the hounds had been withdrawn for the day.

His nervousness bordered on stark terror, his only consolation that the police would have surely found the Volvo in London by now and the manhunt had been switched from the city. Maybe it was a good move on his part. Maybe not.

Whatever the outcome, he had no choice. He needed money, therefore he had to have a gun. As he was unable to purchase one, he must steal one. Ed knew of only one place where there was a gun for the taking. *In the pigsty at Mitchell's farm on the outskirts of the city.*

It was raining. He contemplated taking one of the taxis which were plying their trade outside the railway station. No, it would be unwise, the driver might become suspicious, might even recognize him; Ed hadn't bought a newspaper since his flight from the city, an oversight he regretted. Judy might have given the police a photograph of him or they might have obtained one from the bank, that portrait of the youngest bank manager in Britain. Or maybe just an artist's impression, something that might jog a memory. It was safer to walk.

The streets were deserted, glinting in the artificial lighting, passing cars throwing up spray. A concrete jungle where he was the best of prey sneaking into cover, fearful of the hunters. All you have to do is to give yourself up and they'll lock you away for the rest of your life in some place where you can't do anybody any harm. Solitary luxury, good food and board and a television thrown in.

But that wasn't Blake Barrett's way, he would fight them right to the end.

Impenetrable darkness now, barely able to discern the overgrown hedges on either side of the lane, once throwing himself full-length in the tall wet grass of the verge when he heard a car approaching. His clothing was saturated, he did not even have a torch to see his way by. But he knew that somewhere up ahead this narrow road forked and immediately on his left stood Frank Mitchell's dilapidated farm. Where there's muck there's money, he laughed aloud at the truth of that worn-out old saying, for Mitchell had made his million out of breeding pigs and lived like them. In squalor. But that did not matter because just behind the main pigsty door a rusty old gun leaned up against the wall; there was also a box of cartridges on the shelf above it.

Mitchell had told Ed once during a tour of inspection, when the bank manager had made a courtesy call on his customer, that he kept the gun to shoot rats. 'Where there's pigs there's always rats and you have to be careful with this old warfarin bait 'cause pigs are like rats, same kind of belly, and you can poison 'em just as easily.'

The gun was all that Ed wanted.

And it was exactly where he had prayed that it would be, the focal point of his destination, worth every tortuous, gut-wrenching mile of that three hour journey from the metropolis.

'You've got your gun,' Blake Barrett said, 'now go and use it.'

Ed had stalked his way to the pigsty cautiously, suspicious because a light showed from within it. The reason for the outbuilding's illumination was obvious as he peered in through the entrance; a litter of piglets in one of the stalls in need of the warmth from a brooder lamp. Possibly the sow had died giving birth. Ed breathed a sigh of relief. He almost shouted his elation aloud when he found the shotgun.

A rusty double twelve hammer gun with pitted barrels, he had to force the action to open the breech. Cartridges in bright green paper cases that, with some renovation, would have graced that antique display board in the London gunshop. The weapon was like an extension of his own body, he sensed a power vibrating from it; a sense of supremacy, invincibility. *A means of instant death.*

The dogs in the farmyard some fifty yards away were barking. Ed stiffened. They had heard him, his scent had carried to them. Whatever, they knew there was an intruder about and yelped to warn their master. And as if in accompanying chorus the pigs in the row of filthy styes started grunting. Angrily, malevolently, bunting the ramshackle doors like they were trying to reach this stranger who had dared to trespass in their stinking domain. Ed shuddered, he had read somewhere that pigs sometimes ate humans. But he had the gun, he would blast them if they managed to break down one of those doors. A charge of shot at close range, ripping, mutilating, tearing the features into a bloody pulp. He would . . .

Somebody was coming, heavy booted footsteps squelching through the mud outside, dragging on the rough concrete.

A bronchial cough, muttered cursings. 'What the bloody 'ell's up wi' yer makin' a rumpus like this?'

Ed pressed himself back against the wall, saw a stooped figure with towsled grey hair enter, a muck-stained smock over grubby shirt and long pants, the latter tucked into patched wellington boots. Heading towards the sty containing the piglets. 'Shaddup, you little buggers!'

Kill him!

Ed had the gun, cartridges, but instead of loading it he gripped it by the barrels, he swung the stock up above his head. A club; shooting was too noisy, unnecessary. An instant reaction. Blake Barrett's thinking.

Ed Cain did not hesitate, he brought the gun downwards with every vestige of strength that his travel-weary muscles could muster; gasped as the force of the impact almost jerked the twelve-bore from his grasp.

A bone-shattering crunch, he saw the back of that head disintegrate, a chasm opening up in the skull like a rock face that had been blasted with dynamite. An abyss that released a mass of grey frogspawn-like substance, the blood tinting it pink, then scarlet.

The farmer never even grunted. For a moment he stood upright and Barrett screamed at Ed to hit him again. But there was no need. The frail form folded, sank slowly down into the mud and lay motionless.

Ed leaned on the gun, breathless, whilst somewhere

in the distant background those dogs were going crazy. I have to get away from here.

Feed him to the pigs!

Suddenly Ed's weariness was gone, fallen from him to be replaced by an unholy zest. He had killed, delighted in it, but there was further pleasure to come. He stooped, grasped the slumped, bleeding form by the tattered clothing, began to drag it across the uneven floor in the direction of the styes.

The pigs were going crazy, grunting and squealing as though they, too, had heard and understood Blake Barrett.

It was not easy to lift the farmer's corpse. Ed heaved, managed to get it into an upright position against the wall of the sty where the young pigs were going crazy; they smelled death and *food*, a delicacy previously denied them.

He was not going to risk opening the door, those animals had worked themselves up into a frenzy, they were hungry for human meat, alive or dead. Lifting, splattering himself with blood, its bitter odour only served to give him added strength. Pushing, he somehow slid Mitchell up on to the top of the wall; a brick dislodged, sent the creatures scurrying in all directions.

'Hang on, my sweeties, nearly there!' He paused for breath. The piglets were jumping up, their jaws snapping at a dangling arm. There was a crunch as a finger severed, came away. They began to fight over the morsel.

One final heave and the body slid, toppled and thudded, splashed in a pool of urine. Ed realized the danger in delaying his flight but the prospect of becoming a spectator to the carnage inside that enclosure was irresistible.

Clothing shredded, it might already have been partly rotten, exposed a dirt-grimed stomach. Tusks gored, ripped and tore. The beasts were milling now, threatening to trample one another in their lust. Flesh ribboned, entrails flopped out and there was a squelching, sucking noise as the ravenous pigs slurped their fill. The watcher was forgotten as they fed greedily. Masticating, crunching on bones; still fighting although there was plenty for all.

Ed turned away, there was nothing to see now, just the bloody remnants and before long that would have gone, too. He laughted softly to himself. Another 'accident', by morning there would be nothing left to prove otherwise. The farmer had gone to feed his stock, had somehow fallen in the sty . . .

He had his gun and there had been bonuses thrown in, it had all been worthwhile. Now all he needed was a bank.

CHAPTER TWENTY—FOUR

Ed had dismantled the rusty old shotgun into two sections, barrels and stock, tied it together with a length of binder twine before leaving the pigsty so that it fitted snugly beneath his sodden anorak. Then came the long trudge back along those dark country lanes; it had stopped raining but that made no difference, his clothing was saturated.

Ahead of him the night sky was aglow with the lights of the cathedral city, a hostile environment yet it drew him on, the hunted animal returning to its home territory.

A thought crossed his mind; load the gun, shove the barrels in your mouth and blow your head off. It wouldn't work, otherwise he would have done it, Blake Barrett would see to that. The cartridges were old, they would misfire. Or else the cocking springs would be weakened with age and the percussion caps in the cartridges would fail to ignite.

You're on a loser, Ed Cain, you have to see it through to the end.

A wan light loomed up ahead, he shied from it until he knew the glass cubicle as a telephone booth. An idea, it was worth a try. He squeezed inside, dialled with a finger that was almost too numb with cold to function. He heard the number ringing out at the other end and then a voice that was only vaguely familiar saying, 'Is that you, Ed?'

He did not reply, slowly replaced the receiver. There was nothing to say; just checking if you were home, darling. He could not return to the close.

He found the demolition area by accident, was not aware that the row of tumbledown houses, the last of the old city beyond the shopping arcade, was being pulled down to make room for further expansion. Mounds of rubble, bulldozers standing silent in the midst, a wooden boundary fence with notices warning the public to keep out. As with that recreation park in London, the vandals had already made an access point for him.

The last of the cottages, tomorrow it would be flattened, defiantly standing for this last night on its precarious footings. He went inside, at least it was dry even if it stank of urine. A last resting place for both of us, he thought.

Morning. The sound of workmen arriving had Ed scurrying from his refuge, out through another gap in the fencing. Crossing a road towards a narrow track that was lined by a thick overgrown hedge on either side. Running scared, stopping when he came upon the towering mountain of crushed, corroding metal. A scrapyard, precariously stacked car wrecks threatening to avalanche at any moment as they awaited collection.

Tiptons' Breakers, Ed knew the place, they had an account at his bank, had been in trouble recently over tax evasion, itinerant scrap merchants who had made this place their home and had defied the council's efforts to evict them. They lived in a big house up on the commuter belt; the yard would be deserted. Another place to lie low in for a while.

He found an old caravan, succeeded in forcing the

door open. There was even a bunk to stretch his weary body on, a rack which would assist his clothes to dry. He began to peel them off.

A respite, it gave him time to think.

You've gotta rob that bank today, Ed.

7 am. He tried to work out what day it was. By a process of elimination he made it Wednesday. He was sure of it. And ironically he knew that he was going to hold up *his* bank. He laughed at the idea; he had gone round in a circle, ended up where he had begun. A cycle, in fact, Barrett's cycle.

No, the bank was bandit proof. Toughened glass screens from counter to ceiling in front of the tills, every cashier had an alarm button by their feet. No chance. *Except that he still had a key to the door of the manager's office.*

Ed's pulses began to race. The bank was wide open to him and he had the element of surprise on his side. It was the last place where they would expect him to turn up . . .

And afterwards he would walk right out and lose himself again. The chief cashier had the reserve cash in a locked cupboard by his till and Ed had a duplicate to that, too. On Wednesdays the big firms collected their wages ready to make up the pay packets for Thursday; the supermarkets paid their employees in cash, £20 and £50 notes, the money would be packeted in that cupboard.

'*You're getting real smart, Ed.*' Blake Barrett laughed.

Ed's clothes were partly dried, just damp. He dressed, knew what he had to do. The bank, *his* bank, was his immediate target. He did not dare think beyond that.

Ed mingled with the morning shoppers along the arcade. Young mothers with prams and pushchairs embarking upon the trauma of trying to stop their offspring crying whilst they went about routine shopping; retired people for whom this was a welcome relief from the boredom of an uneventful day. An aroma of freshly baked bread from the Sunblest shop, a view of an open plan hairdresser's salon. Young clerks dressed in trendy office suits hurrying on various errands. A normal weekday morning in the city. Except for Ed Cain.

He scrutinzed faces from a distance, turned to gaze in a shop window when he saw a woman, probably a bank customer. Clutching the shotgun beneath his anorak, his heart missing a beat when he spied a helmeted policeman strolling casually with his hands behind his back. They wouldn't expect to see Ed Cain back in the city, they would not glance twice at a scruffy tourist. That was his trump card and he still had it to play.

The cathedral bells were ringing. In all probability today was a saint's day and there was a special service. A congregation of half a dozen in the main aisle, visitors looking on from the back as they toured the holy place clutching their guide books, buying souvenirs from the stall in the west doorway.

Ed moved out into the cobbled square, paused as if intent on reading a plaque beneath one of the statues. A couple of market stalls on his left selling fruit and vegetables, across the street on the opposite side . . . *the bank.*

Customers were pushing their way in and out of the entrance doors, a security van with helmeted officials loading up bags of coin from a trolley, pedestrians having to step into the road because the pavement was obstructed. He glanced up at a public clock; 10.20. Anytime in the next five hours would do, there was no hurry.

Coward!

He was procrastinating; like the time a few years ago when he had a routine dentist appointment and had arrived quarter of an hour early. He had walked up and down the pavement outside telling himself that it was too early to go inside yet. He didn't really need to go, there was nothing wrong with his teeth. In the end he had walked away, gone back to the office. A week later he had suffered an agonizing bout of toothache, had to phone for an emergency appointment. An abscess that had gone septic because he had not realized it was there. If you don't rob the bank today, you'll have to do it tomorrow. Or the day after. And in the meantime you don't have any money nor anywhere to sleep.

He crossed the street, headed towards the bank. They had finished loading up the coin, the pavement was clear and the driver was starting up the van, preparing to move off. Ed glanced in through the plate glass doors of the bank. About a dozen customers queued for the tills, each cashier was fully occupied. At the other end of the counter was the door to the manager's office. A nameplate. E. CAIN, MANAGER. They had not removed it, it was just as though nothing was wrong. And I'm still the bloody manager, I should have come in a smart suit!

His foot was on the step, arm extended to push the door open when it swung back. A man in white overalls, Ed recognized him as the assistant manager of the big supermarket in the shopping precinct, held the door wide, stepped back. After you, sir.

Ed's stomach churned, he grunted an unintelligible 'thanks', stepped inside and felt a rush of air as the door bumped shut behind him. Face to face and that guy hadn't recognized him, that was good. He moved on to the end of the queue.

Nobody was interested in him, they were either reading the bank's hard-sell leaflets or staring blankly at the cashiers. Beyond the heavy transparent counter screens he watched a bustle of activity in the main office. Houghton had his head down amidst trays of documents up on his rostrum, broke off to sign something which one of the female clerks handed to him. So far, so good.

Ed's fingers jangled the bunch of keys in his pocket, he felt out the one he wanted, clutched it clammily.

'Next please.' The queue moved up one. He could not linger here.

He turned away, walked towards the office door, held the key in readiness. A surreptitious glance to right and left; nobody was watching him. A click as the door opened, another click as it closed behind him in the empty manager's room. He experienced a momentary sense of euphoria. Back in his own room, his name on the outer door. As though nothing had changed. Jump to it, you bastards, I'm the boss!

A wave of nausea, he fought it off, withdrew the gun from beneath his anorak, fitted it together with trembling hands that had steel clanking on steel. He had to force the action, it was rusted badly. Two cartridges, faded green with a deep brass base, scuffed lettering that said 'Eley Acme'. Oh, Jesus, they didn't fit!

Panicking, he became weak with relief when the shells finally went into the chambers, the cardboard casing swollen in the damp of that pigsty. There was no guarantee that the powder wasn't damp, too. But he didn't have to fire the gun, he wouldn't need to because everybody would obey him just like they used to.

He laid the gun on the desk, sat down. Power in a different way. There was a buzzer close to where his knee rested, for security reasons, to summon help in case a bogus customer drew a pistol or tried to hold the manager hostage. Arse about, you fuckers, this time the manager's calling the tune! Ed had made a habit of using the device to summon Houghton when he needed him, brought the accountant on the run. Like *now*. He pressed the button, heard the buzzer out in the main office.

Ed cocked the gun, rested it across his knees and watched the opaque glass of the interior door. Come on, I don't like being kept waiting, I never did.

Ed recognized a hurrying silhouette as Houghton's, the other pausing *en route* to answer a clerk's query. Almost panicking, never once wondering why the summons had come from the vacant office of a manager who had fled the bank and the city with every police force in the country looking for him. Even knocking before entering, closing the door behind him before the awful realization filtered through to his harassed brain.

'Yes, sir? Oh, my God!'

'Just stand where you are and you'll be all right,' Ed let the wavering gun barrels come to rest pointing at Houghton's stomach. 'Nobody will get hurt if you're sensible. You know the drill, give a raider the money rather than risk injury or death. No heroics. Now, let's not do anything in a hurry.'

'No, sir!' Still the 'sir', Ed Cain was back in charge even if he needed a gun to enforce his authority.

'You're a creep, Houghton, a real turd!' Ed's lips curled in contempt. 'And, just for your interest, when I wrote the staff reports last month I said that you couldn't run a piss up in a brewery, that you'd never make managerial material!'

'Yes, sir,' the other's head nodded in terrified agreement, he was starting to shake uncontrollably.

'Pull your fucking self together, man!'

A pathetic effort to obey, hands crossed in front of him like his zip had suddenly come undone.

'Now,' Ed rested both elbows on the desk, aligned the shotgun on Houghton's chest, 'I want the money out of the reserve cupboard by the first cashier's till. Get it?'

This time Houghton's 'yes, sir', was a mime, his adam's apple bulging and bobbing.

'Good, now you're going to open the door into the office, tell Priestly that Grindleys have come for your wages, you've got Grindley in the room here with you. A hundred and fifty grand in fifties and twenties, in cloth coin bags. Tell him you'll give him the cheque in a few minutes. Now, straighten up that bloody awful face and stop where I can see you with the door open just enough to put your head round. Any tricks and I'll level those humped shoulders for you. Right, *now*!'

Houghton tottered towards the door, pulled it open, bumped it against his foot and had to try again. Peering round into the general office, his voice a hoarse whisper. Ed was listening intently, his forefinger touching the front trigger of the shotgun. Houghton gave his orders, a whispered whine, had to clear his throat, leaned on the door otherwise he would have fallen.

'Two minutes, sir.' He turned back to Ed. 'I did my best, sir.'

'Good. Take it from Priestley at the door, don't let him see into the room.'

An agonizing wait; through the opaque glass Ed Cain could just make out bodies moving, bustling. They didn't suspect a thing. Everything was going to plan.

He thought Houghton might faint, the lanky

accountant was still hanging on to that door, jumped when the glass was tapped, spun round.

'The cash, Mr Houghton. We're five hundred short in fifties, we'll have to get it out of the strong-room if you'd like to come downstairs with the keys, please.' Priestley's voice; he never hurried, was methodical in everything he did, worked not just to the book but to the letter.

Houghton's head turned, a questing expression. I'm sorry, sir, but if you'll hang on a minute or two I'll go and get the rest. You wouldn't like me to hand the safe keys over, would you, sir, because that's against regulations?

'Tell them to carry on and you'll be with them in a minute,' Ed gestured impatiently. 'And shut that bloody door!'

The money sack was placed on the desk, light-weight with its large sterling denominations but it was almost too much for Houghton to lift. He stood back, wiped his brow.

'That'll do,' Ed wheezed a laugh. 'In fact, that's admirable. Have that five hundred as a tip from me, Houghton!'

The other was cowering, anticipating another order.

'Now,' Ed did his best to hide the shotgun under his anorak, it was too risky to dismantle it. 'I'll be leaving you and if you so much as make a squeak before I'm out of that door I'll come back and blast any guts you have all over the wall. Got it?'

A puppet-like nod, Houghton glanced down at the chair. May I sit down, sir, I don't feel well.

Ed moved fast, the cash clutched in one hand, the other holding the gun beneath his outer garment, opened the door and stepped out into the banking hall. The queue had swelled right up to the main doorway. Heads turned in bored curiosity.

Faces he knew, customers who had sat on the opposite side of the managerial desk pleading for loans, overdrafts. Mutual recognition, shocked horror, the murmur of idle conversation dying to a silence.

'Hey,' somebody at the back yelled, 'that's *him*!'

The tail-end of the counter queue was blocking the door, too frightened or too surprised to move. Huddling because that was Cain who used to be their bank manager and was wanted for questioning by the police. The guy who had killed Canon Holland.

'*Move aside*!' Ed brought the gun into view, those barring his escape tumbled to one side. A woman started to scream.

Then he was out into the street. More shouting, shoppers and tourists alike diving for any available cover on the cobbled square. A trestle vegetable stall collapsed, showered its load, oranges and apples rolling and bouncing like a pool table gone berserk.

Ed's elation was suddenly replaced by terror. Fear of crowds just as he had felt at that football match a quarter of a century ago; they closed in on you, threatened to trample you. Pulled you down.

Hostile faces everywhere. But he had a gun and that made all the difference.

The deafening report sent a flock of feral pigeons clattering from the rooftops. It seemed that everybody was screaming now.

'*Now run,' Blake Barrett whispered, 'and hide*!'

Ed ran, brandishing the gun; spectators parted to let him through. On down the street, not even a pursuit, just eyes followed him. The traffic was snarled up at the lights, he took an alleyway to his right. Not a soul in sight. The money bag bumped against his thigh as he ran, the gun was a leaden weight in his other hand. Aching limbs, a constricting tightness in his chest but somehow he kept going.

'Where to?' he grunted aloud.

'I know how it ended last time,' Barrett's whisper trembled as though the terror of the hunted had filtered through to him, too. 'You work it out this time, Ed, and maybe we'll be okay.'

From that moment onwards Ed Cain was the loneliest man in the world. And for him there was only one place to go.

CHAPTER TWENTY-FIVE

Judy was jerked out of her exhausted slumber by the resounding thud of the front door. Still fully-clothed she leaped off the bed, her brain confused, ran for the landing, down the stairs.

'*You*!' She stopped half-way, told herself that it must still be part of that awful nightmare she had had earlier, the one in which Ed had dragged himself from the crushed Volvo, crawled home. Unrecognizable, crouching there in the hall like some mangled beast of the chase that had forcibly torn itself free from its attackers' jaws. *Just like he was now.*

For a fleeting second there was self-pity on his upturned unshaven features, then the lips formed into a leer. 'Surprised to see me?'

God, he was in a terrible state and that was a gun under his arm! She wondered what was in the bag he carried in his free hand. It didn't matter.

Her initial reaction was to flee back upstairs, lock herself in the bathroom, open the windows and scream and scream until somebody came. Only the fact that that . . . *creature* down in the hallway was, by some narrow and treacherous link, her husband. In body if not in soul. Which was why she descended, a hesitant step at a time.

'Ed . . . what's happened?' Don't tell me because I

don't want to know, I didn't mean to ask. 'You look ghastly. And what are you doing with a gun?'

He spoke in monotones as if his vocal chords functioned but his mind was elsewhere. 'I robbed the bank. Here's the money.' The sack thudded on to the floor.

'Oh, no!' Anguished, recoiling, she thought she was going to faint. It was stupid of her to have come back to the close, there was always the possibility that Ed might return. She didn't care for herself, it was the children she had to think of. Your father's a murderer. He's also a bank robber.

'But *why*, Ed?' She went through to the kitchen, heard him following her. 'Just tell me why.'

'Because I'm Blake Barrett,' he sounded very tired, slumped into a chair. 'That's why, all along. He's gone for the moment but he'll be back.'

She did not understand, only knew that her husband was mad. 'Did you kill Canon Holland? Tell me the truth, please, Ed.'

'Yes.' There was even a hint of remorse. 'Like I killed John Cutler. Lawson fell into the river and drowned. He was lucky, I would have murdered him if I had got to him first. I killed a farmer last night, his pigs ate the body, they might think that was an accident, too. It was different with Holland, I thought he was Blake Barrett, I didn't realize until afterwards that Barrett had tricked me. That was when he finally got me in his power, when I couldn't dodge the issue any longer. He made me rob the bank.' Pleading, close to tears. But he still had the gun propped up in between his knees.

'You'll have to give yourself up,' she said at last. 'They'll put you away, give you treatment. You never know, one day . . .'

'I'll never be free!' He shouted, his anguish hurt

her. 'From that night when I died on the life-support machine I've carried Barrett around with me. And when he gets the urge I have to obey. That was when it happened, his astral found a body it needed. Mine. Only by some freak my soul didn't desert me. *I'm two people, Judy*!'

It was crazy, she almost believed him. 'They'll find you here, Ed. It's the first place they'll come looking . . . '

She was interrupted by a faraway wailing that was becoming louder by the second. Blaring sirens like you heard on a hot summer's day when you had the windows open and there had been an accident somewhere. *Except that now the police cars were screeching into the close, contemptuous of that raised ridge, bumping over it.*

'The police are here, Ed,' she was nervously stretching out a hand, hoping that perhaps she could snatch that shotgun away from him.

'Stop it!' He slapped her arm away, grabbed up the gun. 'Get under cover, blast you!'

It was Blake Barrett talking; he was back again.

Ed ran for the stairs, some instinct warning him that when you made a last stand you stood a better change from an elevated position. From the landing window he could watch front and back; they would not risk rushing the house, not whilst they had a gun. And Judy.

He looked out of the front window. Two police cars, some unmarked vehicles, parked in a line at the bottom of the close. An ambulance had followed them in. Police marksmen, two in riot gear, one taking up a position behind the old well on the cathedral lawn. Deploying their forces with speed and efficiency. And only when they were ready did the message come over the loud hailer.

'*Armed police. We have you surrounded.*'

He did not reply, instead called downstairs for Judy to join him. He did not expect her to obey but a minute or so later her footsteps came pattering up the stairs.

'Ed, you'll have to give up at the finish, why not now?' She was close to breaking point. One half of him wanted to insist that she walked out through the front door, left him alone, the other reminded him that she was a valuable hostage; Blake Barrett's half.

'It's going to be a long siege,' he grunted as he struggled to extract the spent case from the gun, forced another live one into the breech. 'We'll play them at their own game, sit it out.'

Judy sat slumped with her back against the banisters, sobbing softly to herself.

1.00 pm. The police had allowed a television camera crew into the close, they were parked with two wheels of the big van on the pavement in front of Norma Pringle's house. Ed Cain found himself wishing that she was still alive, that she had saved herself for today so that he could have been responsible for her death. She would surely have had a heart-attack. He felt the killing urge coming on him again.

Euphoria because they were scared of him, they had to be otherwise they would have rushed the house, there were enough of them and armed, too. He was holding them at bay. Like those cowboy comics that had fascinated him as a child, Buffalo Bill holed up, surrounded by hordes of Comanches, picking them off one by one every time a feathered head showed from behind the rocks. One man against overwhelming odds. Just like it was here.

Ed smashed the front window with the barrels of the gun, heard the glass tinkling on the porch below.

He could have lifted the sash, fixed it open, but somehow this was . . . *macho*.

'Is there anything you need? Food, drink?' A senior police officer used the hailer again, sounded almost friendly. All part of the siege procedure, these officers were trained to avoid a shoot-out.

Ed thought, what a bloody silly question, the larder and the freezer are full. He did not reply.

3.15. More vehicles, more men had arrived. There were probably twice as many beyond Ed's vision, all the way down to the city centre. Doubtless they had cordoned off the Close to keep the crowds back.

'Make some coffee,' he saw that Judy was still sitting up against the stairs. 'I could use a sandwich, too.'

She looked at him blankly, his words took time to register with her. The only sign that she had heard was when she pulled herself up by one of the rails, turned for the stairs. She would do as her husband asked, she did not have any choice.

Except . . . she stood on the bottom stair looking at the front door. A Yale lock, the chain wasn't even fixed in place, nor the bottom bolt. She could walk right out, there was nothing to stop her. Instead she went on through to the kitchen; because the gunman upstairs was still her husband and it was her duty to stand by him. It wasn't his fault, he was sick, and she did not altogether discard his theory about an astral. A freak, there were things beyond human ken which mortals were not supposed to understand. Once she had been religious, went to church every Sunday; that was years before they came to live in the cathedral city. Since then she had become disillusioned, her faith had wavered. She still believed in God even if He was doing all this to them.

She cut some ham sandwiches, sliced a couple of tomatoes. The kettle came to the boil, cut out. She was in the process of spooning instant coffee into two mugs when the shot shattered the stillness with the force of a grenade thrown into an enclosed space. The jar spun from her fingers, left a trail of instant granules in its wake before it rolled off the table and smashed on the floor. She jerked, knocked over one of the mugs. But for some reason she did not scream, just stood there transfixed as the report echoed and slowly died away.

An awful thought, one that was in its own way a relief. Oh, God, he's shot himself! *Just like Blake Barrett did*!

Trembling, afraid to go upstairs for fear of the scene which would surely confront her. Ed lying on the landing, half his head blown away. I don't want to see it.

Let the police find him. She leaned up against the table, watched the front door through the hall. When they arrived she would let them in. Go on up, see for yourselves.

But they did not come. The awful silence was back, the atmosphere heavy with tension. She thought she heard voices far away but nobody came down the drive and banged on the door.

'How's that coffee doing?' Ed's voice from the top of the staircase, he sounded almost jubilant. And that was when she had to fight back her scream.

'What happened?' She climbed the stairs hesitantly, saw him with the gun, using his penknife to extract a swollen cartridge case, forcing in another shell.

'Just a shot to let 'em know I haven't dropped off to sleep,' he laughed harshly. 'Keep 'em on their toes.'

She placed two mugs of steaming coffee on the landing table, went back for the sandwiches.

A stalemate that might go on for days, a week even.

Judy was thinking about her mother and the children. Doubtless the first television pictures had gone out, they would know all about it by now.

'I'm going to ring Mother, just to let her know I'm . . . we're all right,' she half-expected him to try to stop her but he made no move to prevent her going back downstairs.

The phone was dead, not so much as a dialling tone. Communications had been severed. And that was when Judy became aware of the loneliness, the terror of all this.

Dusk had started to creep in beneath the shadows cast by the cathedral; night always seemed to fall earlier in the Close than elsewhere in the city, Judy thought. Ed was no more than a silent silhouette standing by the front landing window, menacingly motionless with the gun propped on the sill. Watching.

Soon she would not be able to see him at all, she was thinking, when without warning blinding white light flooded the house. She gasped, threw up her hands to protect her eyes.

'Floodlights,' Ed was calm, as if he was giving a documentary for those television cameras at the bottom of the Close, 'they've got their own searchlights as well as the cathedral illuminations.'

For the Cains this was to be the longest day. Night would not fall in the cathedral Close.

'I've been thinking,' it was well after midnight when Ed broke the long silence, turned back from his lookout post, 'there's no reason for you to stay, Jude.' He had stopped calling her Jude about a couple of years after they had been married, a term of endearment that had become worn out. Hearing it now brought a feeling of sadness. 'I mean, I'm not holding you *hostage*, am I?'

She refrained from replying, 'Oh, I see.'

'You just happened to be home when I arrived. Look, I think you'd better go. The kids will be wondering what's happened to you.'

'No, they won't, they'll have seen it all on the television if the police haven't already been round to Mother's. I don't want to leave.' Yes, I do, but I'm going to see it through, whatever the final outcome.

'I want you to go,' his voice was terse. 'Now, this minute!'

She caught her breath, asked 'Why, Ed?'

'Never mind why,' his tone was harsh. 'Go downstairs and walk right out of that front door. And close it behind you as you go.'

Another fear, she had been through it a few hours before when that shotgun blast had boomed through the house. When she had been afraid to go upstairs in case she found . . . *I know you're going to turn the gun on yourself, Ed.*

She did not trust herself to speak, her words would have been shaky, she might have broken down. A dilemma. It was Becky and Richard who swayed her. If Ed really was Blake Barrett then it could only end one way, whether she was here or not. And in his madness he might shoot her before he shot himself. That was becoming a fashion these days, crazed fathers and husbands murdering their families before committing suicide. Staying here wasn't going to help anybody.

'All right,' she spoke at last with only a hint of a quaver. 'I'll go.'

'Good. Thank you, Jude.'

They stood there for what seemed an eternity in a kind of mute farewell. She was hoping he would kiss her, but he made no move to do so. He just nodded, did not even say 'good-bye, darling' and then she was on her way downstairs, along the hall and clicking that Yale behind her.

As she walked out into the dazzling brilliance of an artificial night she braced herself for the sound of the shot in the house behind her.

But it did not come.

Ed Cain stood watching at the window until an armed escort of police converged on Judy, led her to the safety of the waiting vehicle. Then he spoke aloud, 'Thank you for that, Blake, if for nothing else.'

Now you know what you have to do, Ed.

The gun barrels were suddenly icy cold in his grip, vibrant as if a current passed through them and set off a trembling in his body. They might have glinted evilly in the glow of the searchlights outside except for the fact that the steel was rusted. A means of instant death, a means to put an end to everything.

Make a better job of it than I did, Ed. You've bungled it all so far, you shouldn't have come home.

It wasn't easy, Ed wished that he had a handgun, one that you could just press against your temple, or suck the end of the barrel, and press the trigger. He worked out how to go about it; stand the stock on the floor, grip the muzzle with your teeth, then stretch your arm downwards . . . you needed to be a contortionist to reach the triggers. Press downwards instead of pulling and . . .

Fuck you, Blake Barrett, I'm not going to do it!

You must. You will!

The gun rested on the floor, Ed's mouth was open; an obscene kiss of death. Push your tongue into me, sweetheart. His shoulders stooped, arms dangling. And then he straightened up defiantly, heard Barrett hiss with rage.

Kill yourself!

Ed lurched towards the stairs still clutching the shotgun in one hand. He snagged his foot on a length of rumpled staircarpet, almost fell headlong, just grabbed the rail in time. Down two steps; three.

The atmosphere was suddenly freezing cold, invisible fingers reaching out for him, trying to drag him back. There was a roaring in his ears, a sense of vertigo like in those dreams where you tumbled from a height, woke up with a bump just before you hit the ground. He had to drag his feet, it was as though leg-irons were attached to his ankles. Darkness where there had been light and amidst the throbbing and pounding he heard Barrett screeching with fury.

This time I'm fighting you all the way, Blake!

Ed was dimly aware that he was in the hall, punching the blackness with a clenched fist. His adversary had a hold on him, cold fingers squeezing his neck so that he could barely breathe. Tearing at them but only raking his own flesh. He tried to pray but it was no good, he had forgotten how and, anyway, the God who had abandoned him to his fate would not be interested in saving him now.

The door; he had to make it out through that door. His hand closed over the knob but was pulled back. He struck out, lost his footing and fell back against the wall. Somehow he maintained his balance, straightened up again. *I have to get out through that door!*

He kicked, cried out with pain as his shoe struck something hard, sent the ornate table rolling and clattering. Barrett was at him again, this time from behind, trying to topple him backwards. Ed mustered his waning strength, the old man of the sea with Sinbad clinging to him, made it to the front door again. The air was heavy with an overpowering stench of putrefaction, the smell of bodies decaying in their graves; gulping for air and swallowing the foulness.

Cold damp fingers closed over his own on the door-knob. A mental and physical battle, Ed screeched his fear and hatred aloud as he pressed down on the spring lock, heard it click back.

The door came open, a shaft of light slanted in. An unseen foot attempted to shut it but his own leg was in the way. A gap, just enough to squeeze through. Pulling, tearing, resisting the force that held him.

Then, without warning, he was free, catapulted out into the porch, staggered and sprawled on the sharp gravel. For a few moments he lay there, tasted blood and dirt in his mouth. Oh, Jesus Saviour, *I made it!*

Barrett was still screeching but now it was a helpless fury, no longer were those hands groping, holding him. I beat you, Blake, in the end, I was too strong for you. Maybe I should have fought you a long time ago.

Blake Barrett was laughing now, a chilling, unnerving sound that had Ed's flesh pimpling. As though it wasn't all over yet, there was still another round to go. That cat and mouse game still being played; you've lost, you've won. You've lost.

Crazy, Ed thought. When I tried to kill myself before he made sure I didn't know, now he wants me to and I fight him. Because he still had a use for me then, now my usefulness has expired. But there was something disturbing about the laughter now, it had a kind of triumphant ring to it.

Tough shit, Barrett, I'm giving myself up to the police. If you want to stick with me then we'll rot together in prison.

With some difficulty Ed picked himself up, swayed unsteadily, unable to see in the direct beam of a mobile police searchlight. Okay, fellers, come and take me.

He was still holding the shotgun. He had clung to it

throughout that terrible confrontation within the house when the weapon was nothing less than an encumbrance to him; holding it out at arm's length in case the evil that possessed him somehow mounted a final assault and forced him to turn the twin barrels on himself.

Shaking it, waving it, keeping it pointed away from himself. *For Christ's sake, somebody take this bloody gun off me!*

Suddenly Ed Cain's head seemed to explode. He felt the splintering of cranium bone, one flash of searing brilliance. And after that there was nothing except infinite blackness.

CHAPTER TWENTY-SIX

'Are you all right, madam?' The tall policeman appeared out of the glare of the floodlights, peered anxiously at Judy Cain. In his right hand he carried a pump-action shotgun, seemed to be trying to shield it from her behind his body.

'I'm . . . all right,' she swayed slightly and the officer's free hand supported her. 'I'm fine, thanks.' She tried to sound convincing as she shielded her eyes against the lights.

'If you'll come with me we'll have you taken to hospital, checked over by a doctor.' Delayed reaction was the worst problem with released hostages, it could hit them hard up to twenty-four hours later even though they seemed all right beforehand.

'No!' She spat out the denial, then made a pretence of relaxing. 'I'm sorry but my . . . husband . . . is still in there. I want to see it through.'

The policeman led her over to the ambulance where more uniformed officers were gathered. They seemed almost casual, were smiling and drinking tea. All part of the play-it-down routine.

'Is there any chance that your husband will give himself up?' A plain-clothes detective eyed her keenly, looking for a reaction. 'How was he when you left him?'

Judy replied, 'He was fine. He . . . oh, goodness, here he comes now!'

Heads turned, they saw the bedraggled figure in the front doorway of the house. He appeared to be having difficulty getting out of the door. As if he was struggling with some unseen person who was trying to drag him back inside. Then Cain stumbled, fell headlong across the porch and into the drive. He lay there motionless, all eyes upon him.

'*Ed*!' Judy screamed, would have run to her husband only the detective grabbed her arm, held her back.

'Don't!' he snapped. 'Let him come on his own. He seems to be . . . '

Ed was up on his feet, was holding out what Judy at first thought was a stick, thrusting it from him, waving it about.

One of the uniformed policemen said, 'He's still armed!'

And even as the onlookers stared a shot rang out. A sharp report; just one, it came from the direction of the old well and pump on the edge of the cathedral lawn, seemed to hang in the still atmosphere.

Judy screamed, it was as though a stage spotlight was focused on the principal actor in some tragedy; she saw Ed jerk upright, his arms flung wide and that shotgun falling from his outstretched hand. For a second or two he stretched, motionless, and she tried to tell herself that the police marksman's bullet had missed.

Then she saw her husband slowly crumple to the ground.

It was the nightmare all over again, Judy thought. Last March it had been reality, they had loaded Ed's crushed and bleeding body on to a stretcher, carried him into the ambulance. A rug covered him; nobody held any hope, they were just going through the motions so that nobody could criticize them afterwards. Certified dead upon arrival at hospital.

Except that Ed wasn't dead. She knelt by his side in the ambulance, held his limp hand, oblivious of the ambulance man, the police doctor, a couple of detectives. She could feel his pulse; it was very faint but there was a beat, nevertheless.

A police motorcyclist cleared a path through the late night traffic, a cavalcade of patrol cars brought up the rear. An escort, a VIP on his way to a function. But they didn't give a damn as long as they did their job, they were hoping he would be dead by the time they reached the hospital. It would save an awful lot of trouble and expense.

Ed felt so peaceful, more restful than she had known him since . . . don't think about it. It's a dream.

The reality of the wailing, deafening sirens disillusioned her, shattered her hopes. This one is for real. Again.

The bullet had hit him on the side of the skull, it might still be lodged in there. The ambulance man was trying to stem the bleeding, the doctor was injecting morphine. Oh, Ed, everything's come right at last, she sensed that that terrible possession, if that was what it had been, had left him. He was hurt, maybe he would die, but that burning tension had left him.

Nobody spoke, there was nothing to say because everybody had seen and understood. Ed Cain had come out of that house brandishing a gun, the marksman could take no chances. Rather a dead murderer than a dead policeman or civilian. No regrets. Except for Judy.

She walked alongside the stretcher into the hospital, down endless white-walled corridors that smelled overpoweringly of disinfectant. Until they reached the operating theatre.

It was Craddock. Judy recognized him behind his mask, the way his grey eyes flicked on to her. You again, Mrs Cain! 'We'll have to operate,' he spoke without emotion. 'The nurse will show you where to wait.'

Dawn was beginning to slink into that small anteroom when the nurse came back for Judy. A different one this time, she even managed a smile, but uncommunicative like the previous one. Walking fast so that Judy could scarcely keep up with her. There seemed to be some frightening urgency.

There was.

Judy saw Craddock first, he looked tired and irritable behind his surgeon's mask. She followed his gaze and her heart seemed to stop for a second, juddered back into life.

That machine again with its multitude of wires and attachments; she saw the body lying on it. She had expected it this way, that in itself was only a confirmation of her worst fears. She had even steeled herself to find a corpse awaiting her, still cherished those precious minutes in the ambulance when Ed had been Ed again, dying but at peace.

But not *this*!

It wasn't Ed on that life-support contraption. No way! Even as she stared that body had changed back to the creature she had known these past few months. A thing that tensed and pulsed, strained as though attempting to escape from the flesh and blood that incarcerated it. The head was heavily bandaged, only the lips were visible; perhaps they moved, perhaps not, but she heard in her mind the way they cursed, felt the sheer evil that emanated from them.

'I'm afraid that your husband is clinically dead.' Craddock was speaking, almost a recitation; words uttered time and again to distraught next of kin. 'There will be no recovery, there is no point in continuing.' We are all wasting our time, but we have to have your permission to switch off the machine.

Judy tore her gaze from the pulsing malevolence, closed her eyes for a moment. When she opened them the surgeon was still watching her intently; hurrying her. *There is no point in prolonging the inevitable, Mrs Cain.*

'You *do* understand, don't you, Mrs Cain?' Craddock asked softly. 'I would strongly advise you to authorize us to turn off the life-support machine.' You would do just that for a dog badly injured on the road, wouldn't you? Euthanasia.'

Judy nodded. One last look at the tormented form lying there, then she wrenched her eyes from it. She felt her features contorting with the hatred burning in her for that monster writhing within her husband's body, for what it had done to him that night. And for what it was still doing to him.

Finally she was able to speak; her words were a barely audible hiss, her lips quivering, her body trembling uncontrollably.

'*Kill it*!'

Guy N. Smith

While the forces of nature create a white hell outside, a satanic force from beyond the grave is at work inside . . .

Into this world step three unwitting travellers, driven by the blizzard to seek refuge at a country house hotel. A 'hotel' where the 'guests' live in a diabolical world of lunacy and madness, where demented creatures prowl the corridors, where putrefying flesh lies in the cellar and blood-curdling screams echo from the bedrooms . . .

And, amidst the horrors, the monstrous spawn of a subnormal girl awaits a virgin sacrifice to bring the Prince of Evil to life . . .

Also by Guy N. Smith in Sphere Books:
FIEND

0 7474 0057 1 HORROR

THE CAMP

Guy N. Smith

The holidaymakers had come from all walks of life to relax and enjoy themselves, little realizing what lay in store at . . .

THE CAMP

They had all been chosen to take part in experiments for a new drug. It was intended to control rioters by producing peaceful fantasies. But for some those dreams would become violent nightmares . . .

And after the brutal murder of a young girl the media began calling it the 'Camp of Death'. But no-one was prepared for the horror and violence that would be unleashed when the antidote failed to work at . . .

THE CAMP

0 7474 0058 X HORROR